YOUR
FINAL
MOMENTS

YOUR FINAL MOMENTS

JAY COLES

Scholastic Press / New York

Copyright © 2025 by Jay Coles

All rights reserved. Published by Scholastic Press, an imprint of Scholastic Inc., *Publishers since 1920*. SCHOLASTIC, SCHOLASTIC PRESS, and associated logos are trademarks and/or registered trademarks of Scholastic Inc.

The publisher does not have any control over and does not assume any responsibility for author or third-party websites or their content.

No part of this publication may be reproduced, stored in a retrieval system, or transmitted in any form or by any means, electronic, mechanical, photocopying, recording, or otherwise, or used to train any artificial intelligence technologies, without written permission of the publisher. For information regarding permission, write to Scholastic Inc., Attention: Permissions Department, 557 Broadway, New York, NY 10012.

This book is a work of fiction. Names, characters, places, and incidents are either the product of the author's imagination or are used fictitiously, and any resemblance to actual persons, living or dead, business establishments, events, or locales is entirely coincidental.

Library of Congress Cataloging-in-Publication Data available

ISBN 978-1-5461-2556-3

10 9 8 7 6 5 4 3 2 1   25 26 27 28 29

Printed in Italy   183

First edition June 2025

Book design by Maeve Norton

TO ELLI COLES, WHOSE STRENGTH AND BEAUTY
INSPIRE ME EVERY SINGLE DAY. LIKE WILDFLOWERS,
YOU HAVE GROWN AND THRIVED IN PLACES MANY
WOULD NOT. THIS BOOK IS FOR YOU.

"Consider how the wild flowers grow. They do not labor or spin. Yet I tell you, not even Solomon in all his splendor was dressed like one of these. If that is how God clothes the grass of the field, which is here today, and tomorrow is thrown into the fire, how much more will he clothe you—you of little faith!"

LUKE 12:27–28 (NIV)

"You may encounter many defeats, but you must not be defeated."

MAYA ANGELOU

CHAPTER ONE

"If you were told that today's your very last day on earth, what would you do in your final moments?" That's a question my old therapist, Dr. Chandler, asked me once. It's a question I think about when I wake up. A question that popcorns around my thoughts during second-period Biology. At the dinner table when I'm picking through the meal that Momma's conjured up even though she's definitely not a chef. At night when I'm alone in my room, unable to sleep, because I'm afraid of the dark.

Not afraid of the dark like when I was six and thought monsters hid under my bed.

It's a different kind of afraid of the dark.

It's the kind that keeps you wide awake because the darkness reminds you of death. Everyone you love the most will die. Your friends will die. Your family will die. One day *you* will die. There won't be any more sunshine or laughter or joy or memes or puppies or rainbows or whatever makes you real happy, only the darkest and loneliest kind of night.

It's been months since I last saw Dr. Chandler, and I'm still struggling to think of something that would be sufficient for my final hours of life. Would I want to conquer my fear and go horseback riding? Would I learn to bake macaroons? Would I fly to Israel to see where Jesus's tomb lies? Would I hook up with some stranger from a dating app just because I couldn't stand to die without having sex one last time? I wonder if Miles felt this way before he stepped out in front of that bus. I wonder if he wanted to pet a baby shark, wrestle an alligator, try the world's hottest pepper, meet Nicki Minaj, memorize the entire script of *Rogue One*. Knowing Miles, he'd do something like that. But I don't know exactly what he wanted to do.

That's the thing about suicide: It leaves everyone without answers.

It leaves everyone wondering and wondering, wishing and hoping, offering thoughts and prayers. That's the most annoying part.

If I'm being real, I hate myself for letting what happened to him happen. Miles and I had a pact. We knew that we were both struggling, and we knew to send a red flag emoji whenever one of us needed to talk. Relationship drama, red flag text. Drank a little too much and needed a ride, red flag emoji. Depressed about the way life shits on you, red flag emoji.

But Miles was hurting a lot, and I couldn't see it. I missed his red flag text. I failed him. He would've never done that to me. He was always there.

Always, always.

Here I stand, staring at myself in the bathroom mirror. Staring at this black suit that matches the black tie and black shirt and black pants that I wear, all matching the blackness in my heart. Here I stand, tears streaming down my face as I'm minutes from seeing Miles, my childhood best friend, in a casket being stuffed into the ground forever.

Someone knocks on the door, causing me to jolt back and wipe at my face.

"Hakeem, are you okay in there?" The voice is muffled by the door, but I know it's Momma.

I get myself together kind of quick. "Yeah, I'm good." I turn on the water and splash some onto my face.

"We're going to be in the car, okay?"

"Yes, ma'am," I say back, a lump forming in my throat as I think about where I'll be headed as soon as I get in the car.

I brush my hair quick and then head outside to the blue minivan Momma's had since I was in elementary school. Dad's in the passenger seat and my little siblings, Jorjah and Judah, are already in the van, buckled up, wearing their Sunday best.

Normally, Momma plays some of her R&B oldies when she drives, but not today. This car ride is quiet, almost painfully so. Minus Jorjah and Judah antagonizing each other. I think, *Do I want to allow myself to think about my favorite memories with Miles? Am I ready to do that? Will I ever be ready to do that?*

I pull out my phone and pop in AirPods. I click play once I load up the "Just Chill" Spotify playlist Miles and I made together during last year's spring break trip to Chicago. The first song that plays is "Levitating" by Dua Lipa. I remember it being Miles's number-one top song on his Spotify Wrapped this year. He was obsessed with her and even made her his phone background. Now he's gone. Damn. This isn't fair at all.

My throat gets tight, and my eyes suddenly are wet, tears pooling and blurring the view as we pass cars and buildings on the road. My eyes feel the same way as when I would help Momma chop onions in the kitchen. My face stings for a moment before things get worse and I'm in pain all over. Just a week ago, I was talking to Miles on the phone, catching up about the NBA, talking about the girls whose DMs he'd be sliding in, and how we were cheating on a biology exam in Mr. Munich's class. I've got no one to call up anymore. Just like that.

Finally, we arrive at First Baptist Church. The church we grew up going to together. Even here, there are memories of Miles and me that stain the walls. Like the time when we were both six and got baptized in the three-feet-deep baptismal. Like the times we would steal extra dinner rolls from the church kitchen during post-service mealtime. Like the times we skipped out on Sunday school Bible lessons and hid in the basement, pretending the boiler was a rocket ship we were building. Miles and I got in so much trouble in this place over the years. I can even see the mark in the carpet from the time we spilled a whole bottle of grape juice during one World Communion Sunday when we were little.

So many of us are wearing black. But I know how much Miles hated dark colors and loved tie-dye. Even though I know tie-dye isn't funeral or church appropriate, it's not like Miles followed rules.

Shuffling inside this cramped church, I notice there are so many people from our community and school, people I haven't seen in years and who don't know him like I do. In some ways, Miles was *my* twin brother, like Judah is Jorjah's. We did everything together. We even asked our parents to buy us matching clothes until we made it to high school. Nobody else here, not even our families, knows what we were like together. Not really.

It's been months since I've come to this church. I almost forgot about all the paintings of the saints and the giant cross hanging from the ceiling like a chandelier and the huge portrait of Black Jesus behind the pulpit. The carpet is the worst kind of vomit green. The pews are wooden, with stained cushions.

It's already kind of warm outside for the beginning of March in Indiana. The air-conditioning has never worked in this church for as long as I've gone here, and they only pass out those little paper things glued to a Popsicle stick to fan yourself when it's high summer. I'm already sweating and my suit sticks to my skin like Scotch Tape.

Momma and Dad find open seats for us near the back. I sit next to Momma, and Jorjah and Judah both sit on Dad's lap, even though they definitely should be too old for that now.

Momma grabs my knee, noticing my shaking. "You okay?" A question I don't think I can answer honestly right now—or maybe ever.

I hope my non-answer will make her stop asking me. I watch as Miles's parents are escorted to their seats in the front. Miles's mom, Mrs. Angela, screams so loud from a place deep within her. Her cries ricochet and bounce off all the walls and hit me in the chest. Suddenly, I'm thinking about not being able to knock on Mrs. Angela's door to ask if Miles is home. Tears pool in my eyes, but I wipe them away quick. For some reason, I keep telling myself that I can't cry, that I must be strong.

Occasionally, I hear people say things to other people that make my blood run cold. *He was such a good kid. Gone too soon. Such a big loss for the world. He was still a young man. He had his whole life ahead of him. He was so good at sports. He was a jokester. I remember when I used to change his diapers. I remember when he would come knocking on my door selling candy bars. I remember . . . I remember . . . I remember . . . I remember.*

Pastor Walt hops up on the pulpit in an annoyingly bright and distracting purple suit, but at least it isn't black. He clears his throat into the mic and the entire church goes quiet.

"We gather today to honor the life of Mr. Miles James Parker. A kind soul and gift from God. A wonderful son to Angela and Rodney Parker."

The church erupts in a variety of "amens."

Pastor Walt gives a whole sermon about how Miles isn't *really* dead. That he's alive in Heaven, that he's in a better place, that he's with us in our hearts, and blah blah blah. I try to tune it all out, resting my head on the back of the wooden pew in front of me. I wonder if it looks like I'm praying to God. Momma rubs my back the whole time, reminding me that I'm not alone, that she's here. And it's kind of nice.

Once it's time to go up to the casket to say our final respects, I'm all kinds of nervous. My feet don't want to work, my legs don't want to work. Momma and Dad nearly carry me as we approach the front of the church. We pass by crowds of people staring at us. Strong smells of old-people perfumes and colognes fill my nostrils, making me feel more nauseous. Or maybe that's just what I'm telling myself.

The casket. It's baby blue. Miles's favorite color. I am thinking about how he would like it when I look inside and see a brown-skinned mannequin.

"That's not Miles," I say to Momma, locking eyes with her.

Tears pool in her eyes and she nods before cupping my chin. "I know, baby," she says with trembling lips. "I know."

I look back at him in this casket. Miles always had a smile. He was even nicknamed "Smiley" all through middle school. He's not smiling in this box. I'm imagining other universes where I can see that smile again, and each time reality sets in, I break at the seams.

Miles had a diamond in his ear, but there's nothing there now. Miles also had dimples, but they're gone, too. This feels so unfair. I want to throw up. I want to punch something. I want to scream, yell, let out all my rage.

"Not Miles," I repeat under my breath instead. "Not you, Miles. Not you. Not you. Not you." Momma leads us back to our seats. The worship band comes up and leads the congregation through a couple hymns like "Amazing Grace" and "Be Thou My Vision." I watch tears stream down everyone's faces like rivers on a globe. Then the pastor comes back up to introduce Miles's dad, Mr. Rodney. Mr. Rodney reads a benediction from the book of Ephesians in his thick New Jersey accent. He takes a bunch of breaths before he reads, and he chokes up between certain syllables. I can tell he won't be okay for a long, long time, either.

For this reason I kneel before the Father, from whom every family in heaven and on earth derives its name. I pray that out of his glorious riches he may strengthen you with power through his Spirit in your inner being, so that Christ may dwell in your hearts through faith. And I pray that you, being rooted and established in love, may have power, together with all the Lord's holy people, to grasp how wide and long and high and deep is the love of Christ, and to know this love that surpasses knowledge—that you may be filled to the measure of all the fullness of God. Now to him who is able to do immeasurably more than all we ask or imagine, according to his power that is at work within us, to him be glory in the church and in Christ Jesus through-out all generations, for ever and ever! Amen.

Mr. Rodney invites Miles's mom to share next. She sings part of "Somewhere Over the Rainbow"—a song that she used to sing to Miles when he was a baby—and that makes her cry a lot.

"Miles was such a good, sweet boy," Mrs. Angela says. "He never did anything to hurt anybody."

The church amens that.

Through sobs, Mrs. Angela continues, "He loved his friends and family so much. If you were close to him, you knew how much he cared about you because he was always there for you, especially when you needed him most."

She's right about that. There's a throbbing ache in my throat now that won't go away no matter how many times I try to clear it or no matter how hard I try to swallow.

Mrs. Angela looks up at the ceiling. "Dear Jesus, I don't know why you had to take my sweet, sweet boy, but please tell him that

Mommy loves him and can't wait to see him when I'm in Heaven one day."

People clap for Mrs. Angela like this is some kind of performance. I feel boiling hot thinking about that. This is all so hard to make sense of. I can't imagine what Mrs. Angela must be going through right now. To give birth to a son, to have so many dreams for him, to think that he would outlive her, and to all of a sudden see him being stripped right from her arms seems cruel. Mrs. Angela deserves better. Miles deserves better.

Miles was a beautiful soul. People would tell him that all the time. I'm determined to help people never forget that fact.

At the end of the funeral, I can't wait to get into the car to drive away. I want to go home. I *need* to go home. I've had enough of being at my best friend's funeral. I have a headache and I'm people'd out.

The moment I get there, I collapse onto my Avengers-themed bedspread and scroll through all the pictures of Miles and me on my phone. It's honestly more torture than healing, but something about it feels instinctive. The world might forget about Miles, but I won't. I'm not done with him yet. I won't delete our texts, our voicemails, our photos. I won't delete his number from my phone.

I stare at the red flag emoji in our text thread and tears gather in my eyes. Something builds and builds deep in my stomach. I can't believe I failed my best friend. He's gone, and I can't help but feel like it's all my fault.

CHAPTER   TWO

Center Grove High School is already one of my least favorite places to be, but everything is so much worse coming here the Monday after my best friend's funeral. Between classes, I walk behind a group of girls who keep going on and on about what happened to Miles and all their theories and predictions, and I just want to yell at them to shut up and to keep his name out their mouths, but I don't. It takes a Herculean effort, but I calm myself down.

The bell rings, and I'm late to second-period Biology.

I stare ahead, listening to Mr. Munich talk about the DNA in a cell, but also not really listening to what he has to say. DNA, the nucleus, the cell wall, mitochondria, aka the powerhouse of the cell, none of it truly matters, does it? It matters even less to me today. I can't stop thinking about the empty seat just rows away from me. People are looking at it now . . . but did they care when he was sitting there? I cared. Or maybe that's just what I want myself to believe. Maybe if that were true, he would still be here with us and not packed underneath the ground in a box.

"Hakeem Lee Hawkins." Mr. Munich calls my whole government name out. "What holds one strand against the other in the double helix?"

The only helix I know refers to a porn site, so I'm not entirely sure what he's referring to. But I go out on a complete guess and say, "Hydrogen bonds?" It's the only thing I remember from last week.

"That is correct," he says with an impressive smile. "I didn't think you had been paying attention."

Classes drag on for what feels longer than usual. I end up skipping lunch because nothing sounds good, and I can't stand to sit at my usual table without Miles. I need a break from everything that reminds me of him, so I'm honestly not sure when I'll be able to eat in that cafeteria again. There are too many memories there.

Fifth period comes around and Principal Samuels calls for everyone to meet in the gym for a convocation. I know it's all about talking about Miles and suicide prevention stuff, so I hide in the band room. I sit on the floor behind the percussion section, plug in my headphones, and play my Spotify blend playlist that I made with Miles. The first song that plays is "Space Cowboy" by flipturn. They're my favorite band of all time. My first and only concert was a flipturn concert with Miles and Mikki. I remember that night like it was yesterday. Banging our heads to the drummer absolutely killing it, smoking cigarettes after the first set, eating footlong hot dogs from the concession stands. Minutes pass by, songs pass by, and I'm safe from getting caught for skipping the convocation.

I suffer through the rest of the day's classes until the dismissal bell rings, which for most kids is relief enough because they get to go home. But for me, I have to head to my Narcotics Anonymous meeting. I hate that I still gotta go there, but I promised Dr. Chandler and my parents that I would finish out the year before I stopped going. The last time I took pills or had anything to drink was almost four months ago. You'd think the death of my best friend might send me over the edge—it didn't. I'm not at all complaining. I'm actually glad that it hasn't hit me in that way, causing me to do something I'd regret. Maybe the meetings have been working after all and this is the proof.

I'm at my locker exchanging books—putting the ones I don't need to take home back and grabbing the ones I do need. I forgot about all the pictures I had in my locker of me and Miles doing the most random things, like chugging milkshakes from Freddie's, wearing our Halloween costumes at Mikki Hawthorne's Halloween party last year. And then there's the photos of us as kids, like the one where we are holding our trophies for coming in first place at our youth flag football tournament. Miles would play sports and could do it well, but he really preferred to watch. I wonder how many people close to him actually knew that.

"Hey," a voice says, catching me off guard.

It's Mikki Hawthorne, Miles's ex-girlfriend, and our classmate since elementary school. She's standing here in front of me with a box in her hands.

"Hey, Mik," I say, wiping away at my face.

"Didn't mean to startle you like that," Mikki says, looking down at the box. Then she looks up at me with the saddest brown eyes I've ever seen. Those eyes—they're exactly why Miles loved her. I remember him telling me about how Mikki had grown up to be this fine Black girl who kept catching his eye. And I remember telling Miles to make a move. And then days (*literal days*) later, they're dating. I'm sad they didn't work out. They were perfect for each other. They were my relationship goals, to be honest.

"No, it's fine," I say. "I was just grabbing my Pre-Calc textbook. Gotta be ready for that exam coming up on Friday, right?"

"Right."

We both stand there awkwardly for seconds that feel more like minutes, until I ask, "So, what's up, Mik?"

"I realized that I still had a bunch of Miles's stuff at my house, and I didn't want to just throw it all away and I definitely don't feel good hanging on to all of it," she says, tears pooling in her eyes. "And then I thought maybe you'd want it? You deserve it. You were there for him way more than I was."

"No, I don't think that's true, Mik," I say. "I couldn't even . . ."

"Hakeem, it's not your fault. You didn't cause Miles's death."

"Yeah, but—"

"But nothing," Mikki says, her conviction stopping me in my tracks. "This world failed Miles, not you."

"I hear you," I say, but there's still a pang in my chest.

"Besides, no matter what, he would want you to have all this stuff. He would want you to have it over me."

"I don't know if that's true, Mik."

"Just take it! Please. Just take it," she insists, pushing the box toward me to grab. I listen to her and accept it.

"Thanks, Mik," I say.

"I'm sorry I couldn't make it to the funeral. It's been hard getting out of bed, let alone going there. Feel me?"

"I understand. No hard feelings, Mik."

She makes this face like she needed to hear that. You know, that tight-lipped smile and eyebrow raise followed by a slight head nod?

"Let me know if you ever need anything," I offer, not believing I can even commit to that. I don't know if I'm in any place to pour out any more of myself for anyone, but maybe there's an exception for Mikki.

"Same to you, Keem," she says, that tight-lipped smile still on her face.

Out the corner of my eye, I see August, her older brother, walking up to us. I haven't seen him around in a while. Ever since he got kicked off the football team for using steroids, he doesn't really talk to many people. Also, specifically, August and I used to be friends with benefits. He's *straight*, but would always hit me up to fool around when he was bored or in the mood. We used to be cordial, but now it's like he doesn't want anything to do with me. I'm Casper the *unfriended* ghost.

"You ready to go, Sis?" August asks, barely looking at me.

"Yeah," she says. "I'll catch you later, Keem."

I wave at her and August as they walk past me. Of course, August doesn't wave back.

After double-checking my backpack for all the stuff I'll need, I pull out my phone to see a dozen missed texts and phone calls from my mom. One click, and I can tell she's just reminding me to not miss the NA meeting. I clear all my notifications and head outside.

The air always smells like an old person's ass crack when I get to support group. The same ten people come every week. Every now and then, a new person comes around, but they never stick around long enough. There's six white people, all of them are between the ages of late twenties and early fifties. There's an Asian guy who looks like he's in his thirties. There's one Middle Eastern man, a Black woman, me, and another girl named Violet who's about my age or a little bit older, but I can't make out what her race is. She's come every week, but never shares unless someone calls on her.

We all sit around in a circle and Yolanda, a Black woman who always wears a pantsuit, leads us in some kind of activity. It's always the world's most awkward activity, but for some people, it seems to help them in their journey, so we all participate, no matter what.

"Hello, everyone, my name is Yolanda, and I'm a former addict. Welcome to the Northside Indy group of Narcotics Anonymous. Can we open the meeting with a moment of silence for all those who are currently suffering from addiction, those who are present and those who are not?"

The meeting always begins like this. Everyone nods an answer to her question and we sit in silence. Some of us even close our eyes. Usually during the moment of silence, I squeeze my eyes shut and imagine I'm on a beach somewhere, being massaged by some hot girl or guy (I don't discriminate). But now, the only image I can think of is Miles's face.

The front door creaks open, and someone walks in. The floors are thin, so you can hear them walk over. In an instant, every single person looks over to get a glimpse at who just came in. It's another girl who looks about my age. She's wearing all black—black pants, a black shirt, black boots, and a black jean jacket. Her hair is brown and long and flowing. Yolanda points to an open seat and the girl takes it, joining us in the circle, staring at her hands.

15

"If there is anyone here attending their first NA meeting, welcome! I won't single you out, but know that this place can be your home and safe haven, if you want it to be," Yolanda explains, with some eagerness evident in her voice. "I only ask that you stay off your phones for the duration of this meeting. Okay?"

Everyone erupts in different monotonous versions of "okay" and "yes."

"Also, if you've used today, please find me or someone else here you might trust and share that with them. Now, shall we begin?" Yolanda's always smiling at us, but no one ever really smiles back at her. I don't envy her and her job. But I admire her dedication to helping people get clean and stay clean. And I'm sure it helps that she has her own complicated history with drugs. How despite everything she went through, she came out victorious on the other side. There's something about her story that gives everyone hope— hope that they, too, can make it out on the other side.

The Middle Eastern man raises his hand shyly.

"Yes, Aram?" Yolanda calls on him.

"What happens if you used right before this meeting?" he asks.

"That's okay. We can talk after this meeting, if you'd like." It's like Yolanda's never disappointed. Nothing surprises her.

Aram nods at her remorsefully, like he did something wrong and is asking to be forgiven.

Yolanda presses on. "Okay, let's start by sharing a highlight and a lowlight of our week! I'd love to hear from everyone. However, if you're new or you don't quite feel comfortable doing that, that's perfectly fine. There's no pressure. We want you to feel safe here first before sharing your truth. Now, who wants to go first?"

We sit in silence for a really long time. And it's like time is marked by deep breaths and sighing, not minutes. Yolanda isn't afraid to let the silence linger, either. Sometimes, I speak up and share something just to kill the awkwardness, but today, I'm beat by the new girl.

"My name is Eliza," she says, pushing her hair out of her face.

"Hi, Eliza," everyone chants back at her, fake happy that she's here.

"A week ago, I was kicked out of the house I'd been staying in. The family was generous enough to let me live with them for the last month, but they had enough of finding me blacked out in the shower, lying there cold, naked, and face down. This is the ninth family I've stayed with. I don't know what happens next. I've been staying at the Motel 6 down the street, and I saw a sign about this group. I don't know why I felt led to come here tonight, but to be honest, I'm afraid. I'm afraid that I'm stuck in a never-ending time loop where I'm forced to relive the same hard shit over and over. For once, I want out."

"Welcome, Eliza. Thanks for sharing that. You're so brave," Yolanda says.

This Eliza girl makes a face like she doesn't believe it, but then goes back to looking at her hands, fidgeting with her fingernails. What she said *is* brave, though, especially with this being her first time. I remember my first meeting. I came early, so I didn't make a scene and have everyone staring at me. I sat there quietly, looking

17

down at my shoes the whole time. I didn't say a word and when I was called on, I gently passed by shaking my head. I haven't shared much here since then, but to be honest, I haven't much to say. Until now.

"Would anyone else like to share?" Yolanda asks, smiling and looking around the circle.

"Yes," I say, raising my head.

"Go ahead, Hakeem. Please share."

I'm already nervous, and once Yolanda calls on me, all of that amplifies. I glance over and Eliza happens to look up. Suddenly, I've got cotton mouth and words whirl around in my head. My tongue holds them back at first. *Breathe*, I tell myself. *Just breathe.*

That's it. I'm ready.

"My best friend died," I tell these near-strangers. "He stepped in front of a bus. It was on Eighty-Sixth Street. You probably heard about it in the news. I'm lost now more than ever. I don't know how to move forward with this kind of grief." I can tell people are listening to me. Like, really listening to me. For the first time since I found out, I feel like I can keep sharing more than what's on the surface. "His name was Miles. We did so much together. We grew up together. He was like my twin brother in a lot of ways. We were both sad and had our own struggles, but we were always there for each other. In a lot of ways, I blame myself for what happened to him. I haven't thought about using again, I swear, but I'm worried that at some point in the future, his death is going to hit me a lot harder than it's hitting right now and I'll slip up. I'm terrified of that. I got clean for Miles. Well, I got clean for myself, but Miles was my accountability buddy and he kept encouraging me to do it. Now he's gone. He's . . ." A huge sob erupts from my gut and I'm a mess, tears coming and pouring out with no end in sight. I bury my head in my hands. Eventually, I feel hands on my back, rubbing in a slow motion, just like Momma did in church.

I can't move, I can't look to check who it is—I just cry and cry and cry. Eventually, I'm able to get myself together and see Yolanda standing over me. There's wetness around her eyes, too, like she can feel my pain. I wonder if she's lost someone like this.

"We're all here for you, Hakeem," Yolanda says with assurance. "Loss has the power to break you, but it doesn't change who you truly are. It reveals your heart. Miles is in your heart, Hakeem. He hasn't left you. He is still there, encouraging you along in your journey, even when you can't see him."

I wipe away at my face. Maybe Yolanda is right. Maybe I've been looking at this wrong. It's not like I'm suddenly running on a ticking time bomb to using again because Miles isn't here. Maybe I have the power to stay clean right inside me. No matter what, I need to hear what Yolanda's saying.

The rest of the group is spent with more and more people sharing highlights and lowlights of their week, affirming one another, and then at the end, like always, we have light refreshments—cheap gas station donuts and coffee.

Group lasts about a little more than an hour. I sneak out in the best and sneakiest way that I can. One of my gifts is the Irish good-bye, which is when you exit some kinda gathering without saying anything to anyone, leaving everyone to wonder where you are.

The moon hangs in the sky with a couple stars. Streetlights are straight trash on this side of town, so this parking lot isn't well lit at all. It takes me a second or two to see the girl leaning up against my car.

"Eliza?"

"Hey," she says, her hands in her black jean jacket. "Thanks for not letting me feel alone in there."

"Oh, yeah, no problem. You actually inspired me to share in the first place."

"Eliza Fitzpatrick," she says, extending her hand for me to shake. I look down and see so many marks, cuts, and bruises. I'm not sure what that's about and I'm not entirely sure I want to ask, either. For one, we're definitely *not* on that level yet, and for two, who knows if she'll ever come back to group.

I shake her hand and she winces like the handshake hurts, so I loosen my grip kinda quick.

"So?" she says.

"What?"

"You never told me your name."

"Oh, um, my bad . . ."

"Hi, My Bad." She winks before smiling.

"Hakeem," I say. "Nice to meet you."

"Hakeem, that's right," she says, reaching into her pocket to pull out a cigarette and a lighter. She lights it up and takes a puff, blowing smoke in my face. I nearly choke. I hate the smell of cigarette smoke. It makes me nauseous. I'm glad we're outside, so I can breathe in some clean oxygen. It's also a reminder of how glad I am that Dad gave up cigarettes, too.

A light cuts on above us and I see her illuminated even more. She's got smooth and clear eggshell skin, dimples, and large green eyes. Honestly, she's a lot prettier up close. Seeing her like this, she reminds me of someone I think I once knew. But there's no way to recall how, when, or why right now. My mind could also just be playing tricks on me.

"Well, that's my car," I say, in case she didn't know. "I'm gonna get home before my parents start to freak out."

"You still live with your parents?" Eliza asks me, her brow bending down.

"Well, yeah," I say, confused.

"That's cute," she says. "I love that for you."

I make a face at that. It sounds like she's judging me for living with my parents like a normal teenager. I mean, she shared some pretty intense stuff in the group, but I'm not going to throw that back in her face. I don't know if I'm reading these vibes between us correctly, but something feels straight-up weird.

"Are you from around here, Hakeem?" she asks, eyeing me up and down, puffing away at the cancer stick.

"Yes, I go to Center Grove High School," I tell her.

"I thought I recognized you," she says back.

Wait, what? "You do?" I ask her.

"I went to Center Grove my freshman year, then I was home-schooled, and now I don't have to ever see school," she says, like she's proud of being through with it.

"Oh, wow. I thought I knew you, too. Did you have Mrs. Harrison for English?"

"God, I hated her!" Eliza says. "Always eating Cheetos and drinking Diet Coke at her desk every hour of the day. Her breath always smelled terrible."

I laugh. "Yeah, I remember it being really bad."

"Like, lady, mints have been invented! I can't believe she tried to fail me."

"She tried to fail me, too!"

"I'm convinced she hated everyone."

I stand there, admiring her laugh for a moment. "Well, I'll see you around, Eliza. I hope you come back to group."

She gives me a nod. "Take care, Hakeem. I'm sorry to hear about your friend. It sounds like he meant a lot to you." She spins around, and I see her walk down the block. I'm not sure if she's walking back to the motel or not, but suddenly, I'm feeling like the biggest dick in the world. I think I just listened to this girl talk about how she's staying there and now I'm letting her walk at night in a sketchy part of town, all alone. This doesn't feel smart. And instead of offering to help her, I get in my car and head out. I look over and see the box that Mikki gave me. I still haven't opened it. To be honest, I don't know if I can. I don't know if I want to.

The cemetery where Miles is buried *and* his house are both on my way to my place. I don't know if that will ever stop being a wild thing to think about.

The whole drive home, it's like I can see him popping up on random corners, in the middle of the street, and even in the passenger seat beside me. I can remember his laugh, I can remember the ways his eyes squint when he smiles, I can remember the way he would run a hand through his nappy curls when he was anxious, I can remember the scar on his right arm from when he got in a bike accident when he was eleven. I remember him so much I can make a Miles Replica with my mind.

When I get home, I bring the box in with me. I pass up dinner and head straight to my room. I'm sure I'll hear about this from Momma or Dad later, but they know how emotionally exhausting group can be and let it slide every now and then. I'm hoping tonight's one of those nights. I hide the box under my bed. I think I'll save it for another day. I don't think I'm ready to go down that path just yet. I pull out my phone and scroll through Miles's Instagram account.

It's only a few hours later, when I climb into my bed and close my eyes, that I think about what Yolanda said. It's not that Miles is gone. In fact, he's with me. That counts for something.

CHAPTER   THREE

My alarm beeps and blares to life at 6:09 a.m. every day. That time is—no, *was*—an insider between Miles and me. Today, everything hurts when I wake up. My eyes, my chest, my lungs, even my teeth. My dentist once told me that I clench them pretty hard when I sleep. He was so concerned that he tried forcing me to sleep with a mouth guard, but it's still in a box on the nightstand next to my bed. I might need to consider using it soon. Pain shoots electricity all throughout my body. It's only ever this bad when I have a bad dream—like the one I had last night.

In it, I was hanging out with Miles. We just finished playing a game of *Fortnite* and then we got pizza at Domino's and milkshakes at Freddie's—our favorite things. We ended up going for a walk downtown, because Miles loved to window-shop even though he couldn't ever afford anything. At first, we're laughing and having a good time and then the sky turns from a bright baby blue to a dark gray. The sun disappears and rain comes. And the next thing I know, Miles is standing in the middle of the street and he's crying and he's just standing there, staring ahead at a bus barreling toward him. I try to run after him, but I'm too late.

Too late, too late, too late.

I make my way to the bathroom to brush my teeth and wash my face. Once I'm done, I get changed into my *Avatar* sweatshirt (*The*

Last Airbender, not the blue people), some jeans, and my black-and-white checkered Vans that I love.

Downstairs, I find Judah and Jorjah eating bowls of cereal. They don't like pancakes or waffles or other breakfast foods. Only cereal. I thought *I* was picky, but Judah and Jorjah take it to a whole other level. Until last year, they wouldn't eat anything else for dinner besides chicken nuggets or mac and cheese. They're real plain like that.

"Good morning, y'all," I say to them, kissing them both on the forehead.

They squirm and complain like they always do. They should be used to this by now. This isn't anything new.

Dad's sitting at the end of the table reading the obituary section of the newspaper. I'm not sure why he does that. It's strange, but he always seems to find someone he knows—or maybe not *knows*, but has an extremely loose connection to. Somebody's cousin's best friend's boyfriend's nephew. That kind of thing.

Dad doesn't look up at me, but once Momma sees me, she gives me a *look*.

I sit down at the table, and she puts a plate of pancakes, bacon, and eggs in front of me. She clears her throat, so I know she has something she wants to get off her chest.

"What?" I say, preparing myself.

"I've been patient with you, and I've not been asking you about college or what your plans are after high school. I know, I know. Miles just passed away and you've got a lot going on, but the whole thing's reminded me that you still have a whole life ahead of you."

"Yeah?" I say. I don't know what else to add. I'm not sure where she's going.

"I'm just scared for you. I'm scared that if you don't find something to work toward, you'll . . ." She stops and turns around to head back to the kitchen. I can hear her light sobs into her sleeve. She wipes her hands on her apron, and Dad gets up to comfort her. He hugs her from behind and then kisses her hair, ears, and neck.

"Ew!" Judah shouts out. "No kissing!"

"Yeah, gross! No kissing!" Jorjah adds.

I know I've put my parents through a lot the past couple years, so I'm careful when I answer my mother now. I say, "Mom, I'll be okay. I promise. I'll think about college soon, I swear. Just not right now. It doesn't feel like the right time." She knows I applied a couple places, but I also made it clear that I'm not sure about going to any of them, even if I get in. I'm just not there yet.

"Okay, honey," she says. "I hear you loud and clear."

"How was group last night, Son?" Dad asks.

"It was good," I say without really thinking about it.

"What was so good about it?" Momma follows up.

"Ummm." I think long and hard. "There was a new girl there, and I got to share about Miles."

"Oh, I'm sure that was helpful," Momma says.

"We're proud of you for sticking with it," Dad adds. "You know you can talk with us, too, if you ever need it."

"Yeah, I appreciate that, Dad."

"Losing a friend is hard," he continues. "Trust me, I've lost plenty of friends in my day. Even for a cop, like me, who gets to see more death than most, it never gets easy."

Dad comes over and wraps his arms around me, bringing me in for a nice and long hug. I rarely hug Dad, so this feels extra special. He squeezes me, and I squeeze back. He doesn't know how much I need this and honestly, I don't think I did, either.

"Okay, you two, time to head to the bus stop for school!" Momma says to Judah and Jorjah before kissing their chubby cheeks.

They fight and complain how much they don't want to go and how much they would rather stay home, but Momma doesn't fall for it. She never has and she never will. We used to try to fake sick, but she would always call our bluff. She would be taking our temperature and sending us to the urgent care just to make sure, but every single time, when we would get busted, we ended up at school anyway. It's like Momma's got her own kind of Spidey senses.

School is more of the same. Listening to boring lectures about stuff no one really cares about and won't actually help us in the future, skipping out on lunch, hiding in the band room, and finding ways to be more and more invisible than I already feel. The thing that is both a blessing and a curse about going to a massive school like Center Grove: It's easy to disappear there. One good hiding spot and it's like you don't exist.

The weekend rolls around. Saturday usually means Momma blasts gospel music and it's time to deep clean the house, but today she's got a whole other plan.

Momma, Dad, and I drop Jorjah and Judah at a friend's birthday party and drive to Miles's house. The whole drive there is sad. We live in a nice suburb where not a lot happens besides garage sales and white kids with lemonade stands. But Miles's neighborhood is a whole other story. There are gang members posted up with guns, abandoned homes and businesses, police cars everywhere, and bullet fragments littering the ground. You can even notice the difference in the way the air smells in my neighborhood compared to theirs.

It takes about twenty minutes before we arrive at the small brown house. Garden gnomes, flowerpots, and Black Lives Matter signs litter the yard and front porch. I remember putting up some of those signs with Miles.

We take Dad's police car over there. At first, I don't even think about things because I've ridden in Dad's police car several times before. But when we pull up, I'm sure it's a bad idea. I'm sure it reminds Mrs. Angela and Rodney of when the police showed up to their house to let them know about what happened to Miles. Dad is even in his uniform, because he has to go to work after.

Momma, Dad, and I all hop out the car. Momma carries a tinfoil pan of a cinnamon bun casserole that Dad made. Dad sometimes thinks he's a chef, but really he's only good for one or two things—meatloaf and cinnamon bun casserole.

Arriving at the front door of this place brings back so many memories, and it's like they're running through me all at once, making my body shake.

Dad knocks on the door, and I can hear Rocco barking on the

other side. Miles loved Rocco, and Rocco was obsessed with Miles. Damn, now I'm crying thinking about a dog.

Rodney comes to the door in a white tank top and showing his gold teeth. He's holding Rocco back by the collar. "Hey, y'all. Come on in. You know he won't hurt y'all. I'm just trying to keep him back from jumping up on folks and getting their clothes dirty."

When we're inside, he lets Rocco go, and he comes right up to me and jumps up on me, licking my hands, face, arms, whatever he can get to. "Hi, buddy," I say as I pet the top of his head. I've missed him.

"Baby!" Rodney calls out for Mrs. Angela. Once she answers him, he adds, "It's Marcellus, Naomi, and Hakeem."

Mrs. Angela comes from some back room in a dress and bonnet. It's like she's waking up for the first time since the funeral. "Oh, thanks for stopping by. It's good to see you all."

"It's the least we could do," Momma says and hands her the cinnamon bun casserole. "How are you doing?"

"Not good, Naomi. Not good." I can tell by the bags underneath Mrs. Angela's eyes that she hasn't been sleeping, that the weight of Miles's absence has been stuck on her. I feel so bad for her. I wish I could take that night back. I wish I could have a do-over.

"I can only imagine," Momma says.

Dad and Mr. Rodney go to the back and talk somewhere. I'm not sure where they go, but I'm sure they're wanting to give space to Mrs. Angela and Momma.

"We just started cleaning out his room and that's been . . . so hard. It's like we're erasing his memory, like he never lived here at all. That's been tough," Mrs. Angela explains.

"I'm sure that would be hard. I can't imagine what you might be going through, Angela. I'm just so, so sorry," Momma says, bringing Mrs. Angela into a hug, rubbing her back. When they break away, I can see them both crying.

Mrs. Angela says, "Hakeem, if you want to go back there to his room and take something, you can have anything in there. I'm sure he would love it if you kept some of his things."

I'm afraid of that. I'm frozen in place like I can't move, I can't think, I can't speak. But Mrs. Angela stares at me and now Momma is doing the same. Eventually, I'm able to regain control of my body, so I nod at them and head back to Miles's room, taking slow steps at first. It's like my body is resisting going back there, but it's also my deepest desire in the world right now. Rocco follows me, wagging his tail and sniffing my legs and feet.

It's exactly the same as I remember it. I was here just a few weeks ago, doing homework with Miles, the two of us lying at opposite ends of his bed. I walk around, remembering just how messy Miles was. Piles of dirty clothes on the floor, empty and half-full bottles of water and Gatorade lining the window ledge. Hanging over the clutter are the posters of his favorite movies. *The Conjuring. It. It Chapter Two. Candyman. Texas Chainsaw Massacre. Final Destination 2.* Miles always said there was something about horror that gave him the same rush as riding a roller coaster.

I open the top drawer of his desk and see random things that I can tell he just threw in there. Loose change, an old watch, random

30

receipts and pieces of paper. On top of the desk are books that he probably never read. God, I'm missing him even more. I didn't even know that was possible. But my stomach is in knots and my heartbeat picks up. I try to blink the tears away, but my eyes are like Niagara Falls within seconds.

I sit down at his desk and give myself a moment. I'm blinking and blinking, wiping away at my face and eyes. I take several deep breaths and drum my leg some more.

His backpack catches my attention in the corner of the room. I get up and grab it. It's already open, so it's not entirely an invasion of privacy. Miles used to be very particular about people not looking into his backpack. You'd think he kept illegal stuff in it but he didn't. He was a good kid, sometimes annoyingly too good of a kid.

One look inside and I can see his textbooks from the last time he left school, homework assignments he never had the chance to turn in, exams he never threw away, and what looks like a journal. I never knew Miles kept a journal. It always seemed like he hated writing. At least, he would always complain about it when we had English assignments. I flip through it and find out it's not just *any* journal. It's his personal diary. Now I understand why he never let me or anyone else look in his backpack. He must've suspected that I'd flame him for having a diary. I don't read anything super closely, and at first the thought of Miles keeping a secret diary makes me laugh and puts a smile on my face But it also makes me think. Miles was a mystery, for sure, but now I'm left wondering if there's a side of Miles I never actually got to know.

"Keem!" Momma calls from the living room. "We're gonna head out. Your father is on duty and has to get going."

"Okay, I'll be right there," I say. I feel like I've only been here a minute, but I check my phone and it's actually been close to a half hour.

I inhale deeply and exhale even deeper. I hide the diary in my waistband and underneath my shirt, so that no one can see it. Then I search through his closet and grab a vintage Steph Curry jersey. I head into the living room, where Momma and Dad are waiting for me.

"I see you found something," Mrs. Angela says to me, cupping my face in her hands. We're the same height, but she still grabs my face like I'm a little kid. She's always done that to me.

"Yeah, it's the jersey I bought for him for Christmas last year," I say. "Nothing major." I hope they don't ask any follow-up questions or realize I have something I'm hiding in my pants.

"We'll see you all later," Momma tells Mrs. Angela. "Just let us know if you need anything, ever. We're just a phone call away."

"Why, thank you, Naomi. You've always been so good to us," Mrs. Angela says. "I'm thankful we're not going through this alone, even if it might feel like it sometimes."

"You're never alone," Momma assures her.

Mrs. Angela and Rodney both exchange looks like they're grateful.

Dad leads the way back to the squad car. I don't stop waving at Mrs. Angela, Rodney, and Rocco until we're down the road and out of sight. I'm sad that I won't be making the trek over to their

32

place as often as I used to. I used to be over there at least twice a week. The rest of the time, Miles and I would be either at my place or out doing something else, hitting the town hard. I can't believe this is really my life now.

Back at home, I flip open Miles's diary. I wonder if I'm betraying him a second time if I read it. Then I think maybe it matters more for me to find out things he never told anyone, so they don't disappear. Maybe it's selfish, but it can be my way of feeling a lot closer to him.

March 10

Hey Miles,

It's me. Well, you. Miles. Words feel like they've abandoned me, so I'm going to try to say what hurts the most here. I hope this helps. Maybe this can be something you come back to over and over again when you're hurting and in pain and don't feel like you have anywhere to turn.

Some days, I feel weak. Other days, I feel less weak. I have a tendency of only talking about the days that are going well, that make me feel good, that make me forget about all the diffi-cult things in my life. Truth is, I'm scared. I'm scared that if I talk about those days—those days that don't go so well—people around me will

begin to worry. But I don't want them to.
Worrying is meaningless. People have bad days,
that's okay. The moon doesn't stay in the sky
forever, the morning comes and will never not
come, so why can't people look at me that way?
Why can't people see that I'm changing? Miles,
I'm nervous that people will get annoyed at me if
they knew the thoughts in my head. I'm nervous
that people will hear all the darkness that's
inside me and they'll run. I might not want people
to worry about me, but I don't want them to
give up on me, either.

Dude, don't give up on yourself. Please?
For me?

Keep on keeping on.

With love,
Miles

Of course Miles wrote to himself. It's just like him to do something like that. But honestly, it's also kinda sad. Something about the words and the way that he writes makes me feel worse than I did before.

I want to read more, but I can't. This will be something I have to take in slowly, because I don't want to rush past knowing Miles deeper. I want to take my time. I want to savor every entry because I know there won't be any new ones.

My mind goes to that place again, where I wish I could go back in time, grab Miles from the road, and replay for him all our happy days, over and over. I want us to sit and eat ice cream and watch whatever horror movie he wants and talk about anything and everything. Nothing would matter besides the fact that we were with each other, like always. I wish I could be transported back to our easier moments, our quieter memories, our sweeter times, or even when things sucked and were hard, but we came to each other, committing to each other that we weren't done with life yet, we weren't done making memories.

Someone knocks on my bedroom door. The door creaks open and Momma pops in within seconds.

"Hey, honey. How are you doing?" she asks.

"I'm okay," I lie.

Her lips tighten and she nods, wiping her hands on her pants. "Look, I don't want you spending all this time in your room, isolated. I don't think it's healthy for you."

Healthy? I don't say anything. I keep my mouth shut.

"I'm making your favorite for dinner. Are you gonna join us tonight?"

"I'll try to," I say. It's the least I can say. I can tell Momma's sad that I haven't spent a lot of time with her or Dad or Judah and Jorjah since Miles died. I don't entirely want to see her like this, either. It's bad enough to be sad about Miles, but now she's sad about me and I don't like that.

"Okay, I hear you," she says. "Also, this came for you in the mail today."

She tosses me a large envelope that says *Indiana State University*. My eyes light up and I swallow hard. Miles and I both dreamed we'd go to college together somewhere. ISU was at the top of our list.

"I didn't open it," she says. "But that took a lot of self-restraint."

I stare at the envelope from ISU. Part of me wants to burn it, for obvious reasons. Part of me wants to open it. Then I think about Miles all over again. He would want me to open it. I would want him to do that if the situation were the other way around. So that's what I do. I rip it open.

The first words cause my mouth to fall clean open.

Dear Mr. Hakeem Lee Hawkins,

Congratulations! We are pleased to offer you admission to Indiana State University . . .

I could puke.

I mean, I'm excited, but I also feel so much guilt. This is too much to take in right now. I shouldn't have even opened it.

I hand it over to Momma, who whoops with joy when she reads what it says. She hugs me so hard, and I hug her back, but it's more for her than for me. She must sense this, because she doesn't ask anything more of me. I think it's understood that she'll be the one to tell Dad and, I'd guess, the rest of the world. I don't have the energy to do that.

I know I should be happy, but I just can't get there.

Once Momma and the letter are gone, I pull the box that Mikki gave me from underneath my bed. I've been avoiding opening it for reasons I'm not entirely sure of. I remove the lid and I see a couple T-shirts, a miniature *Star Wars* lightsaber, a bottle of cologne, and a bunch of other random small items that Miles may have gifted Mikki throughout their relationship. I'm not sure why she didn't keep any of this stuff. Their breakup was mutual, so I'm sure she's not holding any hard feelings.

I pull out the bottle of cologne to smell it. Well, shit. It smells just like Miles. Miles had this distinct smell that no one else I know has. I could pick him out of a lineup of people while being blindfolded. It's this cologne.

I spray a bit on myself, imagining that he's here with me. I take a breath and fall back onto my bed, staring up at my ceiling. *Miles, I miss you.*

Smothered chicken fried steak and mashed potatoes. That's what Momma makes for what she's now calling a celebration dinner. It's my favorite thing she makes. We rarely have it because she usually only makes it when something bad happens. When Granny died, smothered chicken fried steak for dinner. When Mom's younger brother, Uncle Peanut, got sent to jail, smothered chicken fried steak. And when Dad got suspended from his job that one time last year, smothered chicken fried steak. I'm sure she's making it tonight not just because of the college news but also because she knows how down I've been and she's trying to pick up my spirits. I'm thankful for the way she shows her love.

Dad was also full of no-pressure congratulations when I came down. Now I look at him and his bald head and full beard, imagining if one day I'll look like him even more. Kind brown eyes and wrinkles around his mouth that he's earned. And I wonder if I'll be like him, too. Dad of the century. A hard worker. Always there for his kids. Dad used to cut my hair when I was a kid. It was nice getting haircuts from him on the weekends. As I got older, he cut my hair less and then one day he stopped altogether, and I had to start going to the barbershop. It was hard not getting to bond with my dad like that, but I guess that's what it means to grow up. He still cuts Judah's hair, which always takes me back.

I wolf down a forkful of steak and mashed potatoes. I'm so hungry. This food is normally fire, but it's on a whole other level right now.

"How is it?" Momma asks everyone.

Judah and Jorjah nod their satisfaction.

"Really good, Mommy," Jorjah says.

Judah can't even stop stuffing his face to say anything.

"It's spectacular, my dear," Dad says to her and winks. Momma gives him a smile and winks back at him. I'm not really sure what that's about, but I'm going to try and ignore it.

"How about for you, Keem?"

"Fire," I say. "Tastes better than I remember."

Momma gives me a big smile. She has the biggest smiles, and I love that they always reveal the tiny gap between her two front teeth.

"ISU hit the jackpot with accepting you," Dad says.

Momma lets out a loud squeal like an animal. "Yes, yes, yes, yes! I'm so excited for you, Keem. It's a big deal. I'm so proud of you."

"Thank you," I say. I can tell I don't match their level of energy.

"My son's gonna be a college man," Momma says with some pride, forking around on her plate.

"What's college?" Judah asks through a mouthful of food, mashed potatoes all over his face. This kid is cute. He's got a short fade, his left ear pierced, a dark complexion, and he's tall for an eight-year-old. He's a cuter kid than I was when I was his age.

"It's the place you go to after high school," Momma explains the best she can to him.

"What? You mean there's more school after that?" Judah asks, his face wearing confusion and sadness.

Momma nods. "You can always be in school," she whispers across the table to him.

"Noooo!" Judah complains. "I hate school. I don't want to go to college."

"EW. Me either," Jorjah says. "I want to be a princess."

"Well, we will cross that bridge later," Dad rebuts before taking a sip of wine.

I'm actually laughing at that, but then, as if the universe doesn't want me to be *too* happy, my phone buzzes in my pocket with a notification for a movie night with Miles. Damn. I forgot all about that. Miles and I would watch a movie together every Saturday night. We'd alternate if we would watch it at his place, mine, or the movie theater. I always liked watching it at his place because he had a projector and we could literally watch a movie on his ceiling or outside if we wanted to. I forgot that it was still in my calendar. I can tell this is the beginning of a long journey ahead. That I'm just at the start of understanding the way that grief creeps up on you in small increments, when you least expect it, reminding you of all you've lost. So many things will remind me of Miles, I'm sure. It just sucks that we're wired like that, to miss someone we love so deeply when we can't ever see them again, no matter how hard we try. One little thing happens, one little reminder, and it's like he's dying all over again.

CHAPTER FOUR

Later that night, I read more from Miles's diary.

March 22

Hey Miles,

It's your boy again. How are you today? I hope as you reread this, you're doing better than you are right now as you write it. Today, I feel like a literal flaming hot piece of shit. I broke up with Mikki. She was sweet. Always wanted to help. Always wanted to make me feel loved. Always wanted to save me from myself. I was important to her. She was important to me, too, but the truth is, I don't deserve her. I'll never deserve her. I'm nothing, but she's . . . everything.

I gotta admit it. I miss kissing her just as much as I miss the feeling of being safe when I'm with her, when we're cuddling or just gazing into each other's eyes. And I miss our deep talks, too—the talks we'd have about everything and nothing at the same time. But I made her deal with things she should have never had to deal with. She's not my savior, my mother, my protector. I couldn't get out of my own ass enough to be able to let her love me. I had to let her walk. I had to set her free. Miles, do you think I'm capable of accepting love? Like, truly accepting it? I heard once that we accept the kind of love that we think we deserve. Do you believe that?

With love,
Miles

April 2

Miles,

You don't deserve to be happy. You don't deserve to be happy. You don't deserve to be happy. You don't deserve to be happy. You don't deserve to be happy. You don't deserve to be happy. You don't deserve to be happy. You don't deserve to be happy. You don't deserve to be happy. You don't deserve to be happy. You don't deserve to be happy. You don't deserve to be happy. You don't deserve to be happy. You don't deserve to be happy. You don't deserve to be happy. You don't deserve to be happy. You don't deserve to be happy. You don't

deserve to be happy. You don't deserve to be
happy. You don't deserve to be happy. You don't
deserve to be happy. You don't deserve to be
happy. You don't deserve to be happy. You
don't deserve to be happy. You don't deserve to
be happy. You don't deserve to be happy. You
don't deserve to be happy. You don't deserve to
be happy. You don't deserve to be happy. You're
such a burden to everyone around you. Can't
you see it?

With no love,
Miles

This . . . this is a lot. And I don't know how to deal with it.

CHAPTER FIVE

Four months.

121 days.

2,904 hours.

174,240 minutes.

That's how long I've been clean. That's how long I've successfully resisted the urge to use. I haven't even taken ibuprofen when I've got a headache out of fear that it'll trigger me into using other things again. Honestly, I'm proud of myself that I've come this far.

The first time I used, I was in eighth grade, and I had just discovered that I was into both guys and girls. I downloaded this app called MatchUps and matched with this guy named Cody. I was fourteen and he was nineteen, which was as exciting as it was risky. He told me I could come over for a good time. It all started that night with edibles and alcohol, but it eventually led to more. Momma had just found out that Dad cheated on her with one of her best friends, Ms. Shonda, who Momma has since completely cut off from her life. The screaming and fighting at home just became too much. I'd come home from school, and they would literally be fistfighting each other in the living room, the house a total train wreck. I even saw Momma break a glass jar over Dad's head and he bled all over the walls, the carpet, and his clothes. And because they kept fighting so much, Momma stopped cooking, stopped working, stopped leaving her bed altogether. She was broken for a long time. Dad was gone a lot, so it was really up to me to make sure I ate, to make sure Jorjah and Judah were okay, too. In a way, I was forced to grow up way too soon. I was just a kid, but that didn't matter to them back then. I'm glad things are different now.

Smoking weed and taking pills in large amounts helped me forget all about my situation at home. It was the idea of being transported out of my own skin, out of my own life, that did it for me. It was enough to keep me coming back for more and coming back for more and coming back for more. I'd use again whenever I felt like I lost control of my life. That's what it was all about—losing control, reclaiming power. It's as simple as that. It was like suddenly I was stuck in the world's worst hurricane, and I couldn't get out, no matter how hard I tried. The water would tide over me and swallow me whole. The wind would be deafening, the rain drowned out my heartbeat. I'd need to take in whatever would get me the quickest high so I couldn't feel hurt by the storm. That's the thing about using: Within seconds, the whole world disappears, and all my problems go away with it. Alcohol usually did the same, but I didn't always like that buzzed feeling and I didn't like the way that my stomach hurt because of the way the alcohol was sitting inside my body. Feeling bloated is next to death in my book.

By the time I started high school, I had found some hookups for pills, and was supporting it by reselling some to people on MatchUps. It was a good business model for me for a while, until Principal Samuels found out that I had shared my pills with a classmate—luckily I hadn't sold them to him, just shared. It was decided that I would do virtual school for the rest of the year while I cleaned up my act, which absolutely sucked balls. I guess things could've been way worse, looking back at the situation. Principal Samuels could've reported it all to the police, but he didn't. Dad, being a police officer and knowing how to sweet-talk just about anybody, was able to convince Principal Samuels that he would take care of it himself. Something about not wanting to ruin my future by sending me to juvie and something about wanting to have a "healthier" and better rehabilitation plan for me.

The rest is history. A stern talking-to from my parents, an intense six weeks in a rehab place, therapy with Dr. Chandler, and dozens of Narcotics Anonymous meetings later, I've given all that up. One of the first things I learned at an NA meeting was that there will always be drugs no matter what. The best way to beat addiction is to think beyond it—to understand that it is not drugs but addiction that's the true enemy. Addiction steals, kills, and destroys, but there's always time to choose life. That is exactly what I did. I chose my life.

School the following Monday is a whole thing. Not only is there yet another convocation about suicide prevention because so many students skipped out or were absent for the last one, but they put up posters all over the school for the suicide hotline and facts about people who are hurting and signs they might exhibit.

Before second period, I'm exchanging books at my locker when Mikki comes over and says in a quiet but high-pitched voice, "Hey!"

"Hey, Mikki."

"I see you're wearing Miles's *Star Wars* drip."

I look down. I completely forgot. I wonder if I'm the only one who finds comfort in wearing their dead best friend's Darth Vader sweatshirt. It's warm, but it's also like hugging Miles.

"You look good in it," Mikki says with a grin, showing her braces. Then she diverts her eyes and goes quiet, fidgeting with her hands for a moment. People walk by, brushing shoulders with both of us, like they can't see we're having a conversation—or standing here awkwardly in silence. Then she spits it out. "This might be a, umm, weird question to ask you. But . . . have you been dreaming about him?"

I don't hesitate on answering that one. "It's not all the time, but yeah, of course. You?"

"I do, too. Some of them are scary, but my mom says that's just him letting me know that he's okay in Heaven."

"Ah, I see," I say, nodding. "That's cool."

"Yeah, I think so, too." She runs a hand through her curly hair and pushes back her bright, hot pink headband. Mikki's always in a headband or scarf. It's like her brand. "Hey, I hope you like all the stuff I gave you. Well, all the stuff that he gave me."

"Yeah," I say. "It's been nice holding on to pieces of him." Maybe if I collect enough pieces, like a puzzle, I'll be able to resurrect him or something.

"Do you think he ever missed being with me?"

I think for a second. I know what she *wants* to hear, so I just tell her, "Yeah, I think he did."

Mikki smiles like I just made her day with this half lie. Miles missed being with Mikki, there's no denying that, but he also loved *not* being with Mikki.

For a moment, I think about telling Mikki about Miles's diary, but then I think that sharing what he wrote would probably cause her more pain. I don't want to be a dickhead right now. I'll save her more heartbreak. Besides, who knows what else might be in this journal? I figure it's best for me to finish it all before letting anyone else know anything about it.

I keep my mouth shut and tell Mikki that I gotta get to class. The bell rings and we go separate ways. She goes toward the east wing for English and I go to the west wing for Biology.

I have the diary in my bag, hidden just like it was in Miles's. Between classes, I find an empty spot in the school and read another entry in secret, when no one else is looking. It's honestly how I'm getting by these days. Reading an entry in this diary, no matter how sad or depressed it makes me, is like reclaiming time with Miles.

There's one entry that I read after third period that completely flips my day upside down—or right side up, I don't know. But it causes my stomach to feel like it's on fire from the inside. It causes every hair on my body to stand up, like when there's a jump scare in a really scary movie.

May 22

Yo Miles,

Can you keep a secret? I think I like Keem.
I mean, of course I like Keem. He's my homie.

We've been homies since we were kids. He always had my back, and I always had his. But I mean, I think I like, like Keem. Like the way I liked Mikki, but a little bit different.

I discovered this last night as we were watching *Final Destination 3* together. We were lying in my bed, watching on my projector. We were sharing a bowl of popcorn (with extra butter, just the way I like it) and we kept reaching in at the same time and our hands would touch. We'd just laugh and look at each other before quickly looking away. And when he left for the night, after the movie was all over, I missed him. I missed him more than I've ever missed anyone else before. You see, Keem knows me better than anyone in the world knows me. He gets me, he sees me. And I get and see him right back. I feel like I'm on top of the world when I'm with him. Naturally, I hold my breath, chills shoot up my back, and butterflies flutter in my belly. Bro. I've never felt this strongly before. EVER.

I'm writing to you because I don't know what to do. I think I'm gonna settle on keeping my mouth shut, like with duct tape and everything. I don't want to make things weird with Keem and me...I *like what we've built and what we have going for us. He's my guy for life. I don't want Ma and Pops pissed at me, either. Miles from the future, if you ever change your mind about any of this, you know what to do.*

With love,
Miles

Holy shit.

Holy shit.

HOLY. SHIT!!!!!!!

There's no doubting what Miles just wrote. He might've been in love with me. Scratch that. Not *might've been*, he was *definitely* in love with me. But he felt like he couldn't tell me. Maybe he didn't want to ruin our friendship or maybe he just wasn't ready, I don't know, but suddenly everything I once believed goes out the window.

My best friend loved me, and I loved him, but now, for the first time ever, I'm left wondering if we loved each other in more ways than one. It's too much of a mindfuck, too much on top of everything else. It's not just the answers to my questions that died with Miles. His feelings died, too. And now I'm stuck wondering, thinking, wishing, on an endless loop.

Does this change anything?

How can it?

How can it *not*?

I hate that Miles never told me any of this. To be honest, I don't know if we would've worked, but it would've been nice to know. I like the thought of us together in that way. I mean, the thought had crossed my mind dozens of times before, but like always, I minimized those feelings and said that Miles and I would always make sense as *just* friends. But that was because I thought he wasn't into guys like I was into guys. Now . . . I don't know what to think. I thought my best friend was going to be frozen in the past, but now I see there's still more of him being thawed out.

I want to hit rewind all the way back to being face-to-face with Miles again, just to ask him about how he really feels. But this is real life and I've got to keep moving forward knowing the truth— truth that I'll never get to hear directly from the source. Truth that I'll never get to pursue further.

Dammit, Miles.

All my words abandon me for a moment.

I'm too stunned, staring at this journal entry.

And then I remember Momma telling me that people are like jigsaw puzzles. You'll always be trying to piece them together. And sometimes you put all the pieces together quick. Other times, it takes a little bit longer. But there might also be times where you never get the full picture because, over time, you get caught up in your own broken pieces and have no time for anyone else's.

And that's the thing about time. It's the fucking worst kind of friend. It's only there when you don't really need it and gone and nowhere to be found when you do. Time just stays still, making all the hurt feel amplified.

I try my best to imagine Miles telling me this to my face, but my imagination won't even work. I'm feeling every emotion at once and my brain is too clouded. If I could hit rewind on life, this wouldn't be so hard.

I'll never be able to hear him say these words out loud, but I still believe him.

After school, I drive to the cemetery to see Miles before heading to group. Well, not to see Miles, but to see his grave. When I get there, his plot is covered in flowers, notes, signs, and pictures of him. Some of the pictures have me in them, but many of them are pictures people drew or painted of him.

I look around and it's just me here, it seems. It's quiet, almost too quiet. And it's like all the dead here are truly resting in peace. It's that time of day where the sun is just about to start setting, so the sky is a mixture of blues and oranges and pinks.

I sit down on the cold ground right in front of this sign where his headstone is going to go. It reads:

MILES JAMES PARKER—
GONE BUT NOT FORGOTTEN—
BELOVED SON, NEPHEW,
COUSIN, AND FRIEND

I don't even care about getting my pants dirty at this point, none of that matters.

For the longest time, I just stare at his name and blink, blink,

blink. I'm blinking too much and then the tears come. What starts as a slow trickle of tears down my face leads into me uncontrollably sobbing in this cemetery. I cry so hard that I give myself hiccups, which causes me to have to practice taking deep breaths just to calm myself down.

"Miles . . ." I say his name, but it comes out with a sob, a groan too deep for words.

I pause and wait, almost like I'm expecting him to respond. But he doesn't. Wind, the road, and birds chirping in the distance are all I can hear right now.

"I've been reading your diary, man. I'm sorry if you hate me for doing that. You haven't started haunting me yet, so I take it there's maybe something in it you wanted me to find. That's like you." I laugh, sniffling a little.

The wind picks up around me as leaves rustle and shuffle on the ground. I shiver.

"I wish you would've told me," I tell him, rubbing my hand over the patch of grass and dirt in front of his temporary headstone.

I pause all over again. Nothing but the same. Only quiet. I think back to the moment I first told Miles that I thought I was gay. We were in the parking lot of a Pizza Hut, leaving from getting free breadsticks and cinnamon bites. I looked at him with tears in my eyes, telling him about how I'd been sneaking around with guys in secret, but I couldn't hold that from him much longer. But then I told him about how I still felt like I liked girls—or at least I had been drooling over Nicki Minaj, Zendaya, Ariana Grande, and Zoë Kravitz. I still had a type like that. That's when Miles told me it sounded like I was bisexual or pan. I had no idea what the difference was, but I remember googling them all night only to find out no label really described me, no box felt big enough for me to put myself in. Miles was so accepting, so loving. He was the best listener and the best friend I could ever ask for. I just . . . I'm at a loss for words.

I take a deep breath.

"I love you, Miles," I say. "I wish we could've talked about us before you died."

I grab a handful of dirt around me and crumble it up in my hands, watching it fall through my fingers, just like Miles fell right out of my life—slowly and then all at once.

"Hey there." My stomach does a dip. I turn away quick and jolt to my feet. It's . . . Eliza. What the heck is she doing here? Has she been following me? She looks me up and down, peeks at Miles's name, and then makes eye contact with me again before adding, "This was your friend?"

I look down at the ground. "My best friend," I say, gulping down fresh air and then wiping away at my face as quickly as I can. "What are you doing here?"

"That's a funny thing to ask," she says, then motions around us. "Visiting the dead, duh."

I guess that was a silly question on my part. I don't know what to say back to that. I just blink.

"My older sister is buried right over there. I came to see her, and then I saw your car," Eliza explains.

"Your sister?"

54

"Yeah," she says with a sad face, putting her hands in the pockets of her jacket. "She died when she was nine. I was five."

"I'm sorry to hear that. What happened?" I ask. It's like all boundaries go out the door in cemeteries. So many stories are here, buried beneath this ground. I don't hold back, I can't.

"I don't exactly remember, if I'm being honest. My parents blame me. Apparently, in their version of the story, I got mad at her and pushed her down a flight of stairs."

"Oh my god. So you—"

"Yeah, I guess so," she says, cutting me off, like she doesn't want me to say any more.

"Holy shit. That's terrible and awful and sad. I'm so sorry," I tell her.

"Talk about trauma, eh?" She takes a breath. "And thanks, but it's okay. Shortly after that, my parents became really abusive to me, and once I made it to high school, I had enough, and they had enough, and here I am. There comes a point when you realize that you can never please everyone, you can never force anyone to forgive you, and you can never stop someone from absolutely hating your guts. The only solution you have left is to not give a shit anymore."

I don't know what to say to someone spilling their insides out to me, but it sucks that this has been her life. "Thanks for sharing all that with me. That sounds really hard," I say. *Really, Keem? That's all you can come up with?*

"It sounded at group like you're having a hard time, too," she says. "You must miss him."

"Yeah, I do."

She leans over and puts her hand on his grave. "Nice to meet you, Miles," she says. Then, straightening up, she says, "They can still hear us. At least, that's what I believe. I tell myself that Paige can hear me apologizing to her about what happened every day. I have to believe that. It's my only hope."

I nod at her, understanding what she means. I'm sure there's something really comforting believing in that. I wish it was true, like proven by some kind of scientific study. Maybe then I wouldn't feel this terrible ache in my chest all the damn time.

"Hey, you should take my number down," she says.

"Um, okay," I say, pulling out my phone, passing it to her.

She puts her number in my phone kinda quick and tosses it back to me like a hot potato.

"I texted myself from your phone so I have your number, too."

I look at my message log and see that she sent herself a flower emoji.

I wonder what that's about, but before I can even think to ask her, she's walking off into the sunset like in some cheesy rom-com movie.

Hey, wait, I want to call out to her. But I don't. I just let her go, heading wherever she's going next. Something in me feels scared that this is the last time I'll see her, but then I think about group. I'll see her there.

Eventually, when I get to group, though, I realize that's all just wishful thinking. No sign of her there, either. Funny enough, at group, we end up talking about the ways that addicts sometimes disappear. We talk about the void addicts leave, how we slip through the cracks of people's lives like smoke. The whole time, I'm half listening, scanning the room for her to show up, hoping the door creaks open. But it stays stubbornly shut.

Later on, I end up at home, staring at my laptop in my bedroom with all the lights off. I make a Facebook page for Miles's memory. Within minutes, I've got a handful of people following it, including Mikki, August, Miles's parents, and a bunch of people from school. I'm hoping the number grows.

It takes a while, but I upload a bunch of photos from my phone onto the Facebook page. There's a picture that I took of Miles from when he was working at a gas station down the road from his house. He's in his uniform and everything. There's another one of the two of us at McDonald's eating the McRib when it came back for the last time. And then there's one of us when we went as Batman and Robin at Mikki's big Halloween bash. I remember us getting really drunk that night, like blacked out, like can't-remember-anything-the-next-day kind of drunk. A drink or two or three or four or even five would be nice right about now if it'd help me forget that Miles isn't physically here anymore. But I tell myself no. *No, no, no.*

I can go another four months.

Another 121 days.

Another 2,904 hours.

Another 174,240 minutes.

I've come along too far to just stop right now. I won't stop. I won't go back.

CHAPTER SIX

I work a part-time job at Cousin Vinny's Pizza whenever I can. The manager, Frankie, is real cool like that. He knows I only want a job because I like having my own money and hate having to ask Momma or Dad. And because I'm in high school, he lets me show up whenever I want to as long as I come in when he needs me and cover shifts for people when they call off.

Cousin Vinny's isn't the worst place to work. Before that, I worked as a sweeper at a barbershop and before that I was bagging old people's groceries at the downtown farm stand. This job is by far my favorite. Not only is Frankie the best boss I've ever had, he knows my family. He and my dad went to college together, but Frankie dropped out after his first year because of partying and drinking. You can see why he felt like he needed to take a chance on me. He could probably see a lot of himself in me.

Frankie used to have three locations in the city. One downtown, one on the south side, and one on the west side. Last summer, he closed his westside and southside locations. He's down to just the one shop now, which is both more manageable and sad. If Frankie's business doesn't pick up, Cousin Vinny's will be just as extinct as the Cuban sandwich shop that used to be next door. And that means I'll be out of a job. I'm hoping things stay afloat long enough for me to finish high school.

It's been mostly dead here all afternoon. We've had a couple customers—a college frat boy who wanted two large pepperoni pizzas and an old Black lady who just wanted an order of breadsticks with nacho cheese. Other than that, I've been standing around and scrolling through videos on Instagram and TikTok.

"Here you go, kid," Frankie says, handing me an envelope with my name on it.

Today's payday. My cash is in this envelope. I grab it and shove it in my pocket, so I don't lose it.

The money I used to make went directly to weed and booze, but now that I've kinda turned my life around, the money goes straight to my savings account. Ever since I learned about how helpful savings can be in the future, I've been putting twenty dollars a paycheck into it. My future self will thank me later. Momma and Dad might make enough money now, but who knows what the future holds?

"Back when I was your age . . ."

I never get tired of Frankie's stories. They're truly one of a kind. Frankie's a type of guy who's been around the world and back. He's seen some things in his day, life leaving a deep mark of wisdom on him in the process. Things that I've learned about Frankie: He used to be in a gang; he used to sell cocaine; he once illegally crossed the border to Mexico and was detained there for a whole year; and he was the first white guy to go to Morehouse College. I don't know how true that last part is, but Frankie's convinced of it, so I am, too. It might be more accurate to say he was the first white guy to go to Morehouse College and drop out within six months. I'm sure not many people are fighting to hold that record.

My phone buzzes.

Usually, it's a text from Miles. Not this time.

It's a text from Eliza.

Eliza: Hi 👋

Me: Hey there

Eliza: 3160 tons of water flows over Niagara Falls every second. Incredible, right?

Me: . . . okay?

Eliza: Gotta go.

Me: Gotta go where?

And that's it, she doesn't respond, doesn't say anything else. I can tell she's read my message, but she chooses to not reply. I can hear Miles telling me all about how this girl is bad news anyway, just based off the way she's ghosting me, but Miles was always the dramatic one like that.

The following Monday, I find the early morning car ride to school particularly annoying. Between almost every single stoplight on my usual route being "out" and made into blinking red lights, which is just a worse version of a four-way stop, and thinking about Miles and how I would often pick him up and drive him with me, it's all too much. Miles should be telling me jokes at the buttcrack of dawn as we cruise all the way to Center Grove High School, annoying me with how hard he tries to make me laugh. Miles should be complaining about some small aspect of teenagerhood that grinds his gears. He should be giving me some kind of lecture about why adults don't understand kids. He should be telling me all about whatever new scary movie he watched the night before and what he put as his review on Letterboxd.

This ride is too quiet.

Walking into Center Grove High School makes me want to turn around and get back into bed. It's another day, another reminder that Miles is not here and I am forced to do the rest of my high school career without him. I will one day walk across a graduation stage and they will just call his name and we will be forced into some stupid moment of silence. He should be *here*, not in the silence.

I pass Miles's locker, reminding me of all the *Fortnite* and *Texas Chainsaw Massacre* stickers still there. Oblivious groups of students chatter and laugh around it, their happy faces almost turning me violent, making me feel more alone than ever with this heavy weight of grief in my heart.

I grab books from my locker that I'll need for the day. Chemistry, US History, and my copy of *The Catcher in the Rye* for Mr. Sanchez's English class.

Mr. Sanchez is waiting outside his classroom before I walk in. He's the type of teacher who always dresses in a relevant style and isn't actually that much older than us high school students. He's a favorite around here because he runs the GSA and lets students listen to music on our phones while we're in his class. He's quite eccentric and his teaching is the same. He clutches his black cardigan closed and gives me a certain look like he wants to talk with

61

me. Sure enough, as I get close he says, "Hakeem . . ." Lines form on his light-brown forehead.

"Yes, Mr. Sanchez?" Something stirs in my stomach. I don't want to be asked about Miles. I'm silently praying that's not what he wants to talk about.

"How are you doing?" he asks me. He pulls out a cough drop and pops it in his mouth. It's a strong cherry medicine smell that meets my nose, but it's not the only reason I want to throw up.

I don't know how to answer that. All my words seem to leave me. All I can think to say as an answer is, "I'm hanging in there."

"That's about all we can do when we lose someone close to us," Mr. Sanchez says, like he's offering me new words of wisdom I've never heard before.

I nod at him, clutching my copy of *The Catcher in the Rye* at my side.

He goes on, "I lost my best friend when I was your age to a similar tragic accident. The only thing that made it easier was, well, time. Give it some time and you'll see that Miles is right here." Mr. Sanchez gestures to his chest, to his heart.

I give a small, faint smile and divert my eyes.

"If you need anything at all, I'm here for you, kid. Okay?" he says sweetly.

I nod again. "Thanks, Mr. Sanchez. Means a lot."

At lunch, as I'm heading to my usual lunch table, Mikki stops me.

"Want to sit with us?" She nods at the table where she, August, and their friends are. Some of them I recognize from other classes. Once upon a time, when Miles was dating Mikki, he would sit there. I hesitate, but then agree. Whatever awkwardness there is between August and me, it'll have to die for at least a little bit.

I sit down at their table and it gets strangely quiet. I know if I weren't here, the conversation would be booming. But now that I'm here, I'm the equivalent to the elephant in the room. I open a packet of mayo and spread it on the bun of my spicy chicken sandwich. It feels like all eyes are on me, which makes me start to sweat nervously, my leg shaking beneath the table.

Through bites of chicken sandwich, I wonder if I'm making the right choice and if it's worth it to just gather my things and go back to my usual spot.

I wonder if telling Mikki about what I've been reading in Miles's journal is a good thing, but then I think . . . maybe that's not exactly the best way to break the ice. I'm just annoyed that I haven't had anyone to talk about his diary with. I wonder if Mikki knows any of the things Miles wrote. I wonder what she would say if she read them now.

I wonder a lot of things, but right now, they will all have to stay in my head.

The next time I'm at group, it's Wednesday and Eliza isn't there. I'm not entirely sure why, but I wait for her to walk in during the whole hour. When she doesn't come, I feel sad. I guess I was wrong. The last time I saw her was *it*. She still hasn't responded to me from the last text exchange we had, and I wonder what's up with that. We're not, like, friends or anything, so I have no room to feel upset or bothered, but something doesn't feel *right* about it. I felt this feeling before with Miles and chose to do nothing about it. And look at where that landed him.

Yolanda leads us through a meditation of some sort where we inhale and then exhale all of our troubles. Some people sob and weep between breaths, but I shut my eyes and all I can see is Miles's face. I see him alive, not dead. Every time I think about him, I think about him when he still had life in him. That's the best version of him.

I inhale and exhale nicely, slowly, and deeply. One thing that comes to mind is the diary. It's like one of the only pieces of him I've got left, but the anxiety and guilt of holding on to it and reading it is becoming unbearable. My eyes find their way, flickering all over the place as I try to distract myself from what I'm feeling all of a sudden, this knot in my gut that's getting thicker and thicker. I look at the walls, stained and peeling, filled with graffiti and signs of years of neglect. I look at the chairs arranged in a circle, each one filled with weary faces and tired eyes. I look at the makeshift podium near the front, covered in old flyers and pamphlets. One flyer catches my eye in particular.

It's for some program called Odds and Ends, an anonymous app that pairs you up with someone who is also going through some kind of loss or grief. I snap a picture of it and save it for later. It's intriguing, but I'm not so sure I've reached that level of desperation yet. I mean, I had a sponsor before. Wesley was his name. Tall, red hair, glasses, a few years clean from heroin. Somewhat metrosexual. He was a pretty cool dude, but the weird thing about having a sponsor was that it always seemed like someone was watching over my shoulder, judging my every move, comparing it to some addictive behavior deep inside me. Maybe that's the whole point of sponsorship—having someone bring to light the things you can't see? Part of me knows how helpful Wesley was, but the other part of me is glad he moved all the way to Colorado.

At the end of group, Yolanda asks if anyone needs or wants to share anything. I wait in the longest stillness kind of silence until no one raises their hand. There are empty seats around me, which means one or two things when you're at a group like this: Either there are people who gave up or there are people who have passed away. It's a harsh reality, but it's what happens at places like this. Some people bend, some people completely snap, losing all the fight left in them. They use again. And it only takes that one time to send them spiraling further and further away from group and having to start from the beginning all over again.

Sometimes you can tell how long people will be here and sometimes you can't because the thing about addiction is that it's unpredictable. It's easy for the biased voice in your head to convince you that the people who come here in dirty clothes and looking rough are the ones who won't make it and that the ones who come in wearing fancy, clean clothes, have their hair combed, and are wearing makeup are the ones who will live to tell the tale of victory, but that's not how it works. The best metric to determine how long people will be here is actually paying attention to what they tell you. Often, they mention their triggers, cravings, and how they're really doing. It's always in the language. That's what I've learned.

Group gets released, and the moment I walk outside, my phone buzzes. It's a text from Eliza. *Finally.*

Eliza: Wanna smoke a joint?

Me: ummm

Eliza: A JOKE. Relax.

Eliza: I can make those jokes when I am in NA, right? Anyway, what I really was going to ask is if you want to get a milkshake later on tonight.

I text back a thumbs-up and she agrees to pick me up at my house. I give Momma a good excuse as to why I'm going to head out after dinner. A school project, I tell her. It's something believable and one my parents won't ask many questions about. They want me to focus on my schooling. They want me to get good grades. It's not like I need to hide hanging out with Eliza from them, but explaining her to them is way more complicated than lying.

CHAPTER   SEVEN

When I get back home, I lie in bed, staring at my popcorn-textured ceiling, thinking about my last text exchange with Miles. I consider texting back, after all this time, but it's not like that'll do anything besides give me an out-of-service message—and that might make the pain even worse. No use to pouring rubbing alcohol on an open wound like that.

I get the idea to scroll through my call log and I see a voicemail that I never actually listened to from Miles. I haven't heard his voice in so long, way too long. My finger glides over the call and I almost delete it on accident, a gasp slipping from deep within me, my heart racing, like I just about did the worst thing I could ever do in the universe. I close my eyes and take a breath. Then I click play.

▶ Yo! It's me. I was just calling you to see if you wanted to go to the mall with me. LeBron just dropped his new shoes. I can't afford them, but I at least want to look at them. Also, answer your damn phone next time. You know I hate leaving these. It reminds me of my grandmother. Anyway, goodbye. Also, play me back on *Clash of Clans* already.

I press play again. And then again. And then again. And then before I know it, I'm on my twenty-fourth listen. Just the comfort of hearing his voice makes life a little more bearable. I'm just about to hit play for the twenty-fifth time when Momma sends Jorjah and Judah up to get me for dinner. I should've known she wouldn't let me leave the house before forcing me to put something in my belly, even if it was for a "school project."

Judah and Jorjah jump in my bed, singing a song that they made up where they just repeat "It's time to eat, it's time to eat" in an annoying voice, the one little kids use for every damn thing.

"Okay, okay," I give in. "I'll be down in a second." This does the trick and gets them to leave, allowing me to regroup before sitting at the dinner table.

When I'm at the table, the whole family is there. Momma, Dad, Judah, and Jorjah. A beautiful platter of baked potatoes and all the toppings you can think of sits before me. A Crock-Pot filled with roast, carrots, onions, and peppers causes my mouth to water.

Despite what's going on in my thoughts, I manage to put enough food on my plate to satisfy Momma. I pick through it, taking small forkfuls here and there, but enough to keep her from asking if I hate her cooking now.

I get a text from Eliza asking for my address. I send it to her and she says that she's a few minutes out. My parents don't seem thrilled that I'm jumping away from the table before dinner is over, but they don't stand in my way, either. I wait for her outside, near the end of the driveway. She sends me her location, so I can track when she'll be here. I kick at a rock on the ground and scroll through my phone's voicemails, searching for another one from Miles but coming up empty-handed.

I remember something I read about someone who lost a loved one and processed their feelings by calling the phone number of the one who died and leaving their own voicemail. I thought it was absolutely insane to do such a thing, but now I'm thinking maybe they were onto something.

Eliza is about three minutes away, so if I'm going to make a move and leave my own voicemail, I need to do it now.

I make up my mind.

I can't wait.

I scroll through and find Miles's contact. I click call and the phone rings. I'm so glad it still rings and doesn't immediately give me an alert that this number doesn't exist.

Of course, no one answers, but the answering machine lady leads me through the process of leaving a voicemail.

When the beep blares, I don't know what to say.

It takes way too long, but eventually, my brain does what it's supposed to do and allows me to form sentences. "Miles . . . it's me. I don't know what to say . . . It's not like you will ever hear this, but they say this might help me feel like things are . . . normal. I don't know what normal is. I don't know if I'll ever know what normal is. I just wanted you to know that I miss you and I think of you often. I don't know if I can survive high school without you. I don't know if I want to, either. Miles . . . I . . . I've been reading your diary. I'm sorry if that feels like a big no-no or like I'm invading your privacy, but it just makes me feel close to you, and that helps me. I know it's selfish but . . ."

A vehicle beeps its horn as bright headlights approach me.

I look up and see Eliza sticking her head out the window. My mouth widens as the gears turn and it hits me that it's a . . . hearse. Eliza drives a hearse, like the thing you drive dead bodies in, taking them to the funeral and then to be buried. Like the thing Miles had to ride in.

I click off my voicemail and shove my phone in my pants pocket. That's it. If I want to say more, I'll have to try again later.

"Well, are you gonna get in or no?" Eliza says, almost cheerfully. My feet do what they're supposed to do. The ten-minute ride in a hearse is painful. It feels like an eternity—every bump, every turn, every stoplight, I'm reminded of the day we buried Miles. I'm sure it isn't hard for Eliza to see my discomfort as I hold my breath as much as I can. For whatever reason, she chooses not to ask about it or even acknowledge the tension clearly filling the inside of the hearse. She cranks up the volume on the radio and allows the latest Olivia Rodrigo album to fill the car instead of conversation.

The moment we pull up at Shake Shack is such a relief. As we walk inside, a chime sounds off, alerting the workers that new customers have come in. A man in a black baseball cap and black apron comes out and approaches the register. It's strangely empty for the middle of the week.

"How can I help you guys?" the man asks. His name badge says *Jim*.

Eliza and I exchange glances, telepathically deciding who is going to order first. She wins.

"I'll just take a chocolate milkshake," she says.

"I'll do the maple snickerdoodle milkshake," I say, after a little while of thinking. I'm usually a plain vanilla type of guy. But the picture of the maple snickerdoodle milkshake on the menu looks too good to pass up.

After asking us if we want anything else, Jim tells us the total. Then he asks, "Cash or card?"

Before I can even offer to pay or anything, Eliza answers, "Cash." She hands him a balled-up twenty-dollar bill. Jim takes his time to uncrumple it, straighten it out against the counter, and verify that it's legit before giving Eliza back her change.

"You two can have a seat anywhere you'd like and we'll bring those out to you," Jim says with a slight smile.

"Take your pick," Eliza says, almost like a joke. Nearly every table and booth is available for our choosing, minus one in the way back right, where an older Asian couple sits, spoon-feeding each other ice cream and laughing. Christmas lights line the wall around their booth, making this look like the perfect Hallmark movie, except Christmastime is a ways away.

I lead us to a table on the opposite side of the restaurant so we don't kill their vibe. I know if I were them and two teenagers sat right next to us when all these other options are available, it would ruin it for me.

Eliza flips her long hair behind her, putting it up into a ponytail. She rolls up the sleeves of her purple fleece jacket, then says, "Okay, you've been weird since I picked you up."

"Sorry," I say, blinking.

"What is it?" She looks at me with big, concerned eyes.

"I hadn't been in a hearse before," I say, reluctantly opening up.

I figure putting us both out of our misery and telling her the truth is the best option at this point.

"Oh my gosh," she says. "I'm so used to it that I didn't even think . . ."

"It's fine," I say, but she cuts me off.

"But it's not, though. I thought I'd said something before that had made you weird."

"You're okay," I mutter. "It's just . . . so many things remind me of Miles these days."

"That makes a lot of sense."

"So why do you drive it?"

"The hearse?"

"Yeah."

"I can give you the real story or the one that I made up," she says, her eyebrows furrowing as if to give me the choice.

"Hell, I want to know both now," I say.

"Well, I bought it from a guy on Facebook Marketplace for five hundred dollars last year. It has served me well. It's super reliable and never has any issues besides the back tires getting flat every now and then. But that's nothing a little air or tire tape can't fix."

"Nice," I say. "And the other story?"

Before she can share anything else, a girl with red hair and blue eyes, wearing a black face mask, comes with our milkshakes. She gives me the chocolate one and gives Eliza the maple snickerdoodle one and we have to do a little switch around across the table that makes all three of us chuckle awkwardly. The waitress walks away and I suck in a bit of my milkshake. It's just as delicious as I predicted it would be. Anything with cinnamon is a win.

"It's all a metaphor for me," Eliza says, looking down and stirring her milkshake with a spoon. Jorjah and Judah do the same thing. They think mixing it makes it taste better.

"Your hearse is a metaphor?" I ask with curiosity evident in my voice. I don't know what I was expecting for her to say, but that was not on my list.

"Death awaits," she says, still stirring, occasionally stopping to look up at me as if to study my reaction.

"Wow," I say. It almost slips out of me. She sounds like some nineteenth-century poet or philosopher. "That's actually really depressing." Shit. That slips out, too, but there's no going back.

"I don't think it's *that* depressing," she replies.

"You have to admit that's at least kinda sad?" I press.

"Sad . . . maybe. But I don't think that's a bad thing," she rebuts.

"Sure," I give in. "But why *death awaits*?"

"Well, it's a hearse. Its whole existence has to do with death."

"I know that but, like, why does it mean that to you?"

"We're all on a continuum that will one day lead us to death. I want to be reminded that life is short and it's best to make it worth it while you're on the earth. You have to make each day count for something, you know?"

I think about Dr. Chandler and the whole final moments thing. The way Eliza's saying it makes it sound darker. And so does driving around in a hearse. I get what she means, but I also can't help thinking about Miles and how that continuum can have a steep cliff at the end.

I get a look at Eliza's right arm. I notice a flower tattoo there. I didn't notice before, but with the way her arm is stretched out on the table and the way the light illuminates her skin, it's obvious. I'm not familiar with my flowers, besides the obvious rose, lily, or daisy, so I think to ask her about it.

"I like your tattoo," I say.

"Thanks, I got it six months ago. It's a wildflower."

"A wildflower?"

"Wildflowers are kind of my thing," she says.

"Is this another metaphor?"

"Almost."

"How so?"

"Wildflowers can be anywhere and everywhere, always. Some people think that wildflowers are just wild, untamed, and beautiful things. But they're simply so much more than that. Wildflowers are resilient. They don't have gardeners who take care of them and replant them when they're in need. Wildflowers are brave and daring and bold. They have to be to survive. That's why I love them so much. They remind me to allow myself to grow in all the places I hid for so long. If wildflowers can grow anywhere and everywhere, then so can I. Wildflowers are wild, but they're free."

"I like it," I say again. "That's actually beautiful."

"Thank you," she says through a smile, showing her teeth. "It's the only tattoo I've gotten so far, but I can't wait until I get another. They say once you get one, it becomes an addiction. I think people really mean that they enjoy it. Though I'm sure there's someone out there in the world who has a legit addiction to tattoos. Painful."

I take too big of a sip of my milkshake and am forced to palm my head. "Shit, that hurts."

"Brain freeze, huh?" she asks, starting to snicker.

"Yeah. This one's a bitch," I say.

"I've been there before. They say to press your tongue or your thumb up against the roof of our mouth."

I try that, and while doing it try to say, "Like this?" But it comes out pretty funny-sounding, which makes us both laugh.

It's quiet again for a beat. Eventually, the silence is broken by the waitress, who comes to take our trash away and ask if we need anything else. We both offer a "no, thanks," which is enough to send the waitress walking away again.

"So, how are you liking group?" I ask. I put my hands under the table so she can't see me scratching my palms. It's one of the many things I do when I'm nervous. Though I don't know why I'm nervous right now.

She hesitates and lets out the longest "umm" before giving her answer. "It's okay. I've only been once and that was weird, but also somewhat helpful."

"Why weird? Did something happen to make you feel uncomfortable?"

"No, it wasn't anything that happened there. It's mainly just me." She draws in a deep breath. "It's just, I've always been so independent, and I knew that getting help would be nice, but then being there, I felt like I was betraying myself."

"Betraying yourself?"

"Like you've got to *want* help to be there, and I thought I did, but the truth was I only wanted help for the sake of other people. I can figure things out on my own."

"I thought that for a long time, but I kept ending up in the same place," I offer. "The bravest thing I did was admit to myself that I needed a hand."

She sighs. "Yeah, I get that. And for the record, I'm not opposed to help. I just want it to be on my own terms and not anyone else's."

"That's very fair. Getting clean for yourself is so freeing." I smile, believing it to be true. But I know there's no way that would have been possible without Miles's intercession.

Eliza pulls out a deck of playing cards. "Wanna play?"

"I don't know how to play cards," I admit. "I've only ever done Uno and Go Fish."

"Let's play Twenty-One. I'll teach you."

"Okay."

I watch her shuffle the cards like she's been a professional at this for years. She shuffles and cuts the deck in ways I've never even seen before. She gives me three cards and keeps three for herself, placing the rest of the cards face down between us on the table.

"So, all you do is draw a card when it's your turn. If the card will help you get close to twenty-one, you should add it to your stack. The key is that you only get to keep three cards in your hand at a single turn, so you'll need to discard a card you don't want. It can be the one you just drew."

"Okay, that makes sense. What if I get over or under twenty-one?"

"If we don't quite have twenty-one, we keep going around the circle until one of us gets close. If we get to twenty-one or close enough to it, you just knock twice on the table and we have to reveal our cards. Now, if you get over twenty-one, you bust and you automatically lose the game. At least, that's the way I play it."

I look at my hand.

"So, wait. What are jacks, queens, kings, aces, and jokers worth?" I wonder.

"You don't play with joker cards, so if you have one of them you can draw again. Jacks, queens, and kings are worth ten points. Aces are worth eleven points or one point—you get to decide. Usually, it just depends on whatever you need and whatever will keep you from busting . . . or going over twenty-one."

"I get it now," I say, kind of telling the truth, kind of not.

"Newbies go first," Eliza says, grinning.

I grab a card and it's an ace. In my hand are a three of hearts, seven of clubs, and king of diamonds. I remember that according to the rules Eliza just explained, I can use it as one point. If I do that, then I will have twenty-one. But then, I remember her saying that I can only have three cards in my hand. Hmm. But if I use the ace as an eleven and get rid of my king, that would still be twenty-one and I will win the game.

I add the ace to my hand and discard the king.

"Wow, you got rid of *that*?" Eliza looks surprised. "You must have a good hand."

"Something like that," I say, unsure what to say to my competition. "When do I knock if I want to knock?"

"Good question. So, on your next turn, if you have twenty-one or are close enough to it, you can knock."

I nod as I watch Eliza draw a card, then immediately make a face as she discards it. Guess she didn't get the same kind of luck that I just got. I knock on the table.

"What? Really? No way! Show me!" I flash my hand. She counts out loud.

"There you go," I say.

"Damn. That's actually twenty-one. How did you get so lucky on your first try?"

"I wish I had an answer for that. I guess I'm just favored by the playing card gods or something."

We play a few more rounds and I don't get that lucky ever again. Each round that we play after that, Eliza wins, and she makes it known that the tables have turned. Eventually, the waitresses start cleaning tables and emptying trash cans, signaling that they're closing.

"Well, want to get out of here?" Eliza offers after putting away her cards and pulling her sleeves back down.

"Sure," I agree.

The ride in the hearse the second time is a little more bearable than the first time. It's been nice being out of the house and being away from getting stuck in my thoughts and my grief. I appreciate getting to just drink a milkshake and talk to another human being without the conversation being about or centered around my dead best friend, something that's felt somewhat impossible to do at school.

On the way back home, I ask Eliza about something that

she shared at group. "Do you really live at the Motel 6?"

We come to a stop at a stoplight, homeless people sitting on the side of the road, traffic crossing paths in front of us. She pulls out a cigarette, lights it, takes a drag, and then blows smoke out the open window.

At first, I think she didn't hear me, but then she answers like she's embarrassed or caught off guard. "Yeah, I've been staying there until I can get on my feet."

"You don't have any other family in the area?"

"No, I don't. My family is gone."

"Gone?"

"Yeah. They're gone. That's it, okay? *Gone*."

I can tell by the way she says that last word that she's not wanting me to press it, so I don't. I'm not sure what she means, but I know that I can take a hint. It's sad that she's dropping me off at my nice house while she's staying at an old, rundown hotel. I wonder about offering her one of our couches, but I know between her and Momma, someone's going to object. Maybe that's a topic I can approach later, but right now, I'll keep my mouth shut.

When we arrive back at my place, Eliza's hearse roars to a stop and it jolts like it's going to shut down, but she seems not to react. Maybe that's normal and it's no cause for alarm.

"I'll see you later," I say.

"Yeah. See you later," she says back. "Sorry we didn't get to talk more. Maybe another time."

I nod and reach into my pocket, pulling out my wallet. I grab two twenty-dollar bills and put them on the dashboard.

"What are you doing?" she asks, looking confused.

"Paying you back for the milkshakes and leaving you something extra in case you need it," I say, trying to be helpful.

She reaches for it and says, "No, take it back. I don't need your money." She responds like she is offended.

"Okay," I say. "My bad."

"Goodbye," Eliza says, tossing the cigarette out the window.

"Goodbye," I say.

I slip the money into the passenger door and then get out of the hearse. I wave at her and she zooms off and down the street, out of sight. Before I head up the driveway and into my house, I pull out my phone just to check it. What I see on my phone screen nearly causes me to scream. I can't believe my eyes. My heart races and it feels like there are fire ants marching in my stomach.

8:32 p.m.—missed phone call from Miles

CHAPTER EIGHT

The rest of the week, whether I'm at home or school or work or group, I can't stop thinking about the strange notification that I had a missed call from Miles. I searched the internet to see if there could be any logical explanation, and the world's best guess is that someone else got the number and was trying to call back. I've been staring at it, unable to bring myself to clear the notification from my phone. Despite what the internet seems to think, I have to believe there's another explanation—one where Miles exists in some other universe and is able to still reach out to me.

I don't tell anyone else about the call. I'll save myself the trouble of seeming like I've lost my mind or that I'm too grief-stricken to see reality clearly.

Come Saturday, Frankie practically begs me to come in because he's short-staffed. He says he'll pay me extra for the trouble, offering to contribute to my future college fund, too. Frankie's lucky I'm loyal to him to some degree, but I know he's been way too gracious to me in the past and allowed me to skip when I need to and not take back any of my pay. I text Frankie that I'll come into the shop and work a shift as long as I don't have to run the front or wait tables. He lets me know that we have a deal, because the only other person who is working today he doesn't want making pizzas anyway.

I head into the bathroom to get ready for the day. I get a shower going, waiting for the water to become steamy hot. I have a routine where I start the water and wait for the mirror to fog up before hopping in. If the mirror isn't foggy, then the shower is not hot enough. Cold showers aren't my thing.

As the water washes over me, warming and cleaning the soap off my body, a memory pops into my head that I almost had completely forgotten about. I think about last spring. It was May fifth to be exact because I remember it being an odd day and I remember being annoyed that Miles was still making *Star Wars* jokes because the previous day was the fourth of May. I remember me and Miles protesting white people celebrating Cinco de Mayo and making fun of people from school who were posting about it on Instagram and Facebook. I remember we decided on watching a scary movie at his place. We were torn between *Midsommar* and *Hereditary* (we were both A24 fans). We ended up settling on *Midsommar*. The movie goes hard on so many levels. It's a genius and beautiful film, which isn't something you hear said about horror films. It has all the things you can ever ask for with a horror movie. Each scene keeps you on the edge of your seat and you never expect that ending. I remember popping popcorn with extra butter and crushing up a bunch of Oreos into the bag of popcorn, then shaking it up to mix everything together. Miles was always the mastermind behind creations like this, swearing that they would be good. And usually, he was right. This time was no different. I remember reaching in the bag and his hand reaching in at the same time but then the jump scare with the grandparents on the cliff happened. When the movie was over, we remained lying across his black-and-white checkerboard bedspread, talking about how insane the movie was, mentioning our favorites scenes, the best characters, the choices that were made, and what we would do if we were there. That was one of our favorite questions when we watched movies together: What would we do if we were in it? That night, he had also randomly brought up having sex with Mikki, a conversation I didn't want any part in. Not because I was jealous or didn't want to be a good friend, but because Miles would always share every single salacious detail that made you want to become celibate. He walked me through what it was like to shop for condoms with his dad, what it was like to have the birds and the bees conversation with him on the ride back shortly after, then how he snuck into Mikki's house later that night and they did the thing while her parents were asleep downstairs. I don't remember exactly what I said, but I do remember the way I responded to him was as if I was annoyed at him. Whatever I said, I wish I could take it back. He said I made it sound like I was judging him for his decision, even though I was having sex, too. If it wasn't sex with whatever easy girl at school who I found attractive, it was the occasional meetup in some abandoned parking lot with August. The one thing that's been true about Miles since I met him was that he was honest. You can't say the same for me. One thing I regret is never telling Miles about what was going on with August and me. I was trying to protect August and maybe a little bit myself, but Miles always told me everything. The least I could do was return the favor.

I wonder what Miles would've said if I told him about the times that I hooked up with August. The first time honestly took both of us by surprise because we had just left a varsity basketball game and walked across the street to smoke a blunt. At the time, August and I both had connections and would hook each other up with weed when we needed it. One thing led to another and we were giving each other hand jobs on the ground behind a totaled car. The second time took me by surprise, when he showed up at my place, visibly angry that he was losing his starting position on the football team to a freshman recruit. Every other time had been a moment of loneliness or desperation or just plain horniness on either of our parts. There were never any feelings. At least, not on my end. I never asked August about whether or not he was bi or gay and just afraid to come out of the closet, but August ended our situationship faster than I could even blink and started dating some cheerleading girl named Ximena. Now that I think about it, I was just being used—and I used him right back. I wonder what Miles would say about that, too.

Looking back, if Miles had been the Miles I've always known, he wouldn't have judged me or made it a big deal, like I was dirty or irredeemable. Would he have made fun of me and thrown in some jokes? For sure, but he was always trustworthy and real.

I hop out of the shower and dry off. I stare at myself in the mirror, wiping fog away to get a better view. In seconds, it fogs right back up. Then I stare at my missed call log in my phone, seeing Miles's name at the top of that list.

But before I can think or react or close out the voicemail log, my phone rings with a FaceTime call. The name that comes across the screen: **Miles**.

I don't want to answer out of fear that it will blow up the fantasy that I've created where Miles is reaching out to me from some alternate universe out there. And not some stranger who happened to get his number.

Shit.

Shit.

What do I do?

My heart beats in my chest. Faster and faster. It'll soon pound its way right out of my flesh. My breathing picks up and the steam in this bathroom doesn't help. I click the green answer button, butterflies fluttering in my stomach.

"Miles?" I say, answering.

The screen goes black, but all I can hear is breathing. It's not heavy or deep. It's very light and faint, but no words.

"Miles? Is that you?" I say with some amount of desperation collecting in my voice. "Miles?"

Static on the other end gets louder, and I hear some slight formations of words, but I can't quite make out what the voice is saying. I can't tell who the voice belongs to, either. The person trying to speak sounds robotic.

"Miles? It's me!"

Nothing, just crackling, hissing, and sizzling from static on the other end.

Some of the static settles for a few seconds and then I hear a very clean, very crisp, "Keem!"

"Miles??" I begin to cry, my chest heaving. "Is that really you?"

Beep, beep, beep.

Just like that, the call drops.

WHAT?

"No! Nooooo!" I yell, slamming my phone down, tears pouring from my eyes now. "Miles. Miles!"

I pick up the phone and call back. No one answers. I call again. No one answers again. There's no denying that that was Miles. There's no denying that he said my name. Unless someone out there is playing the cruelest joke possible on me, my dead best friend said my name through the phone. Even thinking this is crazy, but I swear on my life that it was him.

I get dressed—jeans with slits at the knees, my vintage 1991 March Madness graphic T-shirt I got from thrifting with Miles, and my favorite pair of Jordan Retro 11s. Dad's off at work already, patrolling the streets in his cruiser. Judah is playing video games in the living room and Jorjah and Momma are doing their nails at the dining room table.

"Frankie asked me to go in," I say.

"Frankie?" Momma ponders. "Does he not care about your schoolwork?"

"I don't have any work to do," I say, not really sure of that. The truth is, I haven't even looked to check what I have due the next couple days for school. School has been the last thing on my mind.

"Will you be back for dinner? Your father and I wanted to have a talk with you kids," she says, looking hopeful that I'll say yes.

"I can try to be back," I say. It's a promise that I mean and she knows it.

"Okay," she gives in. "Please try your best to be here."

I nod, grab my keys, grab my jacket at the door, and head out to my car. My phone buzzes and I frantically pull it out of my pocket, thinking it could be another attempt from Miles to reach me. Instead, it's just Frankie. I answer it and put it on speakerphone.

"Hey, Frankie," I say.

"Hey, just checking on your ETA," he kind of grumbles. Frankie has a muffled voice, but talking over the phone is worse.

"I'm about ten minutes away," I tell him.

"Perfect. See you when you get here. Be safe, kid."

I click off, feeling some sadness that it wasn't Miles calling. I make a sharp turn onto Washington Street as the light turns yellow. Miles used to say that I drive like I'm racing to get somewhere, but I told him I'm just a *determined* driver. It made things sound a lot nicer. Miles was just jealous that he never got his license. He got his permit, but then settled on not taking his driver's test. He said, "Why would I go get a license and waste money on a car when I have you?" I guess he had a point there. I did drive him everywhere—and I mean *everywhere*—when he was alive.

I get stopped by a red light. Nervously, I tap along on my steering wheel as if it counts the seconds that I wait. I see Miles standing on the corner across the way. Or at least I think I do. Naturally, my foot presses on the gas a little too early before the light turns green. I have to swerve my car hard to the right to avoid getting T-boned. The other car, a blue minivan, honks as they drive off to their final destination. I pull over to the side of the road, out of breath. I hop out and scan the same corner where I saw Miles. I don't see him anywhere all of a sudden. Convenient,

I guess. All this anxiety lately must have me imagining things, I think. I haven't had a trip like this since trying shrooms that one time at Kourtney Johnson's birthday bash. I hop back in my car and bright red-and-blue lights flicker behind me. The *whoop* sound of a siren gets closer and closer. One look in the rearview mirror and I know that I'm getting pulled over. *Shit.*

I watch the cop get out of his squad car and pull out his flashlight, shining it into my car.

"License and registration," he says.

My dad is a cop, but he still had the talk with me. The talk most Black and brown parents have with their children about what to do when you get pulled over. The one where they walk you through where to place your hands, how fast to move, what words to use, and when to shut all the way up. Dad always told me to memorize their badge numbers in case something ever happens that's a little fishy.

"My license is in my pocket, sir. Can I grab it?" I ask without looking at him.

"Go on ahead," he says. He has some kind of Southern accent.

I reach into my pocket and grab out my wallet. Getting pulled over wasn't something I had on my agenda today, and here's one thing that will make me late to work. I can't even call Frankie to let him know what just happened. He would just give me a lecture like Dad would, and then would turn around and make me work a double. I keep the registration in the pocket of the door, so I reach for that and hand both over to the officer. This time, I get a good look at him. He's a white guy, somewhat young. He wears sunglasses, despite it being a little bit overcast. He has a thick handlebar mustache and a coffee stirrer in his mouth. I recognize him, but can't place him. With my dad being a police officer, there are always friends from his work that stop by. Maybe he came by once before.

"Hawkins? You any kin to Officer Hawkins?" the officer asks. I squint to read the badge number on his uniform. 18798.

"That's my dad," I say. "Do you know him?"

"Yeah. Real good friend of mine. I thought you looked familiar," Officer 18798 says and removes his sunglasses. "What are you doing nearly causing a collision in the middle of the street?" His accent seems like it gets thicker the more he talks.

"I'm sorry, Officer—"

"Officer Eugene," he says, interrupting me.

"I'm sorry, Officer Eugene," I say. "I thought I saw something."

"You thought you saw something, eh? Like what? It better be pretty damn good."

"I thought I saw my best friend," I say reluctantly, looking forward and avoiding all eye contact. "But he died a few weeks ago."

"I remember your dad telling us about that down at the station," Officer Eugene says, handing me back my license and registration. "Listen, kid, your mind sometimes plays tricks on you when you're in mourning. Maybe you shouldn't be driving in the daze that you're in."

"But I'm on my way to work," I say.

"How about I give you an escort there," he offers. "You won't get a ticket today, but if I catch you in a daze like that again, I'm going to have to have a talk with your father."

89

I guess I deserve that. "Thank you," I say to the officer.

"Where do you work, kid?"

"Cousin Vinny's Pizza."

"All right. You just wait there and I'll lead the way. Stay close behind."

I nod at him. I slip my license back in my pocket and toss my registration back where I keep it.

The officer hops in his car, keeping his lights on, and whips around in front of me. He extends a hand out of his window, signaling me to come and follow. He escorts me all the way to work. We run through red lights and stop signs and hold up traffic in all directions. I make it there within just a few minutes. Luckily, Frankie doesn't see this escort. He's in the back, and focused on being upset that I'm five minutes later than I promised over the phone.

"There are six orders waiting for you back there," Frankie says, staring at me. He's covered in flour and sauce, and I know that he's been busy. I also know it's only a matter of time before we match.

I quickly slip into an apron and gloves. Then I get started on the next order. Three large pizzas. One cheese, one pepperoni, and one Hawaiian with barbecue sauce. The whole time I'm making pizzas, Miles's voice fills my head. I think about the way I heard my name on the other end of that FaceTime call. Then I think about how I randomly saw him on the corner and nearly crashed the only car I've ever owned. Something is going on, but I can't explain it.

When I'm working on the third order, which has a record number of strombolis, Nick, my coworker, comes to check on me. This is a sure sign that things must be dead out front. Most orders, I guess, are coming in for delivery or carryout and not dine-in.

"How are you doing back here?" Nick asks, genuinely curious. He wears a *Naruto* graphic tee and some khakis. He's not covered in flour like I am now.

"Fine," I say. "Gonna run out of cheese soon because of all these strombolis. We should've ordered a special cow to provide all the dairy for this order."

Nick laughs. Then his face goes serious again. "You sure you're okay?"

"Just a lot on my mind," is what I settle on.

"Like what?" He's really poking at it, I see. I've known Nick for a while. We've only worked together for a bit, but he goes to Center Grove. We're in the same grade and have had some classes together in the past, but none this year. We've never been *friends*, but we've been *cordial*.

I think for a moment. "You ever lose someone and you can't stop seeing them everywhere or hearing their voice? Fucking crazy, right?"

"Not crazy at all actually," he says. "I think that's pretty common."

"Really?"

"Hell yeah, dude. You know the place between sleep and awake?"

"The place between what?"

"There's a place between sleep and awake. It's where reality begins to warp. It's the place where dreams meet real life. Where you don't quite know if what you're seeing and feeling is fiction or true. Just read Charles Dickens and you'll understand."

"Charles Dickens?"

"Yeah, you've never read *Oliver Twist*?"

"No." I shake my head.

"*Peter Pan*?"

"Charles Dickens wrote *Peter Pan*?" I question.

"No, but both Charles Dickens and *Peter Pan* talk about the place between sleep and awake," Nick says. "Anyway, I just thought I would help you not feel so out of your mind. Grief sucks and it makes total sense for it to make you feel strange. It's just grief."

I get it, but I don't know if grief is *just* anything.

My shift lasts a couple more hours, and I get to go home right before the dinner shift comes in. Frankie asks me to come work another shift in a week, but I tell him about a paper I have to write for class (which is a perfect excuse). He understands and just asks me to promise to come work a shift sooner rather than later, even if it's not a full one. To that, I agree.

On my drive home, and over dinner, and back when I'm in bed and trying to doze off but the moon won't get the hell out of my face, I think about what Nick said—about the place between sleep and awake—and I wonder if everything that has happened is just because Miles is trying to send me a message. If there's still some way that I can reach out and touch him, to talk with him, to see him, to hear him, anything. It seemed so real to see him on that corner today. Just as real as hearing his voice on the phone earlier. But it's all been too much at the same time. I need to sleep. Even if I can't, I need to try.

And that's exactly what I do. It takes way too long, but eventually,

I fall asleep. I slip into a dream that's more like a re-creation of a memory with Miles. In it, Miles and I are both fresh out of sixth grade. It was a record-hot day in the middle of summer break. Miles and I had conducted a plan to create our own amusement park in my backyard. Armed with nothing but cardboard boxes, duct tape, a laundry basket, some string, and our imaginations, we transformed almost anything we could get our hands on into some kind of exciting ride. Miles, always the mastermind, took charge of the roller coaster—a rickety contraption of wobbly chairs and a laundry basket—while I manned the Ferris wheel, a makeshift structure of broomsticks and old bicycle wheels. As we spun and soared in our fantastic world of our own imagination, the world outside faded into nothing, straight meaninglessness, and for once, we were the rulers of our own kingdom. However, our multimillion-dollar grand amusement park was short-lived when Miles was attempting some kind of stunt on the roller coaster, only to crash-land into a pile of cushions and grass, sending us both dying with laughter. It was moments like this that were so pure and joyful, etched into the fabric of my being, a testament to the boundless creativity and camaraderie we shared. Though Miles may be gone, his spirt lives on in the memories we crafted together, forever cherished in my heart. I could dream about our memories forever.

CHAPTER   NINE

I toss and turn through the night as the memories that were such lovely dreams become nightmares that all end with Miles dying. I think at this point, I've dreamed every possible scenario about Miles's death. There's nothing original left. Luckily, I wake up to my alarm at around eleven on Sunday morning. That means I've slept through church, which isn't all that bad because I've slept through a few Sundays since what happened to Miles. I don't know if I can ever step foot back into a church. Not at least for a long time. I'm thankful that Momma and Dad didn't try to wake me, force me up or anything. I'm even more thankful they didn't send either Judah or Jorjah to get me.

The first thing I do is reach for my phone, hoping I got another call from Miles. But when I don't see anything, I sigh out of sadness and fall back onto the pillows for a bit longer.

I get up out of bed, noticing my shirt is soaked with sweat. I slip it off and slide into my house shoes, which are just black-and-white-striped Nike Slides. I also put on a clean plain white T-shirt.

It's strangely quiet for a weekend afternoon in our house. I head downstairs and notice that everyone is gone. There's a note waiting for me on the marble counter in the kitchen that reads: *Going to church, then grocery shopping, and then taking Jorjah and Judah to a playdate. Call if you need anything. <3—Love, Mom.*

I'm all alone in this house. This feels big, in some way. Momma and Dad stopped leaving me alone after finding out I was an addict. At first, they said they couldn't trust me to be by myself out of fear that I would drink all the alcohol in the house or smoke something under their roof. Then they said I couldn't be alone because they were afraid—afraid of what could happen to me, afraid that I would overdose, afraid that I would die if they weren't around. I gotta admit that now I can see where they were coming from, when things were really bad. After I got clean, they still treated me like I was an addict. Hell, maybe once an addict always an addict—I'm still not sure how it works, but what I do know is that I didn't want them to give up on me. I want them to trust me again. So being home alone is actually a big fucking deal in my book.

There's no telling when everyone will be back, so I head back upstairs to get ready for the day. I reach into my walk-in closet and pull out some black jeans, my retro Toronto Raptors hoodie, and my rainbow Vans. Once upon a time, Miles would have joked on me for my rainbow Vans, but that's even more of a reason to wear them today.

I head to my car and get in. Before I start the car, I pull out my phone and notice that the last person I texted was Eliza. Usually, it would be Miles and now it's not. Things were left off in such a weird way the other night. I feel bad and she hasn't reached out to me, so I'm sure she's hurt or at least annoyed at me—understandably so. One thing I can already tell about Eliza is that she's real good at showing how she feels, even without words. I text her, apologizing, and I wait for her to read the message. Seconds turn into minutes, and still . . . nothing.

Eventually, I get tired of waiting and start the car. The radio immediately kicks on and a song by Stephen Sanchez plays. I turn it all the way down because it's not really the vibe that I have today—or ever. Besides group later tonight, I have a pretty open schedule with nothing to do. Usually, I would like the sound of that, but now it means being alone with my thoughts.

I wonder what Eliza is up to, so I check her location on my phone only to find out that she stopped sharing it with me. Guess I really messed things up between us by whatever I did the other night. And by the looks of it, my apology isn't quite enough to undo the damage I've done. I notice my backpack on my back seat. I reach for it and sift through to find my laptop. Before I get to my laptop, I come across Miles's diary. I don't remember putting it there, but it's one of those things that's become out of sight, out of mind. There's no use in obsessing over its contents when I can't do anything about them to begin with. No matter what love notes or suicide notes or stream-of-consciousness entries exist in this diary, I can't bring him back to ask about them. I make a mental note to do something with it in the future, whether it be burying it next to him, giving it to Mikki, or disposing of it in some glorious candlelit vigil followed by a bonfire.

I take out my laptop. The battery is low and desperately needs a charge sooner rather than later, but for now, what little life it has will have to do. I google Eliza, typing her full name into the search engine. There are many Eliza Fitzpatricks in the world—if only I knew or had thought to ask her middle name. That would give me a better lead.

I scroll through pages of searches until one catches my eye on the fourth page. It's a news article. The headline reads *Father and Son, Robert and Jonathan Fitzpatrick, Sentenced to Death Row for Murder of Local Businessman.*

"Holy shit," I say out loud. I read more and see that the article mentions a girl named Eliza, sister of Jonathan and daughter of Robert, and a mother whose name is Maryanne. The article shows a picture of the whole family and in it, what's clearly a young version of Eliza is sitting on her father's lap. They all look alike, it's almost uncanny. Like carbon copies of the parents, but maybe that's how genes work. The article gives extensive detail about what all happened that night. It says some local businessman named Thomas McNally was found dead in his own home, stuffed in a trash bag. The evidence is all pointing to blackmail and a break-in gone wrong, which turned violent fast. The article also mentions that Eliza's testimony was crucial in convicting her father and brother.

I close out the article and look for more information about her. I find a blog called *Wildflower Wanderings: Exploring Life's Beauty.* Scrolling through, I can see that she's been updating it pretty regularly. Most of the posts are just pictures that she's taken of wildflowers in nature, with a single word as the caption. Things like, *joy, peace, hope, love, freedom,* and *growth.* Her last post was an hour ago. There's a picture of an open field. The background is blurred but I think I recognize one of the signs in the distance. It's a billboard with a Bible verse on it. If it's where I think it is, she might still be there.

I close my laptop, tossing it and my backpack in the passenger seat, and I head from my driveway toward Oakwood Avenue and then down Magnolia Street, which takes me just a few minutes away from the billboard in the photo.

When I get near the billboard, I see an open field and a gas station. Parked at the gas station, there's a hearse. I park my car on the side of the road and head into the field. I weave through wheat and corn and then to a patch of flat land, where there are different kinds of flowers—a colorful burst of flowers, especially for Indiana. And then there she is, sprawled out on the ground, a towel beneath her, in her bathing suit. It's warm out and the sun's out, but it's not *that* warm out.

She opens her eyes and squeals. "Oh my god," she says, reaching for her clothes and covering herself up like I saw something I wasn't supposed to. Out of respect, I shield my eyes.

"Um, I'm sorry," I say. "I didn't know that—"

"What are you doing here?" she says, interrupting me. "This is such an invasion of privacy."

Between my fingers, I can see she's sliding into her pants, and I also notice red welts on her legs that look more like thin cuts than bruises. Then I remind myself I shouldn't be seeing any of this. "How did you even find me here?" she asks, furiously and frantically grabbing her things and stuffing them into the dirty duffel bag that's lying on the ground.

"I . . . I googled you," I tell her, taking my hand from my eyes and running it down the side of my face. "I saw your blog."

"You WHAT?" She seems genuinely shocked. "My creep-o-meter was going off five minutes ago and now it's really going through the roof. You googled me?"

"Yeah," I say. "You didn't answer my text message. And I thought something bad . . ." I stop mid-thought, watching her facial expression change. She relaxes a little, just a little.

"I'm fine," she says. "And I saw your apology. I was planning on answering when I was done . . . never mind."

She pushes past me and heads straight back through the field.

"Where you going?" I question.

"Home!" is all she says back.

I run after her.

"Look, I also read about what happened to your family. Your dad and your brother. I'm so sorry that you went through that. I'm sure that would be tough. Plus your sister. I just can't imagine. We can't pick our family, so I hope you don't blame yourself for any of it."

"Stay away from me," she says, snapping around, a husk of corn slapping me in the face.

"Eliza, I can't," I say. "I don't want to stay away."

"What? I will call the police and report you as a creepy stalker person," she says. She picks up her pace, running through the field. I follow as close behind as I can, out of breath as I try to keep up. We make it back across the street to the gas station where her hearse is.

"I don't mean to be creepy," I say. "But I might need your help."

"My help? With what?"

Just when I am about to give her an answer, I think about how crazy I might seem if I tell her the truth. But then I realize I've got nothing at all to lose here.

I tell her, "I think my best friend is trying to communicate with me."

"What? Like, the one who died?"

I clench my eyes shut when I say, "Yes."

She snorts a little. "Okay, that's wild."

"Please, I'm begging you to believe me," I plead. I pull out my phone, pull out my recent calls log, and flash it to her. "See, look, I'm not kidding."

"There are so many possibilities about why the number would call you. Your friend being alive is absurd."

"No, I don't think he's alive. I mean, at least, not in this universe. I think he might be somewhere else in the cosmos, trying to reach me. I just want to know why."

"Okay, Hakeem. I think you—"

"Please," I say, begging even more, seconds from getting down on my knees to sell it.

"If I were to help you, what exactly would that look like?" she asks, giving me a look like she's both intrigued and skeptical at the same time.

"I'm not entirely sure yet, but when I know, you'll be the first to know," I say back, relieved to have her on my side.

"My blog is all I have," she says. "It's what keeps me going. Don't take that away from me."

I think I get what she means. "I promise not to google you again or look at your blog."

"It's public, I know, but I don't want my blog and real life to mix. Something about that is just . . . weird."

"I understand," I add, saying it but not believing it.

Eliza opens the back of the hearse, where they usually keep the caskets. She throws her stuff there, like it's a trunk.

"By the way, if you think you can figure me out, know that you will always be wrong."

"Noted," I say, swallowing. "Will I see you at group tonight?"

"I haven't decided if I'm going yet. After this stunt, I'm not sure I want to ever go back. I may just have to find another group that meets somewhere secret."

"Listen, I'm sorry," I say. "Don't let me ruin group for you. If you go, I promise I won't even say anything to you." I surprise myself with this one. I used to hate group.

"Well, whatever." She gets in her hearse, starts the engine, which takes a few seconds too long to roar to life. And then she drives off, the sound of the tires screeching along the way, dust and debris kicking up behind her. I turn around and head to my car, thinking about everything that just went down and what I would do differently if given a do-over.

I pray in my car when I pull up to group that I'll see Eliza. There's no sign of her hearse anywhere, which at first makes me sad, but then I remember she walked the last time because the place where we meet is pretty close to the place where she was staying. When I walk in, I see her. There's an open chair next to her and one way across the room. I pass on the one next to her, giving her the space that I somewhat promised.

Yolanda holds a coin in one hand and a framed certificate in the other. She wears a proud expression and smiles big as she sits down in her usual spot. An unseen air-conditioning unit kicks on loudly and Yolanda has to talk over it.

"Today's a very special day, everyone," she says. "For this very day marks five months of being sober for one of our members and a whole year for another."

People clap and cheer, including me. I scan the group to see who it could be. Usually, I would get an inkling because people normally share how many months along they are when they're here. Then . . . *wait.*

Oh, shit. I check my phone's calendar. I used to put a little green flag next to each day that I didn't use. That was something Miles helped me set up. I've since stopped doing that after he passed away. But if I do the math correctly, today does mark five months exactly.

"Give it up for Hakeem," Yolanda says, calling my name like I'm entering a professional sports game. She loves anniversaries, and while I don't think all NA groups give out five-month certificates, Yolanda makes a big deal of it. She waves me up and points to the podium near the front. "Give us an update about how you're doing and maybe a few words of encouragement to keep going."

I walk up, but my feet feel weighed down. Each step feels like I'm walking through thick mud or sand. This is a nightmare scenario, having to stand up and deliver an impromptu speech. I look over at Eliza as she sits there, part keeping herself from laughing and part cheering me on, like everyone else.

The clapping settles when I make it up to the podium. Now I'm forced to be stared at by everyone in the group, including Yolanda, all waiting for me to say something profound or helpful. I just hope I don't completely drop the ball and derail the night. I remember the old advice about making it through a speech—to imagine everyone here naked, but with Eliza being here, something about that feels like a violation.

"Hi, everyone," I say.

"Hi, friend," some people say. Others replace the word *friend* with my name. *Friend* is just custom for group.

"I totally did not remember that today marks five months for me," I say, holding the framed certificate that Yolanda left on the podium. It has my first name on it and underneath where it says *Accomplishment*, she has handwritten: *Five months free*. I think about that word and let it fuel the rest of my speech. "Despite not using, life has been pretty tough on me. You all know about my best friend dying and what that did to me. Life hasn't gotten any easier. I wake up and I feel as if I relive every single moment I spent with him, except he's gone, and I'm here. But then there are times where I remember that I wouldn't be here without him and I can't help but smile. Miles taught me a lot while he was still on the earth. One of those things being that using isn't a grab for attention. It isn't always selfish. And it doesn't mean we need saving. It just means we're temporarily stuck in the darkness and need to be shown the light. Sometimes, people—friends—come into your life at just the right time and show you that light. I hope we all find it," I say. "Thank you."

People clap and cheer for me again as I take my seat. Yolanda clutches her chest and wipes away tears from her face with a hand-kerchief. "We appreciate your words, Hakeem. Thank you." She takes a deep breath before continuing. I watch her chest move under her bright yellow suit. "Ladies and gentlemen, let's also celebrate Violet for her one year of being sober. This chip serves as tangible representation of her commitment to sobriety. We're so proud!"

More applause as Violet nervously tiptoes up, her head down like all the attention is too much. I can empathize with her, but for her, it seems like it's almost painful.

She takes the sobriety chip from Yolanda and smiles awkwardly at everyone and gives a slight wave. "Thank you, everyone," is all she says, in a quiet, anxious, raspy voice. And then she walks off to take her seat. There's a brief pause of silence before people offer a final, hearty applause.

The rest of group, Yolanda passes out our daily reading. It's an article about the book *Living Clean: The Journey Continues*. We frequently read excerpts from this book, which offers insights and inspiration for achieving and maintaining long-term recovery and personal growth. The selling point of the book is that it's a book for addicts, written by addicts. I'm not a big reader, but reading through this book at times has been like little confidence boosts that I need to keep going when I'm away from this place. I look over at Eliza and hope it's doing something to her on the inside. She seems invested in what she's reading. I can only hope that it makes her want to stay.

At the end of group, Yolanda brings out cupcakes and refresh-ments to continue celebrating me and Violet. Just as I go to catch

Eliza as she waits by the door, Aram comes up to me, placing a hand on my arm. His touch is cold. He looks frail and thin and he's shaky. His brown skin looks a little bit gray. Usually, those are signs that he's using something, but he's here and getting help and that's all that matters.

"You're an inspiration to me," Aram says. "One day, I will get one of those." He points to the certificate in my hand.

"I think you'll get one, too," I tell him. I believe in him. He's been here since I started and he's relapsed more than anyone at group, but I believe getting clean is somewhere in his future. He wants it badly—more than most.

I give him a nod and he walks over to Violet to congratulate her. I grab a soda from the refreshment table and meet Eliza at the door.

"Hey," I say.

"Hey," she says. "Congratulations. You've done it."

I nod. "Thanks."

"What? Already sick of people congratulating you?"

"Just a little," I say and laugh. "I'm gonna get the brunt of it from my parents when they see."

Eliza matches my laugh and tucks hair behind her ear. "Look . . . about earlier—" Her voice is sympathetic and apologetic, but I cut her off, placing a finger in the air.

"It's okay," I tell her. "I understand. If I'm not fucking up one thing, it's another these days."

"I can admit that I was a bit harsh, though."

"Sure," I say. "I hear you."

"Besides, that's not the way you talk to your friends."

I perk up and make a face. "Wait, did you say . . . friends?"

"Friends. But don't let me regret that I've said that, Hakeem."

"You won't."

"Promise?" she asks, putting her hand out, giving me the nod to take it.

I grab her hand tightly and shake it.

On the way out the door and to the side street where I parked, Eliza adds, "Today wasn't bad."

"Like the day, or . . . ?"

"No. At group. My goal is to read that book from start to finish. Seems like there's a lot of good stuff in it."

"Yeah, I've enjoyed the days we read it as well."

"I didn't think reading a book *about* addiction would be at all helpful. But when I saw that it was written by other addicts, and replaying your speech in my thoughts, it made me realize that there are people out there who have made it out of their own tunnel of darkness. That maybe there's hope."

"Yes, exactly. Hope."

"Wanna sit with me on the curb for a bit?" she offers. "I'll have to go in a few because I want to grab a sandwich from the little deli in the lobby of my motel, and they close at a time that should be illegal."

I nod and we find a perfect spot to sit, underneath a streetlight that glows dimly but just enough so that we can still see each other's faces. Her face looks washed in the moonlight, highlighting her features up close. Plump lips, perfectly pointed nose, eyelashes that are longer than most.

"When my dad and brother killed that old man, I died, too," she says. "Or at least some part of me did. My life would never be the same. No one ever saw it coming. Not even my mom. We both knew Dad and Jonathan spent a lot of time together, but we thought it was just normal father-son duo things. Not them plotting to hurt someone. My mom's response to everything was the nail in the coffin for me. Instead of mothering me and keeping me safe and moving us away after they were locked up, she decided to stay in that house, looking out the window as she wept for days that turned into weeks that turned into months. She eventually drove herself absolutely mad. She stopped speaking entirely after six months. She stopped eating, too."

Tears puddle up in Eliza's eyes. She turns her head and blinks them back so that I can't tell, but it's too late. "Eliza . . . I'm so sorry. That sounds so difficult."

"I was invisible to my family way before any of that happened."

I want to tell her my parents don't see me, either, to make her feel less alone. My parents see me as this boy who managed victory over addiction. But I'm still just as sad, just as depressed. I'm still a boy who every single day has to fight not to use again. I want nothing more than to fill my body with just enough painkillers to feel like I'm floating through time and space, not feeling anything anymore. But every damn day I tell myself I have to make them proud, I have to make Miles proud. I have to do this for me *and* them.

This feels like too much to say out loud right now. So I let Eliza keep talking.

"My mom's at some mental health facility now getting

treatment," she tells me. "I haven't seen her since. God, I hope she's alive, but I guess she's dead to me already in a sense." She wipes away at her face. "Ugh! Why am I crying about all this?"

"It's okay to cry."

"I know it's okay to cry—you don't need to lecture me about that. I just don't want to," she says, sniffling.

"I understand."

"You see, I used to think that I just didn't care, that I was apathetic about my life, about my past, about my struggles. But when you started digging up my skeletons, I realized it was a lot worse than that. It was hopelessness. Hopelessness is like a shadow that sneaks up on you. It latches on to you and refuses to let you go. It drains you, consumes you, and destroys you from the inside out. It even makes hope feel like the most hopeless thing in the universe. But . . ." She trails off, then pulls out a cigarette, lights it, takes a drag, and blows out the smoke. She offers me a drag, but I say no thanks.

"My family are like burning bushes and I'm the fiery mess left behind," she says.

"I hear you. I'm sorry you've been going through all that alone for so long."

"I didn't mean to talk your ear off," she says, taking another puff of the cigarette. This puff makes her cough, so she puts the cigarette out on the ground nearby and tosses it back in the carton she pulled it out from.

My phone buzzes. I'm getting a call. I quickly pull my phone out of my pocket . . . and it says *Miles.*

"Look," I shout, swiftly shoving the screen in Eliza's face.

"Holy shit," she says, her eyes widening. "You weren't—"

"No, I wasn't lying!"

"Well, answer it."

I hit the little green button and hit speakerphone. "Hello? Miles?"

"Hakeem? You there? Can you hear me?"

"Yes, Miles! It's me! What's going on?" I'm taking in huge gulps of air, my chest heaving. Every hair on my arms rises and a wave of warmth tides over me.

"Look, Keem. I don't have a whole lot of time. They won't let me talk long. And I don't know where I am, but I know that I'm dead."

"How are you able to call me?"

"I don't have answers to that, man. But I have something important to tell you."

"What is it, Miles? Anything."

"I didn't do this to myself. Someone else did it."

"Did what?"

"I didn't . . ."

Hissing static ripples through the call, making it hard to hear anything.

"Miles? You there? I can't hear you."

Then, nothing. Just total silence.

Beep, beep, beep.

The call ends before he can finish his sentence. Just like that last time. I don't know if it's on my end or his, but I try calling back. Nothing. I call back again. But still, not even a ring.

"FUUUUUUUUCK!" I scream at the top of my lungs. "What is going on?" I toss my phone to the ground in a moment of frustration, my skin feeling red-hot and my stomach churning.

"That was one of the strangest things ever, if that was really a dead guy on the phone," Eliza says. She tries pinching herself, testing to see if this is real or not.

"That was *really* fucking him, I swear that on my life. I swear it. I know Miles's voice. I can pick it out of a lineup any day," I say, my voice rising in pitch and volume. I pace in a circle around where we were sitting just moments ago. "What did he mean when he said he didn't do it to himself?"

"He also said someone else did it," Eliza adds.

I search my brain and I instantly lose all the breath in my lungs. "Is he saying that . . . he didn't kill himself, which means that . . . someone else did it?"

Eliza shakes her head. "I can't be sure. But if another call happens, maybe we can get confirmation. When does he normally call?"

"It's not like that," I say. "I have no idea when I'll hear from him next."

I look up at the moon and stars, wondering where Miles could be, wondering what he's trying to reveal to me, and wondering what I'll do.

CHAPTER TEN

Back at home, I don't want to talk to anyone, yet Momma waits for me at the dinner table with her arms folded, which is never a good sign. It's later than usual and maybe that's what has her pissed, but the twins are asleep and it's not like I walked in causing a ruckus, waking everybody up. The lights cut on and Momma examines me like I've been hurt. She sniffs my clothing, like she suspects I might've been smoking or doing something that I wasn't supposed to.

"You smell like cigarettes," she says, frowning.

"I was around someone else who was smoking them. I would never—"

"Oh my gosh!" She notices my certificate in my hand and grabs it, reading it out loud. "This is incredible. Five months, sweetie. Your dad and I were thinking that the whole family should get baptized together at church. Baptism symbolizes death to life, new beginnings. This is the perfect time for all of us. This certificate only solidifies it for me, honey."

Getting baptized is the last thing on my mind right now. But I can't say that. "Mom, I heard from Miles tonight. He called me."

"He called you?" She looks at me like she's seen a ghost.

"It sounds strange, but . . . yeah."

"Honey, that's not possible," she says, cupping my chin tenderly. She kisses my cheek, her lips cold, and continues, saying, "I think it's best for you to get some rest. I think that's just your exhaustion talking. You've had a long day doing whatever it is you did with your Sunday."

"But even Eliza heard it."

"Eliza? Who is Eliza?"

"Never mind," I say with a sigh.

"Get some rest, honey," she tells me a second time, her voice almost a whisper.

I don't fight her on it. There's no use. She'll never believe me. Even if she heard his voice, she would deny it. Whether it be her spiritual beliefs or something else entirely, she won't have the right ears to hear what I hear. I just oblige and head up the stairs to my bedroom, passing Judah's and Jorjah's bedrooms on my way. I peek in and they're both sound asleep.

I slip off my pants and shoes and bury myself beneath the blankets and sheets on my bed. I stare at my phone, turning on the ringer and waiting for a call back at any moment. I wait so long, minimizing my blinking for as long as I can, and by midnight end up dozing off completely.

I'm woken up around four in the morning to the most annoying ringtone possible. It takes a minute for my brain to work, but I remember assigning the specific ringtone to Miles's contact, which makes me lunge up from the bed, searching for where I placed my phone. I find it after a few rings and hit answer.

"Miles?"

"Keem, yeah, it's me again. I'm sorry if I woke you up, but

I'm gonna get straight to the point because I don't have a whole lot of time."

"Okay, Miles, I'm listening."

"What I was trying to tell you is that I didn't walk in front of the bus. Someone pushed me," he says. "I don't know who, but I need you to find out for me. If you can."

"Wait, what are you telling me?"

"Just please find out who did it, okay? Can you do—"

Beep, beep, beep.

The call drops again.

I'm too stunned to react. I stand still for the longest moment, thinking about what Miles just told me. He didn't jump in front of the bus like everyone thought and like the news articles said and the detectives put out there. He was pushed. He was *pushed*? Who would push him? Was it on purpose? Was it on accident? So many questions flood my thoughts. I don't know if I'll get another chance to talk to Miles, but I'm left with this overwhelming new realization and I don't know what to do with it.

Find out for me. If you can, Miles said, his voice now replaying on a continuous loop in my head.

He wants me to find out who's behind his . . . murder. Thinking about this almost makes me want to pass out or throw up or both. My best friend was . . . murdered? Who would do that? Miles didn't have any enemies—or so I thought.

I text Eliza, but her phone is on Do Not Disturb. I explain everything that just happened, and press the little option it gives me to force the notification through, so that she'll see it if she's up.

113

I wait and wait and wait for her to read it, but she doesn't. It's the middle of the night, so it's all understandable. I'm sure she's deep asleep.

Now I'm left to wait even longer. This is the worst. *Waiting.* It's pure torture. I stay awake, staring at the darkness of my ceiling, a stream of moonlight shining in a single corner. Eventually, I start crying. I cry for Miles and I cry for what happened to him and I cry for the lies everyone else believes and I cry for the truth. I cry so hard I get the type of headache that requires medicine, like ibuprofen or Tylenol. But I don't want to go down that trail right now.

Instead, I let the pain keep me comfort through the night, keeping me up even when I try to rest my eyes for a moment.

CHAPTER ELEVEN

We're reviewing about exponents and logarithms and rewriting equations in exponential form in Mrs. Li's Pre-Calculus class the following morning. Normally, I would keep my phone in my locker for Mrs. Li's class because she's got a tough no-cell-phone policy and will hold your phone in the "phone jail" bucket in her desk drawer, but I need to keep it on me just in case. If I get another phone call from Miles, I'm running out of the classroom to answer it, and there's nothing Mrs. Li can do to stop me. This is bigger than learning about some arbitrary math thing that I'll never have to use in life anyway.

My phone vibrates. I see it's a message back from Eliza, replying to everything that I told her.

Eliza: HOLY SHIT.
Eliza: Meet me after school? Text me when you're free.

I type back "yes" and hit send.

Eventually, the bell rings. While I'm in the hallway, Principal Samuels comes on the PA. "Students, please be on time to your classes today. We are noticing a record number of students in the hallway between classes after the bell rings. Teachers, please begin closing and locking your doors once the bell rings. Students, starting today, if you are late and in the hallway after the bell, you will be sent to the tardy room. That room is Room 125. You will receive a referral and a phone call home. If this happens a second time, you will be suspended. Your teachers work too hard for you to be fooling around in the hallways. Get to class."

I get to my locker and exchange my Pre-Calc textbook for my AP Chemistry one. I can't remember if I need it or not, but it's better to be safe than sorry. When I close my locker, Mikki's there. She nearly scares me.

"Hey," she says softly, fidgeting with her fingernails and avoiding eye contact.

"Hey, Mik. You okay?"

She sighs and scratches the top of her head before going back to fidgeting with her nails. "I don't know," she says. "I feel like I'm losing my mind."

"What do you mean?"

"If I tell you, do you promise you won't judge me or look at me like I have three heads, like August and my parents did when I told them?"

I nod. "Of course, Mik."

"So, it all started a few days ago. I pocket-dialed Miles on my phone. I didn't think anything of it at first. I just canceled the call. But then—"

"The number called back," I say for her.

She lights up. "What? How did you know?"

"Something similar happened with me," I tell her, looking around and checking to see if anyone is eavesdropping into our conversation. I lower my voice just to be sure.

"But then I answered," Mikki says. "And it was . . . him. It was really him."

"I believe you," I tell her. "I've talked to him on the phone a couple times now. I have thought through almost every possibility and I have no clue how it all works, but what's absolutely undeniable is that I talked to him." I thought it was just me. I'm so glad he reached out to Mikki as well.

"I couldn't understand what he was trying to tell me," Mikki says. "Every time he would get close, the call would randomly end."

"He told me that he didn't kill himself. He told me someone pushed him. He asked me to figure out who."

Mikki looks right now like I must have looked last night—gasping and grasping and more than a little confused. "Do you believe that?" she asks.

"I don't know what I believe anymore."

Mikki exhales deeply. "But even if that were true, how would that help him?"

"I don't know," I say. "Maybe it's for our sake? So that we know the truth and the world does, too. Or maybe it's just so that his soul has peace in the afterlife. I wish I had answers."

"Same," Mikki says, tears falling from her eyes. She wipes them away quick. "Part of me really hopes all this sadness and anger about losing Miles is just messing with our imaginations. But I have a feeling things are about to get messy."

"Yeah," is all I can say. I toss my backpack over my shoulder.

"What do we do next?" Mikki asks, looking lost.

"I'll think as hard as I can and get back to you, Mik. Let's talk later, okay?"

She nods and gives me a tight-lipped smile.

The late bell rings. *Fuck.*

"Talk to you after school? Gotta get to class," I say. I run as fast as I can down D hallway and E hallway, until I get to where the Chemistry classes are. Right as I turn the corner where Ms. Eastman's class sits, she's shutting the door.

"Wait. Ms. Eastman, please!" I say, flagging her down before she shuts it all the way.

She pauses, noticing me. "Hurry, Mr. Hawkins. This is your one-time pass for being late. You heard Principal Samuels on the intercom. It is your responsibility to get to class. On time!"

"I know, I'm sorry, Ms. Eastman," I tell her. "It won't happen again, I promise."

After school, Mikki meets me at my car. She's got all her textbooks in hand. That's one thing that I've always admired about her. Mikki is a good student. She's gotten all As since I could remember. Normally, people make fun of nerds and people who try at school. But people don't mess with Mikki because they know that she could whoop their ass as well.

"What do we do?" Mikki asks me, pulling down her jean jacket, her dress flowing in the wind.

I rack my brain for any answer because nothing came to me during the school day like I had hoped. Then I say, "Maybe we talk to Mrs. Angela and Mr. Rodney?"

"They haven't left their house since Miles died," Mikki reminds me. It stings to hear that, because I can feel their pain. I know they won't be okay for a long time. But to cut themselves off from the world? It shows they have an unimaginable type of pain.

I wonder what would be the right thing to say to that. "I think they would want to know the truth about what happened to their son. They deserve to know."

"Yeah, I think you're right," Mikki says. "Do you want to head there now?"

"Uh, sure," I say. "Do you want to ride with me?"

"That would be great," Mikki responds. "August is usually my ride, but he's staying after to get help on some project with Mr. Sanchez."

"Hop in," I say, unlocking the passenger side when I get in.

As we drive toward Mrs. Angela and Mr. Rodney's house, there is a heavy silence between Mikki and me. The weight of what we are about to do hangs in the air, filling the car with an unspoken tension too complicated for words. I steal glances at Mikki, her usual confidence faltering slightly as she plays with the hem of her dress.

When we finally arrive at the house, it looks just as desolate and abandoned as it has for the past few weeks. The windows are dark, and there are no signs of life inside. Taking a deep breath, I make my way to the front door with Mikki, nerves churning in my stomach.

I raise my hand to knock, but before my knuckles can make contact with the wooden frame, the door swings open slowly. Standing before us is Mrs. Angela, her eyes red-rimmed and weary, but there is a spark of curiosity in them when she sees us. Rocco starts barking wildly.

"Hi there, Mrs. Angela," I begin, my voice cracking.

There are bags under her eyes and she's wearing pink hair rollers. "Hakeem? And . . . Mikki? What brings you two over here? Shouldn't you be in school?"

"School's over for the day," I remind her gently. "We get out at three o'clock."

"Guess I forgot that since . . ." She stops and tears pool in her eyes. She swallows hard and shuts her eyes for a moment.

"We have something to tell you," I say, my heart skipping a beat. "It's about Miles."

Her eyes widen. She wipes them, closes her bathrobe, and opens the door wider, taking a step back. "Come in," she says. "Would you guys like anything to drink?"

I shake my head and say, "No, thank you."

"Tea, if you have some ready," Mikki says.

"I've got peppermint, lemon-ginger, and vanilla chamomile," Mrs. Angela says. Rocco licks my legs and then goes over to greet Mikki.

"Lemon-ginger sounds good," Mikki answers with a nervous smile. Mrs. Angela leaves the room for a few minutes and then returns with a mug of tea for Mikki and Mr. Rodney, who follows her in. He's wearing a red-and-black plaid shirt and light jeans. Miles didn't get his style from his dad. That's for sure. Mikki takes a sip of the tea and winces at how hot it is. She reaches over and places it on a nearby coffee table.

"So, what brings you two here?" Mr. Rodney murmurs, his face wearing suspense.

Mikki and I exchange glances, unsure who should talk first. We didn't have time to rehearse lines in the car. Nor did we think to do so.

"You said it was about our Miles?" Mrs. Angela questions, sitting on the couch next to Mr. Rodney, gripping his hand as if to be comforted.

"We think that Miles was pushed in front of that bus. He didn't walk out in front of it," I say.

"Are you trying to tell us that Miles was murdered?" Mr. Rodney says. Mrs. Angela shrieks a little, cupping her mouth with her hand.

"We don't know if that's a hundred percent true, but we have reason to believe something else happened to Miles than what we all assumed," Mikki tells them, interceding on my behalf.

Mrs. Angela's face drains of color, her hand trembling as she squeezes Mr. Rodney's hand tighter. "Murdered? But how—why would anyone want to hurt our Miles?" Her voice quivers with a mixture of anguish and disbelief.

Mikki leans forward, her expression somber. "We're not entirely sure yet, but we both got a . . ." She hesitates. "A phone call."

"A phone call?" Mrs. Angela's voice wavers as she questions, more tears welling in her eyes.

"We both got . . . an anonymous tip," Mikki says really fast, like she's trying to get the lie out without feeling guilty. I figure she's too afraid to tell them we talked to Miles, that maybe saving them from

121

the full truth is wise or the best option to get them to believe us.

Mr. Rodney's brow furrows in confusion. "An anonymous tip? Did Miles ever mention anyone who might want to harm him?"

"I can't imagine anyone wanting to hurt him," Mrs. Angela responds, her voice barely a whisper.

Mikki and I both shake our heads slowly. I answer, "No, he never said anything about having enemies or people who might be out for him."

Mr. Rodney and Mrs. Angela look at each other like they are both befuddled and are trying to communicate with each other using only their thoughts.

"What *exactly* did this anonymous tip say?" Mr. Rodney wonders, scratching his beard.

I tell him, "He—I mean, *they* said that there was someone out there who pushed Miles in front of the bus and that Miles didn't take his own life." Maybe this time things will register with him.

"No! Pushed? What? None of this adds up," Mr. Rodney says. "I just don't—"

"The anonymous tip came from Miles himself," I add. Mikki looks like she wishes she could grab my words from the air and shove them back inside me.

Both Mr. Rodney and Mrs. Angela perk up with wide eyes. "What—Miles?" Mrs. Angela's tears turn into a deep, guttural sob. She collapses and unravels, sobbing into her hands loudly.

"I think it's best if you two leave," Mr. Rodney says after a moment, with sadness and frustration evident in his words. "That's enough nonsense that we can handle for one day."

"I know it sounds ridiculous, but both of us heard from him," Mikki says, trying to make it right.

But Mr. Rodney just shakes his head. "I know you two mean well, but if you're expecting us to believe this . . . that's just too much. Really, you need to leave now."

I wish we had some evidence, some recording we could play. But all we have is our call logs and our word, and I know that's not going to be enough.

"I'm so sorry," I say. "We didn't mean to make things worse."

Mr. Rodney nods, but it's clear he still wants us to leave. Mrs. Angela is a wreck, and he needs to tend to her.

Mikki and I are silent as we leave, and silent in the car. Mikki stares out the window, her forehead pressed up against the glass as the city of Indianapolis blurs past her.

Mikki is the first to break the heaviness hanging between us. She turns to me, her face a mix of fear and uncertainty. "Do you think we did the right thing by telling them?" she asks, her voice soft.

I glance at her, seeing the sadness in her face. Taking a deep breath, I reply, "I don't know, Mikki. But they deserve to know the truth, no matter how painful it may be. They might be in denial, but Miles told us the truth."

"Yeah," Mikki says with a sigh.

"I was secretly hoping that he called them, too," I add.

"Miles knows his parents," Mikki says. "They've always been the same way. They would've shrugged it off as a prank or something else."

"Maybe you're right. It's just us, I guess," I say.

As we pull up in front of Mikki's house, she lingers in the car for a moment before turning to me. "What do we do now?" she asks, her brown eyes searching mine for an answer.

Closing my eyes briefly, I consider our options. "We need to find out a way to see what happened that day. And we need to uncover the truth about what really happened to Miles, even if the adults think we're making it all up," I say with some amount of confidence.

Mikki nods slowly, determination sparking in her eyes. "We can't let Miles be alone in this. We can't not help him."

"Yeah," I agree.

"We can't go to the cops or the news people. We may have to Sherlock Holmes this shit," Mikki says. "Look for clues, trace steps, do our own investigation, you know?"

"Wait, I might have an idea of where to go next," I add.

"You do?" Mikki looks relieved.

"That bus hit Miles on the same block where Cousin Vinny's is. I wonder if we can somehow get our hands on video surveillance footage and see if there is someone with Miles before everything happened."

"That just might be it," Mikki says. "When can we go check?"

"Let me make a phone call," I say. I call up Frankie and he eventually picks up. I beg him to give us permission to come into the shop and check the cameras. I owe him a shift in exchange for getting access to the video footage. I tell him deal before I hang up. I text Eliza and let her know about everything, the plan, how things

124

went with Miles's parents, and where we're off to next. She texts back that she'll meet us there.

"There's something I should tell you before we go," Mikki says, grabbing my arm. "I'm pregnant."

"You're pregnant?"

"Yeah." She half smiles. "It's Miles's baby, but I don't think I have what it takes to be a mother and obviously I don't want the baby to grow up without its father. So I don't know what I'm going to do, but if he calls me again, I'm going to tell him."

"Wow," I say. "Um, congratulations, Mikki . . . and I'm sorry." I don't entirely know what to say—I'm stunned. I decide on not thinking about it and keeping my mouth shut, focusing on getting to see the video footage of what happened to Miles.

We arrive at Cousin Vinny's. Eliza is waiting for us at the entrance. Frankie is in the middle of helping a customer when we barge in, heading straight for the camera room. Frankie leaves the customer, tells the other worker, Nick, to take over what he was just doing, and we go in.

As we enter the camera room, the screens flicker with images, capturing different angles of the street outside. My heart races, knowing that the answers we seek may be just a few clicks away. Frankie has to scroll through hours, days, and weeks of footage. But eventually, the room goes all the way silent. Frankie gestures for us to take a look, and with trembling hands, I zoom in on the footage from the day of Miles's accident.

After what feels like an eternity, we reach the crucial moment. There, on the screen, we see Miles walking alone, his hands shoved deep into his pockets. But then something unexpected catches our eyes. A hooded figure lurking in the shadows, following Miles at a distance.

"He's being followed," Eliza says, stating the obvious but saying it from shock and curiosity.

"But why?" I say.

Mikki gasps beside me, her eyes widening in realization. "And who is that?" she whisper-shouts.

I focus on enhancing the image, trying to get a clearer view of the mysterious person. As the pixels sharpen, a chill runs down my spine.

"Wait, rewind it," Mikki says sharply. "I think I noticed something that might be a weapon."

I quickly do what Mikki requests, furiously rewinding the footage to the moment where the hooded guy first appeared. We watch intently as the person moves closer, stepping into a flickering streetlight for just a moment.

"There," Mikki says.

I freeze-frame it.

And that's when I see it. A glint of metal, unmistakably a gun tucked into the figure's belt. This is a dangerous person. They meant what they did.

"They were armed," I say, my heart pounding in my chest.

"No one warned Miles," Mikki says sadly.

I hit play again.

The scene on the screen changes abruptly. Miles and the hooded figure both turn a corner, and that's when it happens:

Miles gets pushed in front of the bus. I'm just relieved I don't have to see all of that happen on-screen. I don't know if I could handle seeing that. I know the bus killed Miles quick. Broke his bones and snapped his spine. I read that there was a lot of blood on the scene.

"We have to find out who that was and why they were following Miles," I say determinedly, already plotting our next move.

"Wait, rewind it one more time," Mikki requests.

I rewind it to the same exact spot we've watched three times now. This time, I don't freeze it. I just let it play on through.

"The hooded man has a red bandanna hanging out of his back pocket," Frankie points out to everyone. Mikki instantly puts a hand over her mouth.

"Holy shit," Frankie says. Because we all know what that means.

Except Eliza, who says, "Is anyone going to fill me in?"

"The red bandanna means he's in the Crimson Brotherhood gang," I explain. "They usually only come after people who are in rival gangs or who fuck over one of their members." I've only heard stories from people and paid attention to news stories from time to time, but I never knew anyone who was in that gang or a victim of them. Until now.

"Miles wasn't in a gang and he didn't hang with that type of crowd," Mikki says.

"I know," I tell her. "That's why this is all so weird. Why would the Crimson Brotherhood want to harm Miles?"

We all fall into a heavy silence, the weight of the situation pressing down on us. The revelation that Miles had somehow attracted the attention of one of the most notorious gangs in Indianapolis is chilling. I can feel the tension crackling in the air as we exchange worried glances, each of us grappling with the implications of what we've just discovered.

"We need to figure out what connection Miles had to the Crimson Brotherhood," Mikki speaks up eventually, her voice edged with determination. "There must be something that links him to them, something we're missing."

"There has to be," I agree, exhaling deeply.

Meanwhile, my mind races with possibilities. Was there a secret side to Miles that we were unaware of? Did he unwittingly cross paths with someone from the gang? Or is there a more sinister reason behind his sudden and brutal demise?

What am I missing? That's the only question popcorning around in my head. I walk down the block, making random turns without a destination in mind, thinking about the information I just learned and the information yet to be revealed.

Eventually, I make it to an abandoned industrial warehouse. The side of the building has a rusted metal ladder that goes up to the rooftop. Without hesitation, I climb up. Pulling my weight and climbing is difficult and leaves me out of breath. But when I make it to the top, there's nothing but gravel and piles of litter and trash. I sit down on the edge of the rooftop, looking over the town. It's naught but three or so stories high, but it's a pretty dope view. The Indianapolis skyline is almost eerie, factory smoke billowing into the air, meeting the clouds, causing a gross almost-gray color to wash over the city.

I look up and see the sun trying to break through some clouds and smoke. What did the Crimson Brotherhood want with Miles? I've only ever heard stories from Dad and sometimes people at school about things that would happen to people who pissed off members in that gang, but now they've gotten to Miles. This makes everything more complicated.

I hear something rattle followed by short grunts, like someone else is climbing up. In the blink of an eye, I put myself in a defensive stance, unsure of who it could be. But it's Eliza. She's out of breath and bends over to take deep breaths once she makes it to the top.

"You followed me?"

"Uh, well, kind of," Eliza says, pausing. "Look, it just seemed like the right thing to do. And I figured you probably shouldn't be alone right now."

I turn my attention elsewhere, looking back up at the sky. "Thanks," I say after some time passes. Birds chirp in the distance and cars honk and fly by beneath my feet. "I just can't piece together everything," I say, my voice splitting like I've just hit puberty.

"I get that," Eliza says. "I'm sure it's all way too much for you. I can't imagine."

"Miles had an edge, but messing with the Crimson Brotherhood is a whole other level of danger that even he would never cross," I say. "What do I do?"

"We. What do *we* do?" Eliza says. She sits down next to me, the gravel making noise as she settles on the ground. "We stick together.

We figure this out. We will find out what happened."

Determination flares in my chest and my heartbeat picks up.

Eliza's words echo inside me. "You're right," I tell her.

"We also must be really careful. If the Crimson Brotherhood finds out we know something that we shouldn't know, we could be next."

"Next?" I say, even though I know exactly what she means. Just the thought of it makes my blood run cold.

Some silence washes over us for a moment, but the whole time, I know that Eliza's point about sticking together is going to be our best chance to find out the truth. I know that we can't back down now. And some part of me feels like Miles is counting on us.

"I'm not usually afraid of heights, but looking down makes me want to throw up," Eliza says, slowly getting up from the rooftop.

She puts out a hand and helps me up as well. I brush off rocks from my butt and point to the rocks on Eliza so she can do the same. It's in this moment that I realize how much Eliza's presence has been just what I've needed. Her steady reassurance helps me trust that I won't be alone in this fight for Miles.

CHAPTER   TWELVE

When it's time, Dad has KFC on the dinner table for everyone. Once every now and then, we get food to eat out. Dad loves KFC more than any other restaurant, so if he's in charge of picking up food, we know what it'll be. Fried chicken, mashed potatoes, mac and cheese, corn, coleslaw, and biscuits with honey. Dad, Momma, Jorjah, and Judah are all sitting at the dinner table. There's an open seat for me when I finally come down from my room, where I've been thinking about everything that's happened without understanding anything new.

I sit down in my usual spot at the table. It's silent, despite the usual smacking from Judah and Jorjah. They like to have competitions from time to time about who can be the grossest eater. I can never look at them when I'm eating. I'd lose my appetite.

The whole time, we just eat, no conversation. Usually, there's *something*, but tonight, nothing at all. It's almost scary that Momma doesn't start a conversation. No asking me about school, about my day. She just sits there across from me, her head down, slowly picking at a chicken wing, eating bits of it.

Near the end of dinner, Momma breaks her silence and the awkwardness at the table. Her words are serious and her tone is angry. And not just normal angry, but Black-mom type of angry, which is a whole other level of anger. It's mixed with disappointment and passive aggression.

131

"I got a call from Angela and Rodney just a bit ago," Momma says, not making eye contact, just putting the lids back on the buckets of food.

My breathing picks up a bit; now everything makes sense why it was so silent.

"Why did you go over there, making their lives worse by spewing all that nonsense?" she says. "I told you it was foolish what you were saying when you told me the other night."

"But, Momma—"

"No, I'm talking!" she interrupts me, standing up from her seat and putting things in the fridge. Dad and Judah and Jorjah all continue to eat. "You went over there and told them that Miles called you on the phone? Why would you do that?"

"But he did!" I plead.

"He did not!" Dad shouts, interjecting with a mouth full of food. "He's dead. I know that's hard for you. It's hard for all of us. But he's dead. He's gone, Hakeem. He can't talk to you on the phone."

I'm fighting a losing fight, I know that. I settle on keeping my mouth shut. There's no use in trying to argue with them or convince them otherwise. They're stubborn and don't believe me. Why don't adults believe kids?

Momma comes over to me after leaving the fridge. She picks my head up by putting her hand under my chin and forcing me to look up at her. "Let me see your eyes," she says.

I allow her to look into my eyes.

"Now let me see your arms and wrists," she says. "I thought

Narcotics Anonymous was helping you. It was supposed to be helping you." She begins to cry as she rolls up my sleeves to search my skin. I know exactly what she's doing. She has a recovering drug addict for a son. She's wondering if I've been using something—anything. She thinks I'm high, out of my right mind, and that she's about to catch me red-handed.

"I haven't done anything," I say. "Please. I'm telling you the truth. All of it. It's the truth."

She slaps me quick and hard across the face, my mouth flying open. Judah and Jorjah watch me, stunned. Dad looks caught off guard, too, lifting from the table and grabbing Momma as she sobs uncontrollably. I have to admit it: I'm hurt. And I'm not just talking about the slap, but the fact that she thinks I'm using again. It feels like she's communicating a lack of trust in me, which stings in more ways than her strike to the side of my face.

One of the most fucked-up parts of being an addict is that everyone is always suspicious of you. How much longer until you snap? How much longer until you snap together? What are you hiding? And it's the worst kind of pain when it's your own family.

I dismiss myself from the table, grab my stuff, and head up to my room. I shut the door behind me, collapse onto the bed, and cry.

I lie on my bed, listening to the muffled sounds of my family downstairs. They're probably talking about me, wondering where they went wrong with me. I know that's what they do when I'm not around. And maybe they're right. Maybe I am a lost cause.

I lie there for what feels like hours, the weight of my mother's accusation heavy on my chest. The tears come in waves, each one washing over me with a mix of anger and sorrow. How can she not believe me? How can she think I would go back to that life after everything we've been through?

As I try to collect my thoughts, I remember the phone call from Miles vividly, as if it's stained into my thoughts. His voice was so clear, so real. How can they think I would make up something like that?

But then doubt starts to creep in. What if I'm wrong? What if someone's just playing with me and Mikki, playing with our desperate longing to hear his voice one last time? The uncertainty gnaws at me, tearing me apart from the inside out.

A knock on my door startles me out of my thoughts. The door creaks open and a head pops in. Dad.

"Can I come in? I just want to talk with you."

I don't budge. "Yeah," I say.

He comes in and sits on the very edge of the foot of the bed. His back faces me.

"Your mother didn't mean to hit you," he says, sighing. "She's just frustrated and scared."

"Scared of what?" I say, curious. I sit up and scoot my back to the headboard for support.

"She doesn't want to lose you again," Dad says. "We both don't want to lose you. When you were on that stuff, it really wrecked your mother in ways I haven't seen before."

"You guys won't lose me," I assure him. "I'm clean. I've been clean for five months."

"I know, I know," Dad says. "You just haven't sounded like

yourself or been acting like yourself. And as your parents, we can't take for granted that it's all about grief. We have to make sure it's not something else. You were your mother's golden boy who got clean. You gave her a reason to even believe in Jesus again, Hakeem. Don't ruin that for her."

"I'm not trying to ruin anything for anybody," I say.

"I hear you, Son," he says, but I don't think he really *hears* me.

There's a beat of silence that lingers for way too long. I stare at my ceiling and Dad stares at the floor. Moonlight sneaks its way through the blinds and casts shadows throughout my room.

"I just want you to know that if something did happen to Miles, we would know it. Some of the best detectives were investigating what happened. Don't doubt them, Son."

"But people make mistakes and get things wrong all the time," I point out.

"I understand, but if something else happened or someone lied, those people will be held accountable. A man always has to pay for his sins."

I don't say anything, just keep listening to him, nodding in the dark. Honestly, everything he says goes in one ear and out the other.

"You'll have to separate the good wheat from the tares. Because if you don't, the tares will ruin the entire harvest. Nurture all the good things, Hakeem. I wish my daddy taught me that sooner than when he did. So I'm gonna impart that onto you."

As the moonlight continues to dance across my room, I speak up, breaking the lingering silence. "So what do I do now? How do I separate the good from the bad?"

Dad looks over at me for the first time, his eyes reflecting the dim light from outside. "You'll know," he says. "It might start with leaving things in the past so that you can move forward in life. You don't look back."

"Hmm," I say.

I think it means something entirely different to me. It means you start by digging deeper within yourself. You don't take things at face value. You question, you investigate, and you trust your instincts, which is exactly what I'm doing.

I nod slowly at him, the pieces starting to come together in my mind, filtering out what he said about not looking back. I know that's his way of telling me not to question Miles's death.

He places a hand on my feet, a reassuring gesture in the darkness. "I love you, Son," he says. "We just want the best for you. Don't break your mother's heart again. I don't think she can take it."

In the middle of the night, I can't sleep. I can't stop thinking about Miles, about the video footage we all saw, about what happened at dinner—what Momma said and what she accused me of. It's all just too much to go to sleep in my bed, in this room, in this house.

I pull out my phone and text Eliza.

Me: are you up?
Eliza: Yeah. Can't sleep.
Me: Me too.
Eliza: Sux.
Me: Can I come over?

Eliza: To the motel?

Me: Yes. Please. I can't be here.

Eliza: Uh, okay. Sure.

Eventually, I arrive at Eliza's room at the Motel 6. The dim light from the neon sign outside flickers through the thin motel curtains, casting a soft glow over Eliza's room. I hesitate for a moment before knocking on the door, unsure of what to expect. The door swings open slowly, revealing Eliza standing there in her pajamas—a crop top and shorts—a concerned look on her face.

"Hey," she says softly, ushering me inside. The room is small and cramped, but it feels like a sanctuary compared to the chaos that has consumed my life lately, especially tonight, as things feel extra heavy. Eliza hands me a bottle of water from a mini fridge under where the small TV sits, and we sit in silence for a while, the only sound being the gentle hum of the air-conditioning unit doing its job.

Finally, I break the silence. "I don't know what to do, Eliza. Everything is falling apart and I'm overwhelmed and now my parents think I'm using again. I feel like I'm drowning."

Tears fill up in my eyes and my throat gets all scratchy and tight like it does when I'm moments away from crying.

Eliza reaches out and squeezes my hand, her eyes filled with empathy. "I'm here for you, Hakeem. I'm sorry your parents are responding like this. That's so unfair to you." And in this moment, I feel like I can breathe a little easier. Eliza's words are a lifeline in the storm raging inside me, a beacon of light cutting through the darkness threatening to consume me.

"I just wish they would listen to me, you know? Understand that I'm trying my best, understand that I have no use in turning back to the old ways of doing things, but it's like they've suddenly made up their minds that I'm not clean anymore all because I went to talk to Miles's parents. How did this all backfire on me?"

Eliza looks at me as she listens intently, taking in my words. After a while she says, "I just think your parents are scared. Fear does terrible things to a person, like, clouds your judgment and makes you believe things that aren't true." She pauses. "But you know your truth, and that's what matters most. You know who you are."

I give a small smile, her words wrapping around me like a protective shield.

"I think what you need right now is just some rest," she says, patting a spot on the bed. She grabs for a pillow and fluffs it up. "This can be your side for the night."

"Are you sure?" I say.

"Of course. It's the least I could do," she says.

We both eventually migrate to the bed. Eliza takes off her shirt, revealing her bra underneath. I look away before she can notice that I'm watching. She doesn't even acknowledge it, just climbs underneath the blanket and sheets, facing away from me.

I climb into bed, shifting uncomfortably under the covers, the closeness between Eliza and me causing a jolt of nervous energy to race through my body. The air in the room feels cool but electric. I turn to look at Eliza, her silhouette outlined by the faint glow filtering through the curtains. In this moment, she's not just my friend; she's my anchor, grounding me in a reality where I'm more than the sum of my struggles. The weight on my shoulders feels a little lighter, as if she shares the burden with me without a word spoken.

She slowly turns her body so that she's facing me, her eyes flickering open as she's centimeters from my face, so close I can feel the warmth of her breath as she exhales.

"One time, I went on a solo camping trip out west. I set up a tent, made s'mores and hot dogs, and then went to sleep around midnight. I ended up waking up a couple hours later because I heard a noise outside my tent," Eliza whispers, as if there are people she doesn't want to wake up, as if it's not just the two of us.

"Raccoons?" I say, preparing myself.

"Gross. Even better," she says. "I grabbed my flashlight and saw a doe and its baby. They were just eating all my leftover marshmallows. I yelled, 'Those are my marshmallows! Go get your own!' They slowly backed up and I swear they made faces like I was the weirdest human being they've ever encountered."

I laugh. "That's a good story."

"The best part was that they came back the next day and brought their friends. It taught me something. It taught me that sometimes it's nice to share something you love with someone or something else, even if they don't quite understand it the way you do. That moment, staring at those deer munching on stolen marshmallows under the moonlight, I felt a connection to nature that I had never experienced before. It was like we were all just creatures of this world, coexisting in harmony for that brief moment in time."

"That's amazing," I say.

"You're like those deer stealing marshmallows. You've been through a lot, carrying burdens that aren't yours to bear. But just like those deer, you deserve to taste the sweetness of life without fear or guilt holding you back."

I swallow hard and stare into her eyes. She stares back into mine. We inch closer to each other like we're pulled by an invisible string, our eyes closing almost at the same time. Our lips touch gently, but Eliza pulls away quick. "Please don't tell me you snore."

"Um, I don't think so," I say, stammering.

"Good night," she says and kisses me quick on the cheek. And just like that, she turns over again. I watch her chest expand and contract, until it gets slower and slower, and I know she's asleep. The taste of her remains on my lips and it's the very thing that sends me dreaming about something entirely different for the first time in a long time.

CHAPTER   THIRTEEN

The following morning, I wake up in bed with Eliza. We are under the same blanket, under the same sheet, and just inches away from each other. She slept facing the wall and I slept facing the door, our backs occasionally touching through the night. I decide not to go to school. What happened last night was just too much. My mind feels way too fried and unable to function properly. I'm in no mood for dealing with teachers or students or learning.

I lie there for a while, listening to Eliza's steady breathing. I check my phone and notice that it's almost 8:00 a.m. I try to ease out of the bed, trying so hard not to wake her up as she looks so peaceful and comfortable.

"Hey," she says. "You're up early."

"I'm used to getting up early for school," I tell her.

"Makes sense. I'm not up until ten most days. Guess that's one of the many benefits of not being in school. You can sleep in every day."

I smile at her and nod. "Yeah, I guess there are many perks to not being in school," I reply. As I start getting ready for the day, Eliza sits up in bed, her eyes still heavy with sleep.

"What are your plans for today?" she asks, rubbing her eyes.

"I don't know," I say. "I really just need to clear my head."

"I get that," she replies. "I totally understand if you just need to go for a walk or get some sun."

"Thanks. I need to figure out what connection Miles has with the Crimson Brotherhood, too, so I guess that's also on the agenda. But first, I was thinking of exploring the town a bit more. Maybe check out a bookstore or get a bite to eat."

Eliza's face lights up at the mention of the bookstore. "I love that idea! There's this awesome used bookstore downtown called White Rabbit. I love it. They have a great collection of rare books. I can spend hours in there."

"I'm not much of a reader, but I'm hoping to find some other things that will help me in my investigation of what happened to Miles," I tell her.

"I'm in," she says. "If it's okay if I join you."

"Sure. But we are not taking the hearse."

She laughs. "I guess that's a deal."

We quickly get ready and head out into the crisp morning air. On the car ride downtown, I turn the radio on, playing Elevation Worship. I might not be as sold on the church as Momma, but there's something about worship music from time to time that's just the right dose of comfort and peace I need.

I'm relieved that I don't have any messages from my parents; since I left after they went to bed, I'm guessing they assumed I left for school early. And maybe the school didn't call them to ask where I was. I guess we'll see.

Eliza and I kill time before White Rabbit opens. When we arrive, Eliza smiles at the sight of the quaint bookstore nestled between two larger buildings. The bell above the door tinkles as we enter, greeted by the musty smell of old books and the soft chime of classical music playing in the background.

Eliza immediately veers off toward the section of rare books, her eyes alight with excitement as she runs her fingers along the spines. Meanwhile, I head toward the section on local history, hoping to uncover any clues that might shed light on Miles's death and what really happened that day.

As I browse through the shelves, a faded, stained newspaper clipping catches my eye. It's an article from a couple years ago detailing a mysterious incident at the nearby abandoned apartment complex—a place rumored to be where lots of Crimson Brotherhood members hide out at. Could this help me find someone connected to what happened to Miles? Could I find that hooded man from the video footage there? I make a mental note to talk to Mikki about it as I take a photo of the clipping.

Eliza finds me in the local history aisle. She holds an armful of books that she's bursting with excitement to talk about. She finds a nearby table to sit them on so she can walk me through what she's going to buy.

"First up, we've got *The Book Thief* by Markus Zusak. A historical fiction novel set in Germany during World War II. Narrator is Death. How cool is that?"

"Hmm, that is kinda interesting," I say.

"Next up is *Agnes Grey* by Anne Brontë. Love a good romance. So I'm excited to read it. Anne is the forgotten Brontë sister. Everyone knows Charlotte and Emily, but no one knows Anne."

"Sucks to be her, huh," I say, a laugh slipping out.

"Right? Especially because societal recognition was a significant marker of success, especially for women writers. Poor Anne was overshadowed by her sisters' more popular books, and she quit writing altogether."

"Wow," I say.

"Here's a memoir by my favorite poet," Eliza says as she pulls out a worn copy of Maya Angelou's *I Know Why the Caged Bird Sings*. She opens the book to her favorite passage and begins to recite it with such passion that I can't help but be drawn in, focused only on her voice—everything else fades away. The words wrap around me like a warm blanket, comforting and empowering at the same time. As she finishes, I look up to see tears glistening in her eyes, like she's feeling the words on the deepest level.

"That was beautiful," I whisper, also moved by the emotion in her voice.

"It's one of those books that stays with you long after you've read it," Eliza replies softly. "Maya Angelou's words have a way of touching your soul."

I nod, listening, admiring all the ways Eliza's coming alive. I'm seeing a different side of her that I don't think I've seen before. Here, she's almost . . . *happy*. I didn't think she was capable of feeling passion like this. I didn't know what was buried beneath all the darkness she's experienced. But now I see. There's always more to a person than what they allow you to see.

"Then, there's Tolstoy! God, I love Tolstoy. But I've never read *War and Peace*. I fell in love with his *Anna Karenina*."

Time seems to slip away effortlessly as Eliza loses herself in the world of books and I lose myself in listening to her talk about them. Next thing I know, a whole hour flies by.

"Want to grab some lunch from somewhere?" Eliza asks me, collecting her books.

"That sounds good. I could go for a bite right about now," I say, feeling emptiness evident in my stomach.

We decide to walk to a nearby café called the Brew-n-Burrito House, the sun shining brightly and a gentle breeze ruffling Eliza's hair. Her hair is long, flowing, and dark—it makes her look majestic.

We settle down at a cozy table near a window in the corner. A waiter, a tall, young white man who looks like he's been working out all his life, comes over.

"Welcome to the Brew-n-Burrito House," he says. "You guys been here before?"

We both shake our heads.

"Well, welcome in. Because you both are new, your drinks are on the house. Our treat to you," the man says, passing us menus. "We're known for our drip coffee, custom lattes, and obviously our build-your-own burritos. What can I grab for you two?"

The combination of coffee and burritos sounds like it'll lead me to spend some extra time in the bathroom later, but I love both coffee and burritos separately so maybe the creator of this place is actually a genius.

"I'll take your strawberry milk latte," Eliza orders. "And for the burrito, I'll take chicken, queso, brown rice, mild salsa, lettuce, guacamole, and pineapples."

Pineapples? I wonder in my head, but then realize it's my turn to order now as both Eliza and the waiter start to stare at me.

I study the menu as fast as I can, unsure of what I want to order. I'm so indecisive. I hate when restaurants have such big menus.

"Um, I'll do a caramel matcha latte and then a bean-and-rice burrito with steak, queso, corn, jalapeños, and extra cilantro."

"Sounds delicious. My name is Charlie and I'll be taking care of you guys today. If you need anything at all, just flag me down. I'll be right back with those drinks." He smiles and winks before putting his notepad in his back pocket and taking off.

I'm wondering if that wink was more than just Typical Waiter Behavior when Charlie returns with our drinks, the steam rising enticingly from the mugs. Eliza takes a sip of her strawberry milk latte, a look of pure bliss crossing her face. I can't help but smile at her reaction. As I bring my caramel matcha latte to my lips, the rich aroma fills my nostrils and I know it's going to be just as good as it smells.

"How are you?" Eliza asks me, taking a sip of her latte.

"I'm . . . okay," I say with some level of confidence, though I'm unsure of the truth. "You?"

"Meh. I think I needed to get out just as much as it sounds like you needed to," Eliza says, running a hand through her hair, showing her wildflower tattoo.

"I can only imagine."

"Being caged up at that motel, I think, has taken a toll on me. I'm already cold, but I think it's only made me colder."

"Cold?"

"Yeah, you don't think I'm coldhearted? Like, a bit of a bitch?"

"No," I lie.

"Truth is, I'm just coldhearted because I'm terrified. I'm afraid about what my life would be like if I didn't control everything," she says, and a silence washes over us before she continues. "Sorry, I need duct tape over my mouth. I keep oversharing, don't I? Geez, like, shut up already, Eliza."

"No, no, no," I say, putting a hand up. "I'm just listening to you share. You don't have to stop if you don't want. Honestly, it's been helpful to think about other things with you, rather than get lost in my own thoughts."

A beat.

"What people don't understand about depression is that it makes you cold," Eliza tells me. "And it's not about everyone else. It's about you. It's not about what happens in the outside world, but in the inside world of your mind, body, and soul. Something in your heart, something in your brain, something in your gut convinces you that you're a burden, that you don't matter, that you're unlovable, that you'll never ever be enough, that this world would be a lot better without you in it. That voice inside you stays and stays, but no one else can hear it but you. That's the loneliest part."

"I hear it, too," I say.

She massages the wildflower tattoo on her arm. "That's another thing about wildflowers. Wildflowers remind me that even in the harshest conditions, there is beauty to be found. They push through the toughest ground, through concrete and rock, just to bloom. It's a reminder that even when everything seems dark and hopeless, there is a chance for something beautiful to come out of it. We're wildflowers, pushing through our struggles to find our own bit of sunlight. And maybe, just maybe, we can bloom, too." Eliza's voice softens as she talks, her eyes glistening with unshed tears. "We may be battling our own demons, but we're still here, still fighting. And that's something to be proud of," she continues, her eyes meeting mine.

I like being here, in the now that Eliza and I are creating. I'm not thinking about my parents. I'm not thinking about how over-whelmed I feel. She puts a hand on the table and then I put a hand on the table. They're inches apart from each other, getting closer, when my phone vibrates multiple times. I check and see it's Mikki texting.

Mikki: I talked with August and we think we might have a lead on who the guy was in the footage. You free after school?
Me: Yes. Where should we meet?
Mikki: 1246 Everwood Rd. Come as soon as you can.

"What's going on?" Eliza asks.

I'm still wrapping my head around it. "Mikki just texted saying she might know who was in the surveillance footage, following Miles."

"What? Wow, she really is a true detective, huh?" Eliza responds.

"We're meeting after school to talk about it. She sent me some random address that I don't recognize."

"Want me to come with?" Eliza offers.

"I don't want to make you do that," I say. "But I'll fill you in on everything."

148

"I don't mind," Eliza says. "There are some things I need to take care of, but they can wait." The way she says it sounds mysterious, but everything about her is a mystery—one I'm not sure I'll ever fully piece together or solve. I wonder if she's even possible to figure out.

CHAPTER FOURTEEN

When school's done, we meet Mikki and August at the location I was texted, on the east side of town.

When we get out of the car, Mikki waves at me and gives a look to Eliza.

"Who's this?" August asks, not making eye contact with me, but looking at Eliza.

I just realized I haven't had a chance to introduce Eliza to anyone—not even at Cousin Vinny's when we were checking the camera footage.

"Eliza, this is Mikki and August," I say. Just awkward smiles all around. "Where are we, Mik?"

"I have a friend who used to be in the Crimson Brotherhood. He asked to get jumped out but now lives off the grid. His name's Jaquan. We think he might be able to give us some help."

It looks like an ordinary middle-class home from the outside, with a messy, overgrown lawn and a couple of bikes lying on the porch that look like they've been untouched for years. As we make our way to the front door, I notice the curtains twitching in one of the windows, as if someone inside is watching us. August rings the doorbell, and we all exchange a nervous glance while waiting for a response. Finally, the door creaks open, revealing a tall, light brown–skinned man with piercing gray eyes and a welcoming smile, wearing a blinged-out grill.

"What's up, G?" the guy says, shaking up with August. "Why you bring so many people to my crib for, huh?"

"You know I wouldn't do this unless I had to, man," August says.

"Whatever. What's up, everybody? I'm Jaquan. But you can call me J-Dog," he says, opening the door all the way, motioning for us to come in. When I'm inside, I see a gun on his waist and a knife in his sock.

Eliza stands close to me, saying nothing, just breathing.

"So what can I do for you?" Jaquan asks, taking a seat in a recliner.

Mikki whips out her phone and flashes it to him. "Do you know who this is?" I didn't even see her take a picture of the video footage when we were at Cousin Vinny's. She must've snuck it when no one was looking.

Jaquan leans in, squinting at the picture on Mikki's phone. Recognition flashes in his eyes before he quickly schools his features into a mask of unconcern. "Yeah, I know this guy. His name's Rowdy. He used to roll with the Crimson Brotherhood until he screwed them over for a better deal with the Night Lords. Last I heard, Rowdy was at their hideout. They've got an abandoned warehouse on the outskirts of town."

My heart races in my chest.

"We need to find him," Mikki says. "Like, now!"

"Why?" Jaquan wonders.

"He killed my . . . friend!" Mikki says, thinking of the right word to call Miles.

"You guys are messing with some dangerous stuff," Jaquan says,

151

his voice low and serious. "The Brotherhood runs the streets. But the Night Lords are on a whole other level."

"What do you mean?" I ask, my hands starting to shake.

Jaquan looks at me, his eyes almost piercing my soul. "That warehouse is filled with rats and pigs," he says. "It's not easy to get in there."

"Rats and pigs?" Mikki and I question, both at the same time.

"Cops, police, ops, that's what I mean. The Night Lords got some kind of agreement with some dirty cops that help them run their whole operation. Rowdy went rogue, is what I was told, and took out a bunch of fellow Brotherhood members. Some kind of Night Lords initiation. Hazing, if you will. This is some tough stuff you're dealing with."

August shifts uncomfortably, a bead of sweat forming on his forehead. "We know, J-Dog. That's why we came to you. You're our best chance."

"Yes. We need your help to get to the bottom of this," I say.

Jaquan lets out a low whistle, clearly impressed by the gravity of the situation. He leans forward, eyeing each of us carefully before speaking again. "All right, here's the deal. I'll help you out, but you're going to owe me."

"Of course," Mikki says before August can stop her.

We follow Jaquan to the abandoned warehouse he mentioned earlier. There are gang members coming in and out, many of them with boxes that come from some unknown source.

Jaquan leads us through a series of dark alleys and abandoned buildings, avoiding the main entrance where the gang members are stationed. As we get close to the warehouse from the back, he signals for us to crouch and stay hidden in the shadows, the moon hanging by its neck in the sky.

"This is it," Jaquan whispers, pointing to a small window that's been boarded up. "If Rowdy is in there, that's where he'll be holed up."

I feel a surge of fear and adrenaline coursing through me as Jaquan starts prying off the boards with a crowbar he brought along. The wood creaks loudly, making me hold my breath, but thankfully no one seems to notice. Without a second thought, almost like it's instinct, or like they're magnets, Eliza and I grab each other's hands, holding tight.

Once the boards are removed, Jaquan gestures for us to follow him inside. The interior of the warehouse is dimly lit with flickering fluorescent lights, casting eerie shadows across the vast space. We stick close to Jaquan as he leads us through stacks of crates and old machinery, careful to avoid being seen.

"This is as far as we can go, before this turns ugly," Jaquan informs us, stopping behind a stack of boxes. "This is a drug ring. And I'm not getting killed because of any of y'all."

I try to quiet my breathing so we don't get caught. "Where is Rowdy?" Mikki whispers.

"There. In the white T-shirt."

I look through a crack between the boxes. I see who Jaquan describes and my blood runs cold, thinking about being in the same room as the man who pushed Miles in front of that bus, taking him away from me and his family and friends.

But then something else happens that makes me want to throw up. Rowdy reaches for a packet and hands it to someone in a cop uniform.

It's the officer who pulled me over. I search my memory for what I remember about him. Eugene was his name. Officer Eugene. Badge number 18798.

"I know that cop. He works with my dad. Oh my god," I whisper. "I've got to go tell my dad."

"But what do we do about Rowdy?" Mikki whispers back.

Before I say anything else, Eliza murmurs, "There's not much we can do at this point. We're here. We can see him. But we are not the police. We can't do anything."

"But who do you call when the police are helping the bad guys?" Mikki says.

"Look, I know there are a lot of people upset about what went down with those Brotherhood members that got ganked by Rowdy. He'll get what's coming to him in time," Jaquan says reassuringly.

We leave the warehouse just as carefully and quietly as we arrived. Jaquan takes off. Then Mikki hops in August's blue Pontiac G6 and they head home.

"How'd you feel about coming home with me?" I ask Eliza. "I'm not sure I can tell them all on my own. They'll never believe me."

"Okay," Eliza says. Unquestioning. It's almost like it was with Miles, which is a weird thought.

I know I need to focus on how to tell this all. The whole time I'm driving, I'm thinking about what Dad will say, what might happen next.

154

I arrive at home. Dad's police squad car's in the driveway so I know he's home. I need to tell him about Officer Eugene and how he's working with the Night Lords gang at that abandoned warehouse. I need to expose the truth. For Miles.

Dad is in the living room, going over some paperwork, when I burst through the front door with Eliza in tow. His head snaps up at the noise, surprise flickering across his face before it settles into a stern expression. I know he's upset. Even if he doesn't know I snuck out in the middle of the night, it's clear he knows I skipped school.

I don't let him get a word out. "Dad," I say, "this is Eliza. She came with me because we have to talk."

"Well, yes, we do, young man. It appears you weren't at school today."

"I'll explain everything," I say. "But right now, I need you to listen to me, Dad! Please."

"Okay, okay. What is it?" he says, his face still wearing concern and anger.

I struggle to find the right words, knowing that there's still a chance he won't believe me. Taking a moment to compose myself, I tell him, "Officer Eugene is working with the Night Lords gang. I saw him at an abandoned warehouse with Rowdy. I saw Rowdy in the video footage from Cousin Vinny's, of the night Miles was killed. Rowdy followed Miles and pushed him in front of that bus. See, it all proves that I was telling the truth. Something else was going on."

"I saw it, too," Eliza says. "All of it. And Cousin Vinny's still has the video, if you need evidence."

Dad stands up abruptly, his chair scraping against the floor.

"Stay here," he orders, already reaching for his police radio. I know he's calling for backup.

It's at this moment that Momma comes down the stairs, having overheard the whole conversation. I expect her to be pissed at me, but she just comes and bear-hugs me. She cries and then I cry, then she cries harder and then I'm crying so hard I can't breathe. I know we're both crying for different reasons, but the moment is nice anyway.

"I'm sorry that I hit you," she says, sobbing into my neck.

"It's okay," I say through tears.

When we break apart, my mom looks over at Eliza and Dad.

"This is my friend Eliza," I tell her. "We met at group. I've been with her." Momma hugs her, too.

"I just called for backup and asked them to meet me at the abandoned Sears warehouse," Dad explains. "We will get to the bottom of this, I promise."

"Please, Dad," I say. "Miles deserves for the world to know what really happened to him."

Dad kisses the top of my head and then Momma's before running out the door and into his squad car. Eliza, Jorjah, Judah, Momma, and me wait on the couch in front of the TV with the news on, waiting to hear any kind of update from Dad or see any breaking news on the TV. After about a half hour, it happens.

A news alert flashes across the screen, causing us all to lean forward in anticipation and nervousness. The reporter's voice is serious as she announces, "This just in: a major operation is underway at the abandoned Sears warehouse, where suspected criminal activity involving multiple Indianapolis police officers and local gang members has been reported. Authorities are on the scene, and a statement from the police chief is expected shortly." My heart races as I realize that Dad and the backup officers are confronting Rowdy and Officer Eugene.

We watch live footage of police cars surrounding the warehouse, officers in tactical gear moving in formation toward the entrance. I feel a mix of fear and determination swirling inside me, hoping that justice will finally be served for Miles.

Suddenly, the camera feed switches to a helicopter view, capturing a dramatic scene unfolding outside the warehouse. A group of figures emerges from the building, their hands raised in surrender. Among them, I spot Rowdy being led away in handcuffs by my dad. It's a surreal moment, seeing the man responsible for Miles's death being taken into custody. Something freeing about that. After that, I see Officer Eugene being handcuffed by some other officers.

The screen flashes back to the reporter. Some white lady in a pink pantsuit. "Authorities have apprehended multiple suspects believed to be involved in criminal activities linked to a local gang known as the Night Lords. The operation is still ongoing, but significant progress is being made."

My heart beats fast in my chest and Eliza brings me in for a hug. Her hug is warm, soft, and perfect. It's exactly what I need to celebrate Miles getting the justice that he deserved. Miles should be here, not wherever he is. He should be with the people who love him most. And though there are still some things that I don't have answers to, like what his connection with any of the gangs in town was, I just hope he gets to have peace now.

CHAPTER FIFTEEN

Later that night, when I'm in bed, I get a call from Miles. I don't let it ring more than once before I answer it, feeling my heart beating in my chest.

"Hey, Miles," I say, thrilled to get a call, lifting up from bed.

"Hakeem!" he shouts in a celebratory voice, his words crystal clear, not even a hint of static. "You did it, man. You did it!"

"No, you did it, Miles," I say. "If you hadn't tried to reach us, we wouldn't have known."

"I don't know how long I've got, how long they'll let me talk to you—*they* being the powers that be wherever I am. It's just nice to hear your voice again, man."

"I can say the same to you, Miles." Tears pool in my eyes. "I miss you."

"I miss you more, man."

"I'm sorry I wasn't there for you," I say.

"You were there for me as much as you could be," Miles says. "I don't blame you for anything. You had your own shit going on."

"I had shit going on, but I could've still—"

"No, no, no." He cuts me off. "But now you need to focus on yourself," Miles continues softly. "Don't waste your time dwelling on the past or what could have been. Live your life to the fullest, Hakeem. That's all I ever wanted for you."

His words hit me like a ton of bricks, because I know Miles is right. I can't change the past, but I can shape my future. Taking a deep breath, I wipe away my tears and straighten up.

"You're right, Miles. I'll make every moment count, for you and for me," I say with determination in my voice.

Miles chuckles softly, the sound warm and comforting even through the phone.

"I always knew you were strong, Hakeem. Keep that fire burning inside you, no matter what. And remember, I'll always be watching over you," he says.

"Really?"

"It's a promise. And you can call me whenever you want. I will answer as long as they let me. Okay?"

"Okay," I say, feeling comforted by him. It's almost like he's really here with me, but I can't reach out to touch him. There are so many things I want to say, so many memories I want to recount, so many questions I want to ask him, but I don't even know where to begin. I just sit here on the phone with him, taking in the fact that I can still communicate with him when I want, thinking about how even though he's gone, I still have *this*.

"Mikki tells me I'm gonna be a dad," Miles says, some emotion evident in his voice. "That shit's crazy man, ain't it?"

"Yeah," I say. "When she told me that, I couldn't believe it."

"Who would've thought one random night of passion after being broken up would end up making me somebody's dad."

"That's kind of how it works, Miles," I say.

"She tells me she doesn't know what she's going to do with the baby. I want her to keep it, but I'm not there and won't ever be there to see it grow up or anything like that. I'll just be here, watching from the sidelines. I hope if it's a boy it's named something like Ashton or Wyshon or even Miles Jr. And if it's a girl, I've always liked the name Natalia."

"Those are dope names, Miles."

"Do me a favor, Hakeem, okay? Look after my kid. Make sure the kid knows that I was a good guy and I wanted to be in their life. Don't let them forget me."

"I won't let them forget about you, Miles. Just like I won't."

It's quiet for a moment, but I can only imagine that it's because he's smiling on the other end. "You there?" I say after a while.

"I'm here," he says. "I'm just picturing it now. Some kid coming into the world with my teeth and nose and ears. I hope they get Mikki's skin and hair, though."

"They will be a cute kid, I'm sure," I say.

"Well, thanks for the compliment," Miles says, laughing. "You think I'm cute."

"Shut up," I tell him, laughing at his silliness. Same old Miles, I see. Death hasn't changed him one bit, huh. After a while I build up the courage to ask about his journal. "Miles . . ."

"What's up?"

"I kept your diary."

"Don't call it that," Miles says quickly. "It's my special book of secrets and stories." He laughs again.

"I read some things in it that made me . . ." My voice trails off, and I feel like there's a knot in my throat. "I just found things that I wish you would've told me."

"About how sad I was?"

"About everything," I say.

"It was just a place where I kept a running log of what was going on in my life. It was my way of coping, of making sense of things. I didn't mean to shut you out, really. It's just that some things were hard to talk about."

I nod even though he can't see me. "I think I get it. But you knew that you could always talk to me about anything, right?"

"Every single day, I knew that," Miles says. "You were—*are* my best friend, my champion, and the only person who knows me through and through."

I smile. For the first time in a long time, I actually feel *close* to my best friend.

"Miles, there was also an entry that you wrote where you said that you might've liked me as more than a friend," I say, struggling to say the words. "I just . . ."

My heart pounds in my chest as the silence stretches between us, heavy with unspoken words and unexplored emotions. The admission hangs in the air like a delicate thread, waiting to be pulled one way or the other.

Finally, Miles speaks, his voice softer than before. "I wrote that a long time ago. We were just kids trying to navigate our feelings and understand ourselves and understand what we wanted from the world. It didn't seem like the thing that I needed to tell. Nothing was ever going to happen."

I struggle to find the right words, my mind racing with memories and missed opportunities. "Miles, if you felt that way, we could've still at least talked about it. Even if nothing was ever going to happen, it would've been nice to know how you felt. Because I think, at one point in time, I felt the same way."

There's a pause before he responds, the weight of his words almost tangible through the phone line. "You felt the same way? Really?"

"Of course I did. Miles, you said it yourself. We are best friends. We did everything together. We spent more time with each other than with anyone else in our entire lives. It wasn't hard to feel like we loved with a love that was more-than-friend love. But if we talked about it, maybe it would have brought us even closer."

"I was scared of ruining what we had. I didn't want to risk losing you, even if it meant keeping my feelings hidden."

Tears prick at the corners of my eyes as I listen to his confession, a mix of emotions swirling inside me.

"I gotta go," Miles says. "Remember, you can call me whenever you need to talk."

The line hangs up with the three beeps like always. I lie back in bed and think about the conversation I just had, replaying it on an annoying loop in my thoughts, nesting myself between my blankets and sheets, wondering about what things would be like if Miles and I had confessed our feelings once upon a time. It's too late for all of it now, but maybe someday, in a different world or in a different lifetime, we would end up more than just best friends. The thought lingers in my mind as I close my eyes, the weight of unspoken words still heavy on my chest.

I close my eyes, letting the tears fall freely, knowing that it's time to let go of the what-ifs and cherish the memories we've created together, cherish that I have him back in at least some way. Miles will always have a special place in my heart, whether as a best friend or a missed opportunity. As I drift off to sleep, I whisper into the air, as if he can hear me.

"Good night, Miles."

CHAPTER SIXTEEN

Mr. Sanchez taps his foot as he waits for an answer from me the next day at school. I completely space out, forgetting what his question even was.

Instead of asking him to repeat it, I just say, "I'm not sure what my answer is." Feels like a safe answer, rehearsed and calculated. I stare down at my desk, my copy of *The Catcher in the Rye* sitting there. I flip through the pages, pretending to search for an answer.

"What about you, Mikki?" Mr. Sanchez says, calling on her and catching her off guard, too. "What do you think is the significance of the hunting hat in the novel? What might it be a symbol for?"

Mikki's smart and she actually reads, so she pulls an answer out of her ass that actually sounds like it makes sense. "It symbolizes Holden's desire for authenticity and individuality. Throughout the book, he often wears the hat when he feels disconnected from the world around him or when he is trying to assert his identity. It also seems like it makes him feel safe and comforted."

"Very nice job," Mr. Sanchez says. "Bonus points for you, Mikki. Great answer."

The bell rings, and Mr. Sanchez reminds the class that the due date for our essays is coming up. I haven't even started on it, which isn't great. And if I don't start soon, I'll be forced to either do it at the last minute or take the zero. Both options sound like I'll be on house arrest by my parents if they somehow find out, which I'm sure they will. When I first committed to get clean, my parents decided they would make some kind of alliance with the principal and one of the school counselors, Mrs. Jenkinson, so that my parents can keep tabs on me at all times. If my grades lower, my parents are the first to be notified.

I make a mental note to start the essay after school.

"Mr. Hawkins," Mr. Sanchez says, stopping me from leaving his class. He waits until the class completely clears out to continue to talk. "I saw the news. I saw about what really happened to Miles. How are you holding up?"

"Um, not great," I say. I think it's the first time I've actually thought about this, let alone said it out loud. Wild that the first person I'm opening up to is my English teacher. "I just keep thinking about what I could've done, what the world could've done to help him. I think there are still questions I might not ever get answers to, but maybe I'll just have to live with that."

"Perhaps," Mr. Sanchez says, tugging at his egg-yolk-yellow tie.

I nod.

"You remind me a lot of our protagonist, Holden Caulfield, Mr. Hawkins. Burdened by the profound grief caused by the loss of someone you love, plagued by always needing to figure things out. Sometimes, life leaves us wondering, without a clear resolution in sight. It's a tough reality to accept, but it's part of growing up and learning to navigate the complexities of the world around us," Mr. Sanchez says with a knowing look in his eyes.

His words hit me in an unexpected way. Holden Caulfield's struggles haven't really resonated with me like that, but now, thinking about what Mr. Sanchez said about facing my own inner turmoil and grappling with loss, his words feel more like a lifeline.

"Thank you, Mr. Sanchez," I finally manage to say. "I appreciate your understanding."

As I gather my things to leave, Mr. Sanchez places a hand on my shoulder. "Remember, Mr. Hawkins, you are not alone in this. There are people who care about you and want to help you through this difficult time. And people here, your teachers especially, don't want to see you fall behind. Your grade in my class has slipped down to the C range because of your lack of participation and missing assignments. I want you to stay on top of things and talk to someone when you need assistance."

Damn. I didn't even know I had missing assignments in here. I also didn't know that my grades were slipping like Mr. Sanchez just said. I nod at him, offering a small smile, and head out of the classroom for my next class.

Thankfully, it's not a tardy sweep day, because I'm late to art, my last class of the day today.

Ms. Oh starts the art class by announcing we will be paired up to work on a photography project. She pulls out a box of disposable cameras that will be given to each group.

The class groans and complains at the mention of a group project. Most people prefer working alone as opposed to with someone else, and I don't blame them.

"You may take pictures of anything and anyone as long as you have their permission. The goal of the project is to tell a story using only pictures," Ms. Oh says, pushing her thick glasses up the bridge of her nose.

People continue to complain, but that doesn't stop Ms. Oh from continuing to explain all the elements to the project and how it's worth 20 percent of our final grade.

"I will be selecting your partners by drawing from a hat," Ms. Oh says, pulling out a colorful fedora. She reaches her hand in and calls out names.

More groaning, some coming from me this time.

"Hector . . . and . . . Kailey," she says. We all wait for them to stand, find each other, and sit somewhere as a pair.

"Tyler . . . and . . . Isabella," Ms. Oh announces with some excitement. Tyler and Isabella lock eyes with each other and roll their eyes in mutual disdain.

I search around the room for anyone that I might absolutely hate being paired with, but before I can even finish thinking about it, she calls my name.

"Hakeem . . . and . . . August!" Ms. Oh exclaims.

August stands and walks toward my desk. I wouldn't exactly claim that we're cool or anything like that, but we seemed on better terms than ever when we were figuring things out with the gangs and Rowdy. We busted a drug ring together, so that counts for something, right? Let bygones be bygones or whatever.

August doesn't say anything, just plops down in the empty seat next to me, silently accepting that this will be our forced reality for the duration of this project.

Ms. Oh pairs up the rest of the class and then informs us of the due date. Conveniently, it's the same day Mr. Sanchez's essay is due. I'll need to hunker down and get my work done if I don't want to fall too far behind.

Ms. Oh hands the disposable camera for our group to August and says, "Good luck, boys. I can't wait to see what you come up with."

August looks at me, holding out the camera. "You want to keep it or you want me to keep it?"

"You can hold on to it," I say.

"A'ight," August says. "When do you want to start?"

"Um, we can start whenever," I say. I don't have another answer for him.

"I'll text you when I'm ready. You have any ideas on what things we can take a picture of or what story we could tell?"

"Maybe we can take pictures at the mall? Or we can go to Funky Bones? That's a story in and of itself? Or we can go to some local garden?"

"Okay," August says. "Whatever is easiest."

"Fair," I say.

When art class ends, I get a phone call from Miles. It catches me by surprise because I didn't think I'd ever get a call from him again. I know he extended the offer for me to call him, but I didn't know that *he* would call *me*.

I answer it.

"Miles!"

"School's out, huh?" he asks.

168

"Yeah. I'm so tired. I feel like I have enough work to supply me for the rest of the year," I tell him.

"That's one thing I don't miss," Miles says. "If there's any silver lining in death, it's that you don't have any school. Ever."

"You say that like it's funny, but it's actually kind of sad," I say, thinking about a reality where school doesn't exist.

"You think being in school is better than being dead?"

"Okay, point taken," I say, laughing with him.

"How was everything today?" Miles asks, curiosity in his voice.

"I just got put in a group project with August," I say.

"You two still beefing or something?" Miles asks.

"To be honest, I don't even know. I never had beef with him. He just stopped talking to me."

"You never spilled the beans as to what you did to piss him off so much," Miles reminds me. I think about the truth and then think maybe sparing it is best for both of us. Spilling those kinds of details with him? I'm not ready.

"Um, I'm not sure," I say, lying. I'm sure Miles can detect that. He always knew when I was lying to his face. He always called me out.

"Fine. Anyway, I'm calling because I've got a surprise for you."

"A surprise?"

"Yes. Go to my old locker."

"Okay, I will," I say, walking toward where his locker used to be.

"The combination is twenty-two . . . four . . . sixteen," he says.

I twist the little dial to all the numbers, making sure I feel the click every time, and then it pops open. Everything inside looks untouched. Just like the last time Miles used it. I wonder why the school hasn't cleaned it out, but I guess maybe it's been the least of their worries these days.

I see Miles's textbooks, the stickers of his favorite horror movies.

"Look at the bottom of the locker," Miles says. "You'll see an old Spanish class binder I never got rid of. Open that."

I do exactly what he says. At first, I only see notes, old graded tests, and homework he never turned in. I flip through and when I get to the back, I run across a Polaroid picture. It's of me and Miles. In it, we are both smiling, arms around each other, standing in front of the old oak tree that used to be in his backyard before Mr. Rodney had it cut down a year ago. We spent so many lazy afternoons there. We even built our very own treehouse there when we were kids. The picture brings a flood of memories from our childhood rushing back—building forts, riding bikes until it was dark out, walking to the corner convenience store to get Flamin' Hot Cheetos and AriZona Iced Teas, and dreaming about all the adventures we would have together.

But as I study the Polaroid further, my heart sinks. There's something written on the back in Miles's familiar handwriting—messy yet beautiful and uniquely his. It reads, *Remember our promise that no matter where we are, we'll always find each other.*

Tears well up in my eyes as I trace the outline of our faces, so young and carefree, so alive and present with each other.

"Miles," I whisper, my voice cracking with emotion.

"I wanted you to have that," he says. "To always remember the good times we had."

"Thank you, Miles . . . it means so much," I say. I clutch the Polaroid to my chest, feeling a mix of sorrow and gratitude wash over me. I shut his locker and remain here looking at it for just a little bit longer. Flashbacks of me stopping by his locker to talk to him, give him pep talks, give him advice, or just to say "what's up" popcorn around in my head.

There was the time where Miles and I were given detention for our explosive debate during Spanish class last year about who would win in a fight: Black Panther or Captain America. Miles was Team Black Panther and I was Team Cap. No matter my love for Wakanda and Chadwick Boseman (God rest his soul), I had to go with my boy Cap. Not only is Chris Evans a very gorgeous man, but he was one of the OG Avengers. Miles's argument was about how Black Panther has vibranium; he thought that was enough to win any battle. I had to remind him that Cap's shield is literally made out of vibranium, too. As much as I love Miles, I'm still sticking with my original pick. I'm sad thinking about a memory like this—I'll never get to debate stupid stuff with him only to see him get really mad, really invested, the vein in the side of his neck sticking out. It's moments like this that I'm reminded that I lost more than a friend. I lost the very thing that gave my life meaning.

If there's anything I've learned over the years, it's that nothing lasts forever. Like the flavor in gum, or the fresh look when you get a haircut, or a good hug, or best friends who you do everything with. Not even love lasts forever. All good things have a terribly small lifespan that eventually fades into nothing. And when it's gone, it's like it was never there at all.

I think about how I'll have to go tomorrow and the day after that and the day after that and on and on and on, making memories without him. And suddenly, I want to throw up. I think about college and I think about the plans that we both had and how the universe or God fucked that up with taking Miles away from this earth so soon.

"Miles . . ." I say, my voice trailing off, weary and heavy. I have a frog in my throat that won't go away, no matter how much I try and clear it.

"Hakeem," Miles says, letting me know he's still here, listening.

"I got accepted into Indiana State," I say.

"Eh, congrats! What a dream, bro. College will be sick, I'm sure. I wish I could be there to experience it all with you. But it looks like college was never in my cards anyway." The way he says it is so fucked up that even I want to push back, but I get where he's coming from. The way those words sound coming out of his mouth makes college feel like a lonely prison sentence I'll be forced to serve without him by my side.

I take a deep breath, trying to calm myself down, a single tear rolling down my cheek. I blink, and blink, and blink, swallowing down hot spit. "I wish you could be there, too, Miles," I finally say, my voice barely above a whisper. "It won't be the same without you. It just won't."

He doesn't say anything back. Before I can double-check to see if he's still there, the call drops. I hate how randomly that happens. How you never know when that moment will happen—the moment where the call just ends and it's like Miles was never there, talking

172

to me on the phone. Something about it makes me feel like I'm drifting through time and space, untethered and alone. I stand here in this emptied hallway for a moment, the silence heavy in my ears, before I gather myself and wipe away at my face. Adjusting my backpack over my shoulder, I make my way out of the school and to my car. As I start the engine, roll down the window, and pull out of the school parking lot, my mind keeps drifting back to the conversation with Miles, the sky and the breeze reminding me that life goes on, whether I want it to or not.

CHAPTER SEVENTEEN

Eliza texts me right after I get home, asking me if I want to do something. I do, so a short time after, she picks me up and we get pizza at Cousin Vinny's. It's one of the few times I'm here and not working. I'm just grateful Frankie doesn't make me pay for the food. It's cheap, but free is always better. Frankie even brings it out to us himself.

We sit at a booth near the back of the restaurant. It's my favorite booth in the whole place. It has the best view of the bathroom, the entrance, and the TV that's always showing the National Geographic Channel for some reason. I'm not entirely sure why Frankie thinks it's appetizing to watch cheetahs and lions hunt and attack gazelles while people are trying to enjoy bread, cheese, sauce, and all the toppings your heart can handle.

"Large pepperoni pizza for you two lovebirds," Frankie says, jokingly with a wink, placing our hot pizza in front of us on one of those little metal stands. He puts down bottles of Parmesan and red pepper flakes as well. I love spice, so those pepper flakes come in clutch.

"We're not *lovebirds*," I correct him. "Just two friends sharing a pizza."

Eliza's cheeks are red and flushed. She looks like she's embarrassed at Frankie's insinuation. She tucks hair behind her ear and sits up. "The pizza smells delicious," she says, as if she's trying to change the subject. I don't entirely blame her. Frankie has a gift in making things awkward. But instead of taking the hint and going away, he stays around, watching us take our first bite.

"I remember back in my day, when I was your age, I would take girls out for pizza just like this," Frankie starts, a wistful look in his eyes. "There was this one girl, Maria, who had the most beautiful smile. We'd come here every Friday after school, just like you two." Eliza and I exchange a glance, both unsure of how to respond to Frankie's unexpected trip down memory lane. But before we can say anything, Frankie continues, "Ah, young love. Enjoy every moment of it, kids." With that, he pats my shoulder and walks back toward the kitchen, leaving us to our now suddenly awkward pizza date. I mean, *hangout*.

We eat for a while in near-silence, as if we're conscious that Frankie might come back at any time and rate us on our lovebird behavior. It's only after I've downed two slices that we can talk real again.

"You hear from Miles again?" Eliza asks me, taking a bite of pizza, a long string of cheese pulling from her mouth, which makes me snort.

"Uh, yeah," I say. "Each time I hear from him, I'm reminded how much I miss him. So, it's almost harder to talk to him than not."

"That seems understandable," she says, swallowing her bite and taking a sip of her drink. "So . . . is he, like . . . a ghost or something?"

"A ghost, a spirit, I don't know. Whatever he is, he's not entirely here, but not entirely gone, either," I explain, swirling my straw around my drink absentmindedly.

"Have you talked to him about all the things you couldn't say before?" Eliza asks, dipping the crust of her pizza in nacho cheese sauce.

"Yeah, a little bit," I answer, reaching for a slice of pizza and taking the tiniest bite before continuing. "I'm sure there will always be another thing I want to talk to him about. But yeah."

"Sometimes I wonder what I'll say to my family if I ever see them again. How can I explain the unexplainable pain they've caused me? How can I explain to them that it's because of them that I hurt myself? I know self-harm is a terrible thing, my addiction to pain, but it's the only thing that feels familiar and comforting in this cold world."

I never really wondered about what addiction made Eliza come to our NA group. I always assumed that if someone walked through those doors, they had some kind of addiction to narcotics and other drugs, but I guess people from all walks of life, all kinds of addictive behaviors, might find something good in coming to NA. After all, the *A* in *NA* stands for *Anonymous* for a reason. Listening to Eliza describe her addiction to pain, I don't know if I want to cry or give her a hug or both. As she speaks, I feel the weight of her pain, her struggle with self-harm. I sit here, still, quiet, but curious. I know firsthand what it's like to grapple with demons that seem insurmountable, to seek solace in destructive patterns when the world grows too heavy to bear. And in Eliza's haunted eyes, I see a reflection of my own battles, my own scars, hidden beneath layers of shame.

I stare at Eliza, her eyes distant and filled with a world of hurt. It's moments like this that make me realize how much she has really been through, how much she carries on her shoulders every day, how much her presence has been nice, to grieve and process all the loss we've experienced together. I reach out and touch her hand, offering what little comfort I can.

Eliza's words stir something in me. I tell her, "You don't owe them anything, you know. Your pain is valid, whether they acknowledge it or not."

"I know you're right," Eliza says. "I just wonder what their faces would look like to see me after all this time. Sorry, I'm always killing the vibe, aren't I?"

"No," I say. "It's not just you. I'm guilty of it, too."

"Maybe what we both need is some fresh air," Eliza says, with a bigger-than-usual smile.

"Fresh air?"

"Yeah, I know a spot," she says, sliding out from her side. I take a large bite of another slice of pizza before getting out of the booth, shouting out thanks to Frankie, and following her outside. We hop into her hearse, which still doesn't get any less creepy the more I ride in it, and we're off to whatever mysterious location Eliza has in mind. If there's one thing I've learned about her, it's that she's full of surprises. Where we're headed could be *anywhere*. But I've grown to trust her. I'm not sure how or why so quickly, but I have. There's no denying that.

It takes about twenty minutes, but we park on the side of a narrow bridge, water in all directions several feet beneath us. There are some people kayaking in the distance, going in the direction opposite of us. The bridge is dusty and gravelly and looks like it's not been used much in a long time. When we get out, Eliza looks over the edge and laughs.

Without hesitation, she takes off her clothes. She removes her jacket, shirt, and pants, revealing the swimsuit she has underneath, like she's been planning this the whole time.

"What are you doing?" I question, not believing my eyes. And not turning away either. There's something about watching her undress that's really nice.

"Gotta stay prepared," she says. "You never know when you'll need to go for a little swim."

"Swim?"

She climbs up on the very edge of the bridge, standing up on it. Her feet dangle over the edge. If she takes the tiniest step, she could fall in.

"I repeat, what the heck are you doing?" I say. This time, more concern leaks from my voice.

"Just take your clothes off. No one's watching. And I promise I won't look at your . . . you-know-what," she says. "Just climb up."

"This seems dangerous," I say.

"What's dangerous?"

"Are you trying to jump in the water from all the way up here?" I ask, feeling my heart beating in my chest.

"Yeah," she says confidently. "I promise this isn't my first rodeo. I've jumped from this very spot several times in my life. You'll be fine. This is the White River. It's several feet deep. The worst part is the free fall on the way down, but when you smack into the water, you'll feel good."

I swallow the knot in my throat and take a deep breath.

"Any day now, Hakeem Lee Hawkins," she says.

"Wait, how do you know my full name?" I can't remember ever giving it to her.

"You're not the only one who can google someone," she says. "Now, get up here. You won't regret it."

I search around for any cars. When I don't see or hear any coming, I strip down. I rip off my hoodie, then my undershirt, pants, and socks. All I'm left in is my underwear. I picked the wrong day to wear light-colored boxer briefs. Just when I get my pants from around my ankles and swing them to the side, I look up to see Eliza looking right at me. I immediately cover myself up, afraid of what she might see, but at the same time, I wonder if she's impressed by what she sees.

It takes both hands to climb up the side of the bridge, which is just rock and brick. Eliza helps me up by offering her hand. Which leads to the two of us holding hands and standing up on the side of the bridge. I wonder if there are people down below somewhere who think we're about to commit suicide or something. I can see the headlines now.

"We jump together on three," Eliza says.

"No, no. How about ten?" I offer, nervous about what she has in mind.

"Three . . . two . . ." She begins counting off, my heart skipping beats.

I close my eyes, taking quick and deep breaths.

"One!"

179

And we both jump! The wind rushes past us as we plummet down, the adrenaline pumping through my veins. I feel alive, free-falling through the air beside Eliza, watching her hair whipping into a mess. The sound of our combined screams mixes with the roaring wind as we fall toward the water below. And as we fall, seconds stretch into eternity, the world around us a blur of blue sky and frothy waves.

And then, with a jolt that steals my breath away, we hit the water. The shock of the cold envelops me, pulling me under before spitting me back out into the sunlight. I gasp for air, my heart pounding in my chest as I search for Eliza, who's behind me, laughing and grinning like this is the greatest thing she's ever done.

She shakes the water from her hair. "That was amazing, wasn't it?" she asks over the sound of water splashing around us, the river sloshing around.

I can't even lie to her. "That was incredible."

She takes a handful of water and tosses it on me. I grab a handful and do the same right back. And suddenly, we're having an all-out water fight. It's harder than one would think, but just as fun as a snowball fight. She swims closer to me and just when she gets inches away from my face, she disappears into the water.

"Eliza!" I call out for her, splashing and searching around. I go under and don't see her anywhere. I return to the surface only to see Eliza getting out of the water near the riverbank. It's almost like a magic trick. Some kind of illusion. She sits in a nearby patch of grass, lying back to allow the sun to dry her.

I swim over to the riverbank and emerge from the water, joining

Eliza on the grassy patch. The sun feels warm against my skin as I lie down beside her, still catching my breath from our playful water fight. The sounds of nature surround us—the gentle rustle of leaves, the chirping of birds, and the soothing flow of the river nearby.

"That was quite the vanishing act," I say, sitting down beside her and flicking leftover river debris off my legs.

"I love that one," Eliza says. "My father taught it to me when I was a little girl. It's one of the only times I remember him caring much about me."

I notice the cuts on her legs again. Some of them look like they're healed scars, but I can't help but notice that some of them seem like they're freshly there. Should I ask about them? I don't want to send her packing up her bags for good, wanting nothing to do with me anymore. It seems like every time I poke a little bit at her, it sends her spiraling farther and farther away. But then I think about what keeping quiet might do to me, to Eliza. "I see you have cuts on your legs," I say, pointing at them.

She searches around for something to cover herself up before the reality sets in that all our clothes are up by the hearse. She reclines back again and shuts her eyes for a long while. For a second, I wonder if she's going to completely pretend like I didn't ask about it, but then she exhales deeply and begins to say something.

"Even before my father and brother's crime, I started to cut. For some people, cutting is a way to stand out. For others, it's a way to hide away. But all people who cut just want to feel something. We self-harm because it can sometimes feel like it's the best way through the messy, dark, and hollow tunnels in our hearts and minds. I cut to hide. And if I hide, no one can hurt me first."

I swallow my spit and nod.

"I ran away, then, maybe I didn't," Eliza says, looking up at the sky, as if she's getting lost in the clouds or something.

"What do you mean?" I wonder.

"Does it still count as running away if you tell people that you're running away, that you hate it here, that you'd rather be anywhere else anywhere else anywhere else and they do nothing but watch you leave, and even close the door in your face?"

"Damn," I say. "I've got no words to say back to that, other than damn. I'm sorry that happened to you."

She gazes at me, her eyes filled with a mix of sadness, anger, and determination. "It's okay. But I can't help but feel like I'm stuck in this perpetual state of running away, even when I'm not leaving anywhere. Something about that is its own kind of sad."

I think about something Yolanda once said at Narcotics Anonymous group. *We are all just walking each other home*, she said. And I realize that maybe, just maybe, that's what Eliza needs from me right now—to be someone to walk with her, to listen, and to hold space for her pain. God knows she's already done that for me.

"You know, we've all been running in some way or another," I say gently, reaching out to take her hand. She looks down at our interlocked fingers, and then back up at my face. "Maybe it's not about running away from something, but running toward something better. Toward healing, toward not hurting yourself, toward a better life, toward people who care—people who don't walk out on you or treat you like you're invisible."

She just sighs and says, "Hmm. Maybe you're right."

I'm admiring the way shapes take form in the clouds when I think to ask Eliza something my old therapist, Dr. Chandler, once asked me. "If you were told that today's your very last day on earth, what would you do in your final moments?"

She doesn't even take a moment to think before she answers, "I have no clue. Never thought about something like that. It's not like when I think about death, I think of wish lists or bucket lists like I'm some cancer patient or terminally ill girl."

"I see," I say, picturing my own dream day, the hours that I'd have just moments before kicking the bucket. I've had plenty of days, plenty of lonely nights to think about my answer, to make slight edits to what things would be like. Unlike Eliza, a bucket list sounds like the perfect thing to have if you know you're going to die. Whether it be a terminal illness, getting randomly struck by lightning during a storm, or natural causes, a list of things to do before you die feels essential to having a life worth living.

I tell Eliza, "I think in my final moments, I'd want to eat cookie dough ice cream on top of the Statue of Liberty, fly to some tropical island, and sip out of coconuts with Rihanna and Lil Nas X. I'd want to visit the seven wonders of the world and sleep with penguins at the zoo. I'd want to learn a new language—maybe Arabic or Mandarin? I'd want to do a lot of things with whatever time I had left."

"Isn't it fucked up that we will never know how much we mean to people until we're gone?" Eliza says.

I remain there, contemplating her words. It's like time pauses for a while. The air feels thick yet still.

Later, when we get dried off and slip back into our clothes, Eliza has the idea to get milkshakes and go for a walk around downtown. I remind her about my essay and my project due, which means I won't be able to stay very long. Still, she convinces me to tag along.

When we're all done, it's jet-black out, not many stars clinging in the sky. The crescent moon hangs there like a loyal companion. And we sit in Eliza's hearse with the windows down, well, as down as they can be, because they're old and don't work as well as they used to. There's that smell in the air that makes me believe that maybe it'll start raining soon. Once we pull up at my house, all the lights are on downstairs, and Jorjah's bedroom light is on upstairs. Judah's bedroom light is off, which could mean he's either asleep or playing video games. Across the street, I can see Mr. and Mrs. Halliburton are watching TV on the couch, their Christmas tree lighting up their window. They're some of those people who celebrate Christmas all year long.

When I get inside, Judah holds his Xbox controller in one hand and rubs the line in his new fade with his other.

"Play with me," he says.

"I can't, buddy," I say. "I have homework."

"You always have something to do," Judah says, visibly upset that

I'm passing up on playing video games with him. I feel bad that I haven't made a ton of time for him or fake tea parties with Jorjah, and I know their young minds don't quite understand the mind of a depressed teenage boy who lost his best friend and is a recovering drug addict. I'm not sure they understand me in that way. Momma and Dad decided to just use the term "very sick" to describe my condition.

"Please!" he practically begs. I can see the boredom and desperation in his eyes.

"Tomorrow," I say. "How about that?"

"Well, okay," Judah says, giving in. "But you'll have to play extra rounds of *Apex Legends* or *FIFA*."

"Of course, Jude," I say, rubbing my hand across his new haircut. He swats my hand away and heads back for his room.

When I get back in my room, I sit on the edge of the bed and grab my laptop out of my backpack. I load up a blank document, staring at the cursor blinking at me. I know what I *have* to write about for Mr. Sanchez's essay, but I don't know where to begin. I've never had writer's block before, but now I see that it's a legit thing.

I remember the picture that Miles had me get from his locker, the one he called a "surprise" for me. I pull it out of my pocket, glancing at it and reading Miles's note once more. Then I reach under my bed and grab the box of things that Mikki gave me. At some point, I'll have to do something with all this stuff, too, but for now, I slide the photo in there. When I reach in, my hand touches something like hard plastic. It makes a rattling sound. I search through the box, moving things around when I need to,

185

only to discover a tiny yellow bottle of pills with no label on it and a blue lid.

I don't remember Miles taking any medications. And I don't remember accidentally putting a whole bottle of pills in this box, either. I have a pill identifier app on my phone from back in my using days. I pull out one of the pills, searching for a manufacturer mark or letter to type into the app. When I do that, the results show Xanax (Alprazolam). I have an urge to dump them down the toilet, flushing them so that I don't do anything I might regret. But then I remember the last time I took a Xanax, after a meetup with August. I was feeling so many things about the double, secret life we were both living that it just became too much to bear. I remember getting them from some guy I met online. I popped one little white savior pill and slid into this mellow, pleasant euphoria.

It was a type of euphoria that you usually only experience when you're dreaming—not a spike but a soak. It's a dangerous type of euphoria that left me feeling invincible yet vulnerable at the same time. The world around me blurred, my worries dissolving into a hazy fog. For a moment, I felt like I could conquer anything, face any truth, but that feeling soon gave way to a numbing emptiness.

I snap out of my reverie and focus on the bottle of Xanax in my hands. I wonder what Miles used them for and when. Heart pounding, I get a good whiff of the pills.

There's a strange, bitter scent as I hold them to my nose. My mind races with questions—not only why would Miles have these, but what had he been hiding from me? My hands tremble as I pour

out a few pills into my palm, the tiny white tablets looking innocu-
ous yet holding a weight of secrets.

My hands begin to shake and I think about them for a long
while. Then I put them back into the bottle and away, hoping to
never have to see them again. I just pray I don't regret not flushing
them down the toilet.

CHAPTER EIGHTEEN

"Keem, did you know that it's impossible to feel pain wherever I am? That crying doesn't exist? Dying doesn't even exist here. I don't know what it is, but isn't that something to look forward to, man? It's like all the things that hurt on Earth suddenly don't hurt as much anymore." This is what Miles says the next time he calls me, Thursday morning before school. I'm standing in the parking lot at school, waiting to go inside.

I don't say anything to him. Between the Xanax I found, cryptic entries in his diary, and ties to a local gang, I'm starting to think Miles wasn't as transparent and open with me as I had thought. It's like everything I thought I believed about my best friend is in question. And it hurts.

"Hello?" Miles says, because I'm quiet, lost in my thoughts, thinking, trying to process and piece the whole puzzle together. But I can't.

"Miles, I gotta ask . . . I'm trying to figure out what the Crimson Brotherhood and Night Lords had to do with you. And the pills that I found in a box of your things that Mikki gave me. I can't help but feel like I'm missing something."

"Look, Keem," Miles begins, sighing. "I didn't mean to hide anything from you. It's just that I couldn't involve anyone else."

"What? What are you saying, Miles?" I feel my nose crinkle up.

"Keem, we were homies since we were kids, man. But you always had things I could never have. Your parents have money, you have a nice house, you have your own car, you have everything you could possibly want. My parents were broke and we often struggled to get by. There were times when my momma had to pick between paying the light bill or the water bill. She had to pick between getting us food or buying us clothes. I got tired of the struggle, man. After a while, it starts to take a toll on you. Your parents' sadness about their reality starts to trickle down to you and then you're left with a choice: Do something about it or don't. And I chose to do something about it."

All my words seem to abandon me. I'm absolutely frozen, arrested in place, thinking about what he's saying. I can't believe it.

He goes on. "Rowdy offered me a way out. If I joined the Crimson Brotherhood, I could make a little money on the side. And by money, I mean, like, an amount of money I've only ever dreamed of. Money can't buy happiness, they say, but it *can* get you pretty damn close. The money I was making kept our lights on, kept food on the table, and kept my parents from fighting. I think it was worth every risk."

"Rowdy?" I say, trying to remember if I told Miles he was the one who pushed him in front of that bus.

"I did minor things like be the lookout for when they were breaking into cars and I made small drug exchanges that were pretty harmless to me. The pills you found weren't things that I was taking. They were supposed to be part of my last delivery. I refused to do the last delivery because I felt like I was losing who I was. Embarrassed, I vowed not to say anything to anybody. Not even you."

I feel betrayed, but I also feel sad hearing what he just said.

He continues, "I quit the Crimson Brotherhood, which put a target on my back because no one quits the Crimson Brotherhood. Rowdy turned on me and ratted me out. The Crimson Brotherhood started looking at him, showing up at his house, sending threatening messages. So he went running to the Night Lords. As a way to save his own ass and cover his tracks, he . . ."

"Killed you," I finish.

"I never trusted him, but I didn't think he was a murderer. But then again, I always knew he was dangerous. Keeping all this a secret was a way to protect you, Mikki, my parents, everyone. I might have even kept it a secret still, but I didn't want you all to think I jumped in front of that bus. I didn't want you to think I wanted to leave."

I stand still a little bit longer, trying to process the magnitude of his confession. My mind races, connecting dots I never knew existed. The weight of everything he's revealed hangs heavy in the air between us.

"Miles, do you have any other secrets?"

"I don't," he says. "I promise."

"I'll take your word, Miles. I gotta go."

"Before you go, Keem, I want you to know that I've always cared about you more than anything. I never intended for any of this to touch your life. I just wanted to do right by my parents and then to protect you and the ones I love, but I see now that I've caused you some hurt. I hope one day you can forgive me." Miles's voice is raw with emotion, I can only imagine he's giving me those pleading puppy-dog brown eyes he's famous for.

Once upon a time, I was the one begging for Miles to accept *my* apology because I was convinced that I wasn't there for him enough, that maybe his death was in part my fault, that I could've been a better friend to him leading up to the moments before that fateful day. But now, it seems like all that has gone out the door and been replaced with something else.

"I do forgive you, Miles," I say and mean it.

I slide into my seat just as the first-period bell rings. I toss my backpack at my feet under the desk and watch others shuffle in late as well, including August. He looks back at me and we lock eyes for a brief second before he looks away. I'm not sure what that's all about. Luckily, first period is always just homeroom, and my homeroom teacher is Mr. Sanchez, so he's chill about what we do. Usually, most people just play games on their school-issued iPads. Some people study and do work for other classes. Others, like me, choose to sit there, staring at the clock, counting the minutes down until school is over. But today, Mr. Sanchez has other plans for the class. Something about getting us ready for the future, for college. "Test prep," he says, which causes the whole class to boo him.

"I'm sorry, guys," he apologizes, putting a hand over his heart. "I wish I didn't have to do this, but the state is requiring it, which means our principal is requiring it." He explains the political game of education to us, which has the class booing Principal Samuels and the state of Indiana instead.

Midway through homeroom, while we are doing test prep practice questions together on the smartboard, someone knocks on the classroom door. One of our guidance counselors comes in and announces to Mr. Sanchez that he's getting a new student. The new student walks in and I instantly lose my breath. *No way. It can't be*, I think to myself.

Eliza?

She walks in confidently and sits in the open seat next to me, all eyes on her. Without even realizing it, I press my pencil into my notebook so hard that it snaps in half.

"What are you doing here?" I whisper-yell to her. I thought school wasn't her thing? She dropped out and started taking care of herself. Why re-enroll?

"I got to thinking. Maybe I missed out on something important by leaving school. And I know my way around a few things now. Maybe getting an education is what I need to do next."

I never thought I'd hear something like that from Eliza.

Mr. Sanchez comes over and brings her a copy of the test prep books we're working out of and a copy of *The Catcher in the Rye.* He says, "This book, we're working on now. This novel is what we're learning in English class. Hold on to it and bring it to class with you later."

"What's your schedule?" I ask her when Mr. Sanchez walks away.

She flashes me a crumpled-up piece of paper that has her full name at the top of it. Eliza Jane Fitzpatrick. *Jane.* I never knew what her middle name was, but I don't think it fits her. She seems more like an Eliza *Raven*, Eliza *Enigma*, or Eliza *Maeve*. But *Jane*?

I notice that we've got some classes together and some not. We don't have next-period Biology with Mr. Munich together, but we do have Pre-Calc, AP Chemistry, US History, and English together. I see that she's taking creative writing instead of art.

"Okay, class! Here's another practice question for you. It's number seventeen in your books," Mr. Sanchez says. He writes a sentence on the board, leaving a blank for us to pick the best word to fit there.

Hands go up, ready to answer the question. But I notice Eliza hesitating, her brow furrowed in concentration. Without any warning, she raises her hand confidently and offers her answer with a slight smile playing on her lips. Mr. Sanchez looks impressed and nods in approval before moving on to the next question.

"When in doubt, pick C, right?" she whispers in my direction, grinning.

I nod at her, also impressed.

As the class continues, I steal glances at Eliza, trying to process this new version of her sitting beside me. She takes notes diligently and participates actively in discussions. She seems like she's not missing a beat, like she's always been a high school student. She's a natural.

Once class is over, I'm just about to dart past August and out the door when he says, "Ay, Keem. Wait up."

I stop and turn around. "What's up?"

"I've already started taking pictures for our art project," he tells me. "I went to the park and took pictures."

Just when I'm about to make a joke by calling him a creeper, he continues.

"There were no kids there," he says. "I just thought the way the swings and slides were graffitied up told a story of its own."

"I see," I say. "Thanks for getting a head start."

"Yeah, we can put everything together later, if you're free."

I clear my throat. "Yeah, I think I'm free. Where should we meet?"

"Mikki and my mom will be gone, so we can meet at my place," he offers.

I nod at him and he walks past me. I meet Eliza out in the hallway.

"I forgot how structured everything is in school," Eliza says. "It's like we're in a fishbowl or something."

I laugh at her point. "Yeah, I guess it can feel pretty suffocating at times. But hey, on the bright side, at least we get breaks in between classes. We can at least say hi to each other and talk throughout the day."

She nods like she agrees with me. Despite her tough exterior, I know that deep down she's just a girl searching for her place in the world. She waves at me as she heads in the other direction for her next class. I watch as she turns her back toward me. She wears jeans, a hoodie that has the flowers all over it, and a simple black backpack.

I run into Mikki on my way to second period. She wears a sweatshirt that's a little bit baggy, but I can still tell that she's beginning to show. I did some research and saw that pregnant people start to grow baby bellies around the fourth or fifth month. I'm not sure what that timing all checks out to, but I don't think I'm curious to know, either.

"Hey, Mik," I say, going in for the hug. She completes it, holding on a little bit longer.

"Hey, have you talked to Miles lately?"

I hesitate, wondering if she's heard more from him. But I settle on the truth. "Yeah, I've talked to him."

"Has he said anything new to you?"

"Um. No, not really," I say, lying this time around. I don't want her to freak out about anything. It's the last thing she needs.

"Well, okay. I've been afraid to ask him about things," Mikki says. "I've just settled on keeping my mouth shut and appreciating that I get to hear his voice."

"Yeah, that's been my perspective, too," I say. "I'm sure not many people get a second chance with their loved one who died."

"At least he seems thrilled to be a dad. Almost makes me want to keep the baby," Mikki says.

"What do you mean, keep the baby?"

"I found a nice family who would want to adopt it at birth," she says. "I was looking online, posted about it anonymously, and they reached out."

"Mikki . . ."

"I'm not, like, one hundred percent certain I'm going to do that, but it's an option. I'm only sixteen. I don't know if I'm ready to be a parent," she says, then takes a breath. "Especially not with Miles gone."

"I understand," I say. What an impossible predicament she's found herself in. Either decision she makes, she'll feel grief.

Mikki's eyes fill with tears and she clutches her stomach. She sniffles, trying to compose herself before speaking again. "I just wish things were different, you know? That we had more time . . . that we were older . . . that this was all just a bad dream."

"Mikki, no matter what you decide, just know that I'm here for you. We all are—me, August, my family," I reassure her, trying to convey the depth of our friendship and solidarity. "You don't have to go through this alone. Miles may not be able to take care of the baby, but you would have a whole village behind you if you choose to keep your baby."

Mikki looks up at me with a mixture of gratitude and sadness in her eyes. I can see the battle raging within her, the weight of her choices pressing down on her fragile shoulders. She nods slowly, as if trying to convince herself that everything will turn out all right in the end.

"Thank you, Hakeem," she says, her voice steady but her hands still shaking. She turns around and walks toward her locker. I watch her, thinking about her and wondering how she will navigate the difficult road ahead. If she will choose to keep the baby or go through with the adoption plan. It's a heavy decision for anyone, but especially for Mikki, given the circumstances.

She turns back and tells me, "Mom and I are meeting with the potential adopters after school today. They live an hour away, up north. Wish us luck. Keep me in your thoughts."

"I'll be thinking of you, for sure," I say. "I hope things go well. Or go exactly how you want them to."

As Mikki disappears into the crowded hallway, I can't help but feel sad. So, so sad.

*   *   *

After school, I arrive at August's house to work on our art project. He's in the driveway tossing his basketball into a raggedy, broken basketball net attached to their tiny garage. August and Mikki live in a neighborhood similar to Miles's, on the side of town where a lot of crime happens and the houses are a lot smaller. This is where the Crimson Brotherhood likes to hide out.

I park my car, making sure to lock it. I head up the driveway and August rolls his eyes as I try to get his attention.

Ignoring his eye roll, I say, "Ready to get this over with?" I attempt to sound somewhat enthusiastic. August turns away from the basketball net, his face a perfect mixture of annoyance and resignation.

He leads me into the house and down the hall to his bedroom, which is the last one on the left, by their back door. The house smells like recently lit incense and Lysol.

He sits down at the desk in his bedroom and props up a folding chair next to him, offering it to me. Looking around his room, I notice it's the same as the last time I was here.

Posters of his favorite NFL players cover the walls, a jumble of vibrant colors and dynamic poses. August's desk is cluttered with art supplies—sketchbooks, markers, and paintbrushes strewn haphazardly across its surface. I didn't figure him as one to be overprepared.

"You've got everything we need and more," I say.

"What can I say? I love art," he says. Maybe I'm getting a glimpse at some secret hobby August has?

He doesn't comment any further, just says, "I'll show you the pictures I've taken so that we can begin piecing together what our story will be." He searches around his desk and finds a stack of photos paper-clipped together. "I made sure to get them developed so we could paste them onto poster board."

"Wow, thanks for your work, August," I say, suddenly feeling like I'm slacking off in this group project. August has done everything so far, and I've contributed nothing. To be fair, I didn't ask August to work without me.

"I'm just trying to get all my work done," August says, like he's reluctantly wanting to open up. "I'm trying to impress my coaches and get back in their good graces. My grades have been slipping a lot lately."

"I get that, man. My grades haven't been the best lately, either. You know, with everything going on, school has kinda taken a back seat."

He nods, like he gets it. I flip through the stack of pictures he took at the local park in his neighborhood. In them, I see images of the park at different times of day—the rustling trees casting long shadows in the early morning, names and hopscotch boards drawn in chalk on the sidewalk in the golden afternoon light, and elderly folks gathered on benches under the soft glow of streetlamps at night, drinking wine coolers, maybe talking about the neighborhood gossip. August has captured the essence of life in this neighborhood, each photo telling a story of its own.

As I study the pictures, a wave of inspiration washes over me. I can see clearly now how we might weave these scenes together to create a narrative that celebrates the resilience and beauty of this community. Excitement and anticipation bubble up within me as ideas start to form in my mind, flowing into each other.

"August, these photos are amazing," I say, turning to him with newfound enthusiasm. "I think I have an idea for our project."

"You do?" His eyebrows furrow and he lifts one up with curiosity. I explain what my vision is—about how we can put the pictures into a collage of sorts that could showcase the diverse moments and people that make his neighborhood special. August listens closely, nodding along and giving suggestions when needed. Within minutes, we're both hard at work on our project. It's not flirty at all . . . but I can't deny that when our bodies get close, I remember them being closer. It doesn't take a lot for all those memories of the fun we had with each other to come rushing back like a flood.

After about an hour of gluing, pasting, and piecing together things on a poster board, August runs out of the room and comes back with brownies. He offers me one and without hesitation, I take one.

"I've got to warn you," he says before we both bite into one. "These are *special* brownies. If you're not into that, I'll take it back."

When he says "special," I know exactly what he means. I haven't had an edible in months. I can go another several months or years or lifetimes without another edible. Besides, the thing about edibles? You never know what your side effects will be. And it's often hard to regulate how much THC is in them, so you never really know what you're gonna get. One time, I had a "special" Rice Krispie treat that sent me into the worst panic attack of my life. I vowed never to do another edible again.

I watch August take a big bite and then another one. My entire sobriety flashes before my eyes. But something in August's gaze, the anticipation twinkling in his eyes, makes me reconsider. Maybe this time will be different. Maybe sharing this moment with him, with our newfound project coming together on the table between us, makes it feel safe. I take a deep breath, ignoring the knot of anxiety forming in my stomach, and bring a brownie to my lips.

The rich chocolatey flavor explodes on my tongue, igniting my taste buds, followed by a subtle earthy undertone that I recognize all too well. I steal a glance at August, who is watching me intently, laughing at me like it's my first time. For a moment, I feel some shame for what I just did. But I know it's too late. There's no going back now.

I feel nothing for way too long. I think for a moment that maybe August is playing some kind of joke on me. That he was trying to get me like bait, but he seems a lot looser than he's been in a while around me. It reminds me of the times when we used to get high together and fool around.

"Not feeling anything yet?" August asks, grinning.

"Not even a little bit," I say. Maybe my body doesn't even react to edibles anymore. Maybe my body's become resistant to them since I started taking other things, harder things. I don't know if that's even possible, but it feels like the drugs have lost their magic touch on me. I watch August take in another bite and then another, his eyes half-closed and a smirk playing on his lips. He looks so carefree, so happy in this moment, while I'm here struggling to find any sort of sensation. What's the point of putting drugs in your body if you don't feel anything, right? That's supposed to be the whole point of getting high. What a waste of throwing away my sobriety.

I stay at August's for a little while longer, until the project is finished. I guess it's better to knock it all out in one sitting than to spend multiple days working on it. Before I leave, August grabs my shoulder and looks into my eyes. He pulls me in close and we're inches apart. He looks at me like he used to before he started avoiding me. I stare back at him, admiring his brown skin, his light brown eyes, the way his lips curve into a smile. I can feel my heart racing, unsure what this moment means. August leans in slowly, his warm breath grazing my skin. And then his lips touch mine, softly at first, then with more urgency. My mind is a whirlwind of emotions—equal parts confusion, desire, and longing. But then I think about his cheerleader girlfriend and then I think about Eliza and then I think about Miles and then I think about Mikki and it's all enough to have me pulling back and saying, "I—I gotta go."

He sighs. "Uh, yeah. I get it. I'm sorry. I didn't mean to . . ." August nearly stutters as he stands there, a flushed look of embarrassment and shock like he really didn't mean to do it, like something took control of his body and now he's all disoriented. "Please don't tell anyone."

I'm used to hearing those words from him. But it's not like I was planning on telling anyone about us before, either. I'd want things to stay as much of a secret as he does. I kept it from Miles, my parents, Mikki, people at school, everyone.

I let him know that my mouth is shut and I head home.

CHAPTER NINETEEN

The edible hits.

Out of nowhere, I'm taken up into a great cloud, with bright lights, some kind of unimaginable rush. It's the kind of happiness that bubbles up from within, unexpectedly and without any specific source. It overwhelms you and takes over your entire being. Everything around you is so stunning, so perfect, that you feel as though you could survive without even breathing air anymore.

I realize I'm near the park where August took the photos. I get out of my car and find a bench. I can't go home like this. As I wait, I admire the birds flying above and the squirrels chasing each other all around me. I never knew black squirrels existed.

The high lasts about an hour. When that hour is up, I'm feeling extreme guilt. So guilty, I want to throw up or shit my pants or both. I was clean, not taking anything or doing anything, for months, almost half of a year. Until now. All my hard work goes out the window, just like that. All the NA meetings, all the months of successfully resisting doing anything, all those conversations with Miles and my parents that helped me along in my journey . . . it's all for nothing now.

But as the guilt threatens to consume me, a calm voice whispers in my mind, reminding me that one misstep doesn't erase all the progress I've made. I take a deep breath and tell myself that recovery is a journey full of ups and downs, twists and turns. I can still choose to learn from this moment and continue moving forward or I can let this consume me.

I head home and immediately barricade myself in my room. I can't let Momma or Dad see me high. I don't want them to be suspicious, either. I can hear them now, telling me about how disappointed they are, telling me that they knew it. I can't let them be right. It only takes one good look in my eyes to see it. So the longer I can avoid them, the better.

I spend what feels like hours pacing back and forth in my room, bothered by what I've done. But I'm also feeling like nothing in the world matters. It's a weird mix of numbness and dread.

I reach for my phone, thinking that I need to talk to someone. I dial up Miles.

The phone rings for what feels like forever. And finally, I'm greeted by a very warm "Hey, Keem!"

"Hey, I need to talk," I say, my voice shaking with emotion. I don't know if it's paranoia setting in from the edible or just my own worry about my actions.

"What's going on?" Miles asks, concern evident in his tone.

I tell him about the relapse, about the overwhelming guilt that's clawing at me from the inside. Miles listens quietly, his steady presence anchoring me in the storm of my emotions.

"Oh, Hakeem, I'm sorry to hear that this happened. I wish I could be there," he says finally. "But remember not to beat yourself up about it. We all stumble sometimes. What matters now is how you pick yourself back up."

I believe him. His words are a soothing antidote to my nerves. "Thanks, Miles," I say.

"Anytime. You know I've got your back," he says, and I picture his smile on the other side of the line. "You're a lot stronger than you think, Hakeem. Don't forget that."

I stand there, taking in his words like they're medicine.

"Where did you get an edible anyway?" Miles asks.

"August," I say, reluctantly.

"August?" Miles wonders. "Mikki's brother?"

I nod, and then remember he can't see it. "Yeah. We were working on an art project and he offered me a brownie and I couldn't say no."

"You *could* say no. You just didn't," Miles corrects me.

"You're right," I say. "But I think that's the worst part. I had the option to say no, everything within me said no, but I still did it. That's what gets me."

Miles falls silent for a moment, as if to process my words. Then he says softly, "Keem, we all have moments of weakness. And tomorrow is a new day. Just look at tomorrow and tomorrow and the day after that as a second, third, fourth chance."

"A new day," I repeat.

"So, about August . . . how did he go from ghosting you to offering you weed brownies?" Miles asks.

"I don't know. I wish I did." Then I joke around. "Why, are you jealous?"

Miles chuckles on the other end of the line. "Jealous? Nah, I'm just curious. Seems like a strange turn of events."

"Well, it was certainly unexpected," I admit. "But to be honest, I think August might have his own struggles, too."

"I'm sure he does. Anyway, you go get some rest and face tomorrow with a fresh perspective," Miles suggests. "I know you can do it."

We exchange goodbyes and click off.

Later when the edible totally wears off, I remember promising Judah that I would play video games with him. I head to his room. As I open the door, I'm met with the sight of him sitting crosslegged on the floor, his eyes fixed intently on the screen in front of him. The room is bathed in the soft glow of the TV, casting long shadows on the walls. Judah doesn't notice me at first, so I take a moment to just look at him, watching him do his thing.

"Hey, Bro," I say.

"Hey," Judah says back, removing his headset from his ears to around his neck.

"Got room for one more?" I ask, sitting next to him on the floor.

Judah smiles big, like this is a dream come true. He tosses me a controller that glows in the dark.

"What do you want to play?" he asks.

"What do *you* want to play?" I ask back.

"How about *Apex Legends*?"

"Sounds good. You just tell me what I need to do and I'm in."

"Just stay alive so that we're the last squad standing," he explains. I'm not really sure how the controls or this game all work, but I can figure it out. I figure most things out.

And so we begin. As we dive into the virtual world of *Apex Legends*, I find myself completely immersed in the game. Judah's a pretty skilled player, despite how young he is. He calls out strategies and points out items for me to pick up. The adrenaline in me pumps as we navigate through the terrain, hunting down our enemies while trying to stay alive ourselves. At first, I fumble with the controls, but Judah's guidance helps me improve the longer we play. I make a mental note to play this game with him more often.

In the middle of us taking enemy fire, Dad comes into Judah's room. "We're having leftovers, so help yourselves with that whenever," he says.

"Thanks, Dad," Judah calls out, not taking his eyes from the screen.

"I'm getting a raise because of you, Hakeem," Dad says. "Chief was really proud that we caught some dirty cops. I couldn't have done it without you."

"Oh . . . yeah." I'm unsure what to say to that. "Congrats, Dad."

"Maybe we can all go out to dinner and celebrate sometime soon," he says. "Celebrate your five months of being sober, too."

I almost pause the game just to see his face, but that would get us killed. But then again, maybe it's best that I don't make eye contact with him at his mentioning my five months being sober. I wonder if my face would hide the fact that that's no longer true.

"Well, I'll leave you two to finish up your game," Dad murmurs before heading out. "But, when you guys are done, you should eat and help your mom straighten things up downstairs."

Judah and I both agree to that.

I feel like I've gotten away with something. And I'm not sure that's a good thing.

CHAPTER TWENTY

I don't tell anybody but Miles about what happened. This is hardest with Eliza, because there's really a part of me that wants to keep things true between us. But bringing it up is too hard and too complicated, especially with August involved.

The rest of the week is a blur. The only things that get me through Thursday, Friday, Saturday, and Sunday are phone calls with Miles, hangouts with Eliza, and cookie dough ice cream, which I end up having a lot of—waaaay too much of, given the fact that I'm lactose intolerant. The way I see it, ice cream is just too damn good to not have. I'd rather pay the consequences later than miss up an opportunity for the rich, creamy, delightful goodness.

Another thing that helps me get through is counting each day that I don't think about weed or edibles. Despite my high, which was actually more pleasant than not, I haven't craved it one bit. Weed is less physically addictive than alcohol, nicotine, or opioids, I know, but still, I remember times when all I thought about was weed, getting one more hit, one more blunt, one more ounce. I remember wanting it with every fiber of my being, wanting it so badly I would have cold sweats, wanting it so badly I would dream of it. But now? None of that.

I even get inspired to also grab Miles's Xanax and flush them down the toilet. I figure there's no use in me holding on to it. It's only going to make things worse if I don't get rid of it now. If it's nowhere I can get to, it'll be less likely that I use it. Miles's voice echoes throughout my head, reminding me that I'm stronger than my addiction, that I always have the power to overcome it, no matter what.

Monday rolls around. It's Prank Day at school. This was Miles's favorite school holiday. He liked pranks, he liked jokes, and he liked making me laugh. I remember one Prank Day prank he did on me two years ago. He had spent weeks planning the perfect prank. He had enlisted the help of some others, like Mikki, August, some people in the drama club, and even some teachers to pull it off. The day started innocently enough, with Miles pretending to be his usual self, not giving away any hints of what was to come. As the day went on, I began to relax, thinking maybe he had forgotten about Prank Day this year.

But just as I let my guard down, it happened. During lunchtime, Miles had mentioned seeing a poster in the hallway of Hayley Williams from Paramore coming to our school to be a guest speaker. Mikki, August, and others had confirmed this by talking about how excited they were to get her autograph. Later, I saw the posters for myself, and they looked so good, so legit. Some of the teachers even talked about how awesome it was that she was coming and how we had to go to the principal's office to buy tickets for fifty bucks. I remember racing to Principal Samuels's office during passing period so fast, pouring out every dollar from my wallet on his desk to score a ticket. Except Principal Samuels gave me a puzzled look, as if I had two heads.

Miles had orchestrated the entire thing, from printing the fake posters to getting everyone in on the prank. As I stood there in disbelief, trying to process what had just happened, Miles walked over and handed me a fake winning lottery ticket.

"Happy Prank Day," he said with a mischievous look in his eyes. I play-punched him and then he play-punched me back. "Got you again."

For a little while, I wonder what prank Miles would play on me today. How elaborate would it be? How long would he let it go on? Would it be his most creative one yet? The reality sets in that I'll never have another Miles prank. Something about that makes me want to cry the world an extra ocean.

I message Eliza and see if she wants to hang out after school. It takes her a minute to reply, but she says that she's down. We exchange a couple texts and decide that she's going to pick me up. I see her hearse outside my window when she pulls up. When I head downstairs, Momma's there waiting for me.

"Where are you going?" she asks.

"Out with a friend," I say. "Eliza."

"A friend, you say?" she says, looking at me like I'm lying. "Seems to me that Eliza is a girl, right?"

"She's a friend. But also a girl, yes."

"Some would just call her a girlfriend," she teases.

Judah and Jorjah come out of nowhere, mocking. "Ew! Hakeem has a girlfriend?" they say in unison.

I think for a moment, picturing Eliza. It's not like I'm offended or grossed out by their insinuation. But I haven't thought about

Eliza in that way. Sure, I like spending time with her and she's been a lot of help as I grieve Miles and pick up all the shattered pieces of my life, but she's a broken girl and I'm a broken boy. There's no way we could work out that way.

"She's picking me up," I say.

"You be careful out there," Momma says. "There's a lot of crazy folks out here these days. You know what happened to Miles."

What she says stings a lot, but I know she's coming from a place of care. Despite the way that she might make me feel sometimes— like a baby who can't do anything for itself—I know she cares about me deeply. One day, I'm her golden child who overcame the odds—the one she's so proud of. The next, I'm the forever addict who always needs to be watched, because everything I do is wrong. By the way she looks at me right now, I'm not entirely sure which version I'm getting.

When I get inside Eliza's hearse, she says, "Heads or tails?"

"Heads or tails? For what?"

"Just pick one, silly," she says.

"Okay. Tails," I say, my face bunching up to show how confused I am.

"I'll vote for heads. Heads is we go to the Garfield Park Conservatory. Tails is the Indianapolis Zoo."

I nod, liking those options. I love giraffes. So anytime I can see them in person feels like a win. And I know how much Eliza loves flowers. I'm sure we would have a great time doing either.

"The winner is . . ." She flips up a penny in the air and it lands in her hand. "Heads."

"Great," I say. "I've never been to a conservatory."

"They're pretty magnificent," she says. "Some of the best types of greenery, plants, and flowers. Plus, I heard they have a room full of succulents. It's like a desert inside a building."

Now I'm even more intrigued.

"What if we do both, though?" Eliza suggests.

"Both what?"

"After the conservatory, we hit up the zoo? I think it's open late today."

"I like the sound of that!"

The hearse putters along the road, the windows down, letting in a warm breeze with a strong smell of some odd mixture of gas exhaust and fresh-cut grass.

When we arrive at the Garfield Park Conservatory, Eliza leads the way, her steps purposeful as she navigates through the lush greenery surrounding us. Everywhere I look, there are vibrant colors and interesting plants I've never seen before. Eliza points out her favorite plants and shares little tidbits of information about each one. She moves with confidence, like she could work here.

We reach the succulent room, and my eyes widen, deeply amazed at the variety of shapes and sizes displayed before us. Eliza's face lights up as she talks about how resilient these plants are, thriving in harsh conditions with their water. The air is heavy with the sweet scent of flowers, and I feel like I've stepped into another world entirely. Eliza's world.

"I love succulents because they remind me of wildflowers," she says, pointing to one that catches her eye. It's a small one, but the leaves on it are in a funny shape.

"How so?" I ask, wondering.

She smiles at me. "Well, they may not look like your typical wildflower, but they share the same spirit."

"Yeah?" I say, standing there, admiring the way she looks at life.

"They're survivors, you know?" Eliza responds, her voice soft as she gently strokes the succulent's leaves. "Maybe my next tattoo will be a succulent."

"I'm sure it would look nice," I say.

We spend another hour wandering around the different greenhouses, seeing rare plants and endangered flowers of the Garfield Park Conservatory. We even see a little pond with turtles and koi fish. There's something about being here with Eliza that's relaxing and makes me feel like I've laid down all my burdens. But I think it's more likely Eliza than the conservatory. Eliza has that kind of effect, I've noticed.

As we make our way out of the conservatory, it's almost like she glows. "Thanks for coming in there with me. I know it's not exactly everyone's definition of a good time."

"I had a good time," I say. "Seriously. I learned a lot, like how vanilla comes from the orchid. I always thought it came from some seed in the ground."

"Vanilla orchids smell so wonderful," she says. "Anyway, I'm glad you had a good time. Should we go see some animals? I'm looking forward to seeing the penguins. What about you?"

"Giraffes, mostly," I answer. "But also the hippos, dolphins, and orangutans."

The sun begins to set as Eliza and I arrive at the Indianapolis Zoo, casting a warm golden light over the whole parking lot. The sounds of animals echo through the air, mingling with the chatter of excited visitors as we approach. I still feel the same way every time I go to the zoo, like there are butterflies in my stomach. Eliza's eyes sparkle with anticipation as we make our way to our first stop. We head down the path that leads to animals from Africa. We pass by elephants, zebras, rhinos, and meerkats before we make it to the giraffes.

The giraffes stand tall and majestic, their long necks gracefully reaching for the leaves on the trees. Eliza points ahead at a baby giraffe, hiding between its mother's legs.

A zookeeper comes over and holds out a bucket. "Would you like to feed them?"

"Yes," I say without any hesitation.

"It'll just be five dollars," the zookeeper says. A real bait-and-switch situation, I see. I reach in my pocket, pull out a loose five-dollar bill, and hand it to her. Then I reach in the bucket and grab a bundle of leaves, shoots, and strips of dried fruit. The zookeeper walks me through how to hold out my hand and feed the giraffes.

One approaches me, nervous yet intrigued.

"This one's named Nala," the zookeeper explains. "She's super friendly. Loves treats!"

Nala nibbles out of my hand. It tickles at first, but I'm too stunned to react. I'm just glad that I can be this close to a giraffe. Eliza stands there, smiling at me. She pulls out her phone and snaps pictures.

"Don't worry, I'll send it to you," she says. "I'm sure you're going to want to remember this moment."

She's not wrong.

As Nala finishes nibbling on the last of the leaves in my hand, she looks at me with big, gentle eyes. I can't help but be mesmerized by her presence, towering above me yet so delicate in her movements. Eliza's phone chimes with a notification, signaling that she has just sent me the picture she took. I somehow silenced my phone, so I didn't hear the notification. I quickly check my phone and there it is—a snapshot of me beaming with joy as the giraffe eats from my hand. But looking at my phone closer, I also notice something else.

"I missed a call from Miles," I say. My phone says that it was nine minutes ago.

I press to call him back. I take a step away from Eliza, for a little bit of privacy, and wait for him to answer.

"Keem!"

"Hey, Miles, sorry I missed your call. I'm with Eliza."

"Eliza? Who's that?" he asks. And it hits me: I haven't told Miles about her. For a second, I wonder why that is. But then, I know that it's just because that's the way I've always been. I've been good at compartmentalizing my life, making sure my worlds don't overlap. It's not like Miles can ever meet Eliza and vice versa anyway, so I felt justified in not talking to him about her. Eliza knows that

Miles exists—or at least, once did—but *he* doesn't know that *she* exists.

"She's a friend of mine," I say. "And before you start teasing me about it, like my siblings and my mom, no, she's not my girlfriend."

"Okay, but do you want her to be?"

I think for a moment about Miles's question. Mostly I have the same feelings I did when Momma brought it up. I enjoy Eliza. I might even say that I've grown to like her. And the truth is, Eliza and I have been spending a lot of time together lately, more than anyone else I know. And each moment with her feels easy, comfortable, almost like we've known each other forever. I even stopped things from going too far with August in part because she popped into my mind. But the idea of crossing that line from friendship to something more feels daunting. What if it ruins what we have now? What if she doesn't feel the same way?

Eliza looks at me with a curious expression, as if trying to read my mind, from the distance we're apart.

She mouths words and I'm trying to understand them. I can't figure it out, so she puts her thumb in the air—up, down, and sideways.

I nod, giving her a thumbs-up.

"You there?" Miles says, and I realize I haven't answered him.

"Um, yeah . . . I don't know," I say.

"You don't know?" Miles questions. "Do you like hanging with her?"

"Yeah, I do."

"Okay. Do you think she's good-looking?"

I look at her. "She's beautiful. Inside and out," I say. "It's not that."

"Then what the heck is it?"

"I don't know about dating," I say. "I don't know if I want to do that. If that's something that's in my cards. I don't know if I'm even the lovey-dovey type. Some people have love lives, some people have Disney Plus. I belong in the latter group."

"Look, Keem. Love is a bitter bitch sometimes. It stabs you in the back and watches you bleed out as you call for help, only to come and patch you up at the last possible second. But even then, that only happens sometimes. You know you're especially unlucky when love convinces you it's worth it despite how it kills you."

"When did you become such an expert on all things love?" I ask him, holding in my laughter.

"Look, you have lots of time to think about a lot of things when you're dead," he says.

"I guess that's fair," I say, a chuckle slipping out.

"It's up to you to decide if love is worth the risk," Miles says.

"All right, all right, I hear you," I say, trying to get him to stop lecturing me about how awesome love is. I didn't remember him being such a hopeless romantic in his living days, but I guess time does change a person. "Also, did you need something?"

"Wow, I gotta need something to call my best friend these days?"

"No, no, that's not how I meant it. I was just wondering—"

"I'm just fucking with you, homie. You're all good. I'll let you get back to Eliiiiizaaa." The way he says her name makes me want to cringe. "You know I had to at least call you on Prank Day even though I can't pull a quick one on you."

I smile. "Happy Prank Day, Miles."

"Back at you, man," he says. Some silence washes over the line for a brief second. And then he continues with, "Just make sure you're honest with this girl and you don't fuck her over. Don't make the same mistakes I made."

I know what he means. And I genuinely do appreciate his looking out for me, making sure that I give love a try and reminding me that I could have love, if I want it. Truth is, ever since Miles died, I've felt like I had to protect my heart. I've almost been overprotective of my heart. I told myself the story that I can't let people in and I can't let people get close, out of fear of losing someone else that gets close to me. I wouldn't be able to handle that.

Miles and I hang up and I walk back over to Eliza.

"Everything okay?" she asks.

"Yeah. Miles was just checking in," I say.

I love that she can just accept this.

Minutes drag along like hours, the two of us getting lost in seeing all the different animals and even getting splashed in the front row of the dolphin show.

As we dry off from the dolphin show, Eliza turns to me with a mischievous look in her eye. I've seen this look too many times before. I know whatever happens next will be wild.

"I have an idea," she says. "Follow me." Curious, I trail after her as she leads me through the winding pathways of the aquarium until we reach a secluded alcove overlooking the shark tank. Eliza grins brightly and points to a sign that says when the next feeding time is. Before I can protest or talk some sense into her, she slips off her sandals and climbs over the safety barrier, dangling her feet above the water.

"What are you doing?" I shout, my heart pounding suddenly, scanning the area for any staff members. But Eliza just laughs and beckons me to join her, the thrill of rebellion lighting up her face. "Come on!" she says in a bit of a shout.

With a nervous glance around, I reluctantly follow suit, feeling the cool mist from the tank on my skin as we wait for the feeding frenzy to begin.

The water below churns with anticipation as the first shadowy figure glides into view. A massive shark, its sleek form cutting effortlessly through the water, its dark eyes fixed on Eliza's dangling toes. My heart slides all the way up my throat.

Anticipation builds with each passing moment until suddenly, a zookeeper appears at the entrance of the alcove, a look of shock and horror on his face. He immediately grabs his radio, I'm assuming to call security and backup, alerting them of our intrusion.

Eliza and I exchange a wide-eyed glance before hopping up and scrambling back over the safety barrier, our hearts racing with a mix of fear and exhilaration. "Get back here this instant!" he shouts, his voice filled with urgency. And we run, we run like our lives depend on it, until we're out in the parking lot. Despite how scary that was, it also felt good. I always wondered what it was like to feel . . . infinite.

We hop back in the hearse and Eliza puts the pedal to the metal, and we skirt out of the parking lot and onto the main road. Eliza laughs the whole time.

"That was amazing!" she says. "Wasn't it?"

I'm trying to catch my breath. "Absolutely . . . fucking . . . awesome," I say, each word spaced out to inhale.

"Hungry?" she asks.

"Yeah. I could go for a good cheeseburger right now," I say.

"To the Shake Shack! Ahoy, matey!" she says, pretending to be a pirate.

"Argh!" I say, joining her.

At Shake Shack, we order cheeseburgers, fries, and milkshakes. We sit in the same place we did the last time we were here. It's a lot busier than before, but we still get our food pretty quick. I take a big bite of my cheeseburger, savoring the juicy patty and melted cheese. Across from me, Eliza grins, her cheeks flushed. She dips a fry into her strawberry milkshake, a combination I don't quite understand until I try it. I start with a tiny fry and dip it into my vanilla milkshake.

"Not bad," I say. "Perfect amount of sweet and salty."

"Delicious," she says. "I've been dipping my fries in my milkshake since I was a kid."

"I never did it. But my younger siblings do it a lot," I tell her.

We're quiet for a while. And as I take another bite of my cheeseburger, I steal glances at her, trying to memorize every detail—the crinkle by her eyes when she smiles, the way her hair falls in soft waves around her face, the way her flawless, smooth skin catches the light.

Out of nowhere, she says, "I've been doing some thinking." It sounds scary, the way she says it. I feel a lump form in my throat.

"What have you been thinking about?" I ask, trying to sound casual.

Eliza takes a deep breath, her eyes searching mine for a moment before she speaks. "I've been thinking about how I used to want to die. I would wake up every single day and ask myself, *Is today a good day to die?* And then you came along. And you gave me a new-found hope. You don't look at me like people who've known me awhile look at me, and I didn't understand how much I needed that. I realize that I'd choose to believe in hope with you, rather than having complete certainty anywhere else."

It feels like the world stops spinning for a moment.

"I had no idea," I say, completely taken aback. "I'm glad you found some hope with me. You've kinda been like a light in the darkness for me as well."

Eliza looks up from her milkshake. "Really?"

I don't know how to explain to her that she's been like an anchor in the storm for me. So I settle with just saying, "Yeah."

"But . . . there's something else I need to say," she tells me. I don't know where this could go from here. My mind races with possibilities and my heart flutters in my chest.

"I decided that I'm going to go and see my dad and brother," she goes on. "I just felt like I needed to see them one last time before I can move forward."

"What do you think that's going to do for you?" I ask.

"I don't know. I just think it's the closure I need," Eliza explains, looking around like she's trying to find answers in the air.

"I'm just worried that you won't find what you're looking for, and will be left more in the dark."

"I think I'm okay if I don't have all the answers, Hakeem. At least I'll know I tried," Eliza says with a determined look in her eyes. "I need to do this for myself."

I know what that's like, to want to do something for yourself. And I can't argue with that point. "Where are they being held anyway?"

"They're at a maximum-security prison in Terre Haute."

"Wow. That's only, like, an hour or so away."

"Yeah, I'm going to leave tomorrow," she says. "I've already called to make sure I'm on their allowed visitors list."

"Well, are you?"

"I am, but an officer has to be with me at all times," she says.

"Do you want me to go with you?" I offer.

"I thought about that. But I think it's best if I do this alone."

"No, I totally understand," I say.

"I didn't plan on telling you today," Eliza murmurs, her voice barely above a whisper. "But I couldn't keep it inside any longer."

There's a sense of finality in her decision, a quiet resolve that shines through her eyes. I admire it about her. Despite my reservations, I can't help but admire her courage.

"Just promise me you'll be careful," I say softly, my voice filled with concern.

"I will. I'll try to call when I can," she says. "But I'm the worst at phones."

"What time are you planning on leaving tomorrow?" I ask, wondering how much time I have left with her before she goes to Terre

Haute. I gotta admit that part of me feels like if I let her go, I won't ever see her again. But again, maybe that's just the fear talking.

"I think I'm going to leave after school," she says. "I don't want to miss my fifth day, you know."

I smile at the mention of getting at least one more school day with her.

CHAPTER TWENTY-ONE

I have to go all day thinking about Eliza leaving to go confront her father and brother in some prison in Terre Haute. The day stretches on for what feels like an eternity. I'm unable to focus on my work in all my classes. My thoughts are only on Eliza, and they are consuming. I think about her determination, her bravery, her vulnerability. I can't seem to shake off the worry that gnaws at me, knowing she's facing her past demons head-on.

The only reprieve I get from my thoughts is at lunchtime when we sit together at Mikki's table. Eliza's so chill about everything. It's like she's trying to pretend that later today won't be happening, or like right now her only focus is being present at school. She even starts a game of Twenty-One at the lunch table, teaching it to Mikki and August.

After school, I meet Eliza at her hearse in the school parking lot. People around snicker and make fun of the fact that she drives a hearse to school, but we both ignore them, knowing that something more important is about to happen.

"Are you ready for this?" I ask, some amount of nervousness in my voice.

She takes a deep breath. "Yeah . . . I think so."

Eliza has tears welling up in her eyes. It doesn't take long for mine to match hers. "You don't have to do this alone, Eliza," I remind her, my voice filled with emotion. "I'll be here waiting for you, no matter how long it takes for you to get back." By the way I'm talking and the way I'm feeling, you'd think she was going halfway across the country.

There's tension in the air for a long while before she steps closer to me and kisses me nice and quick on the lips. Her lips are soft and velvety, like rose petals. One kiss doesn't settle it for me, so I lean in and kiss her back, pulling her in close. She kisses me harder and the world suddenly spins in slow motion. Sparks go off in my stomach and my skin nearly melts from the warmth pulsating between us. Everything is sweet and nice and I'm reminded that despite how I sometimes feel like there's a black slug in my chest, turning me into the walking dead, I'm actually the best kind of alive.

When we break apart, she's smiling and I'm smiling. "You're a good kisser," she says. "I didn't expect that."

"Wow," I say, laughing at that comment. "You really know how to flatter me."

"Ha! Don't take it personally."

"You really thought I was going to be a terrible kisser, didn't you?" I tease, nudging her playfully with my elbow.

She shrugs, a certain look in her eyes. "I like to keep my expectations low," she mutters.

"Low, huh?" I raise an eyebrow at her. "Well, I guess I just exceeded those low expectations, then."

"You did," she tells me.

It's quiet for a moment. The school buses leave and the student parking lot clears out, leaving just the two of us.

"Well, I should get going," Eliza says. "I want to hit the road before it gets dark."

"Yeah," I reply, my eyes diverting to the ground. "You should get going."

"But before I go, I have something for you," she says. She opens the back part of her hearse and tells me to close my eyes.

I oblige. I squeeze my eyes shut really tight.

"Hold your hands out," she instructs me. This feels scary, but I do as she says. I feel her place something in my hands. It's not too heavy, not too light. "Okay, open them!"

When my eyes flicker back open, adjusting to the daytime, I see a card and a flower that looks freshly picked.

"I'm gonna guess that this is a wildflower?" I say.

"Of course it is." She smirks and tucks a strand of loose hair behind her ear. "But for the love of everything holy, do not read the card until I'm gone. It's always so cringey to have someone read the card I just wrote right in front of me."

"Understandable," I say. I know just how cringey that would be. "I'll hold on to the card and read it when you go."

"Which is now," she says. "Goodbye, Hakeem."

I can't bring myself to say goodbye to her, not to another person. I settle on, "See you later, Eliza."

She opens the door to her hearse and slides inside. The engine roars to life, a comforting sound that fills the silence that's killing me.

I watch Eliza drive off toward Terre Haute. I can't ignore the feeling of unease that settles in my gut, turning it sour, as she disappears from view. Suddenly, I feel a deep emptiness in me that I don't know how to treat.

I walk over to my car and hop in. The stereo clicks on, automatically connecting to the Spotify app on my phone, shuffling through my saved songs. "Astronomy" by Conan Gray plays. I take the card out of the white envelope. The front of it says, *Oh, the places you'll go*. I try to figure out why she chose this specific card, and I know I'll be thinking about it all night. I open the card and see the picture she took of me at the zoo printed out. There's also a poem she's written in red ink, drawing little wildflowers around it.

IN THE DUSK'S EMBRACE, WHERE SHADOWS LOOM,
MY HEART, A CHAMBER OF IMPENDING DOOM, GLOOM.
IN FIELDS WHERE WILDFLOWERS BLOOM AND SWAY,
I PEN THESE WORDS, MY SOUL'S ANGUISH AND DISARRAY.
BENEATH THE MOON'S COLD, UNFORGIVING LIGHT,
I WANDER LOST, CONSUMED BY ENDLESS NIGHT.
AMONGST THE BLOOMS, WHERE BEAUTY HIDES ITS STING,
I MOURN THE LOSS OF EVERY FLEETING THING.
OH, LOVE, A SPECTER HAUNTING MY DESPAIR.
AN ABSENCE LEAVES ME GASPING IN THE AIR.
LIKE WILDFLOWERS, WE BLOOM AND THEN DECAY,
IN THE GARDEN OF DREAMS, WE FADE AWAY
YET IN THIS DARKNESS, A FLICKER STILL REMAINS,
A FRAGILE HOPE, A THREAD THAT SOFTLY STRAINS.
BUT SHOULD IT SNAP, AND ALL MY WORLD DESCEND,
LET WILDFLOWERS MARK WHERE MY JOURNEY ENDS.

I never understand poetry and I'm not sure hers is any different. Poetry always seems like some kind of riddle you have to salvage through to find its meaning. I don't know what Eliza's trying to say to me in this poem, but it's beautiful and makes tears pour from my eyes. I didn't know she was a poet. It's another layer of her I'm just discovering.

At home, I read and reread the poem, but I still don't think I understand it. Suddenly, I'm wishing I paid more attention during the poetry unit in English class. I settle on telling myself I'll just have to wait for Eliza to come back. Then I can ask her all about it and she can tell me herself what the meaning of it all is.

An hour and a half passes, still no sign of Eliza reaching out to say she made it to Terre Haute. I text, call, and FaceTime her, but she doesn't answer.

I'm home alone. Dad's working an all-day, all-night shift. Momma's doing parent-teacher conferences up at Judah and Jorjah's school. It could be a while until they're all back. I wonder about what Eliza's up to. I wonder how she's feeling as she confronts her father and brother. I wonder if she'll have the courage to finally speak her truth, to stand up for herself after years of hiding, running, and pushing away what happened. I wonder where things will end up for her after all is said and done. I wonder what she'll be like upon her return.

For a little while, I pace around my room and wait by my phone. When she still doesn't call, I feel like I'm going to lose my mind. Once upon a time, I'd take something to settle my nerves.

Right now, I need to clear my head. Going for a run sounds like a good idea.

I lace up my running shoes, slide into my joggers and a T-shirt, and head outside. My regular route starts down my block but ends near Cousin Vinny's.

I take off at a fast pace, my heart pounding in sync with my footsteps. I usually find it's best to start slow and then gradually pick up my speed, but now running as fast as I can helps me break the sweat I need. The familiar rhythm of my breathing grounds me as I pass by houses with neatly manicured lawns and blooming flower beds. The sun hangs low in the sky, giving me warmth.

I reach the entrance to the trail, a winding path through the woods that always makes me feel like I've entered another world. The trees loom overhead and birds chirp in the distance. I run, jumping over sticks and rocks when I need to, trying to control my breathing as I pick up the pace. I run like I'm being chased. I run like I've got something to prove. I run until I reach Cousin Vinny's. I wave at Frankie through the window and then immediately begin my trek back home, running as fast as I can, the whole world blurring as I go.

The whole time, horrible images flash before my eyes of things that could've happened to Eliza. Maybe her brother and father said something horrible to her, maybe her car flipped over on the way there, maybe she got kidnapped by some old man and her body is discarded in a random river. Thinking about something happening to her makes me want to pass out right on the pavement.

I'm so out of breath once I make it back home. And now

I desperately need something to drink. I search through the fridge—seeing skim milk, orange juice, chicken broth, and a half-drunk bottle of lemon-lime Gatorade. Once upon a time, this fridge would be filled with PBRs and vodka because Dad loves light beers and Momma likes mixed drinks. I reach for the orange juice and take the biggest swig. I grab a cup and pour some orange juice inside it. I open the freezer side for some ice. As I reach in, I notice something hidden behind where different cartons of ice cream are. I reach in the back and pull it out.

The bottle is big, fat, and see-through. There's some kind of brown liquid in it and it's filled halfway, like someone's been drinking it. That's strange because I haven't seen my parents drink since before I started NA. I guess maybe they've been drinking in secret, when I'm not around. I guess that makes sense, in some way. But it also stings. I twist off the cap of the bottle and smell its contents. It's strong, but it's also . . . nice. The label says *Crown Royal*.

Suddenly, there's a war going on within me between my flesh and my mind. My mind tells me to put it back where I got it, to leave it alone, to stay away—far, far away. My mind tells me dealing with this stuff could be the start of a long spiral down to the beginning. My mind tells me that this is no good, that I'm no good if I drink it. But my flesh? My flesh tells me just one sip, just one taste, and it'll all be okay. Just one sip won't hurt.

I bring the bottle to my lips, remembering back, in an instant, to the very first time I tried alcohol. I lift it up, allowing the liquid to pour into my mouth. I take a mouthful and swallow hard and fast, not wanting to taste much of it. That's the thing about alcohol: I was never much a fan of the taste. One sip won't do much, so I go in for one more. Then, another. Then, another. With each swallow, I push away the voice that tells me to stop. There's no use in stopping if I've started, right? But then, I think about Momma and Dad. I don't want to drink so much that it becomes noticeable, so I stop there and put the bottle back in the freezer. It takes a while to get a buzz going on, but when it hits, it's like a wave crashing over me, washing away all my worries and doubts. I feel lighter, freer, like I can take on the world without a second thought. The warmth spreads through my body, numbing the ache in my chest that has been a constant companion for as long as I can remember.

I head back up to my room and try and sit down to work on Mr. Sanchez's essay. The blank document I've been staring at has been blank for days at this point. The cursor blinks at me as if it's mocking me. My hands feel all jittery, but I know it's just because I want more alcohol. I struggle to focus on the screen after a while. I try to type a sentence, any sentence, but my fingers fumble over the keys, the letters coming out jumbled and meaningless. I think about the bottle in the freezer again and the calming effect it has on me.

Maybe just a little more wouldn't hurt. I push myself up from the desk, swaying slightly as I make my way back to the kitchen. The cold air from the freezer hits me as I reach for the bottle again. As I take another swig, the burning sensation down my throat is almost comforting. The worries about my parents and the essay fade away with each gulp. After a few minutes slip by, a sudden wave of nausea hits me, and I realize I may have had one drink too many. Panic sets in as I struggle to keep everything down, but it's a losing battle. I run to the bathroom as fast as I can, and before I know it, I'm throwing everything up until I'm dry heaving on my knees.

My head hurts from throwing up and my throat is sore from stomach acid coming up.

My phone rings.

Sloppily, I search around for it, pulling it out of my pocket. I wipe away at my mouth with a piece of toilet paper and flush the toilet before answering. I don't even check to see who it is. I hope it's Eliza, telling me that she's okay. I hope it's Miles, giving me encouragement and not judging me for the thing I just did.

"Hello," I say, sitting on the floor of the bathroom, remembering why alcohol was my least favorite thing for a quick high.

"Keem, it's me," Miles says through the phone. Relief washes over me. "Are you okay?" he asks.

I take a deep breath before responding, trying to sound more composed than I feel. "I've had better days," I say back.

"What's going on?"

I consider lying, but don't. "I had something to drink."

"Okay," Miles says. It takes him a second for things to register. "Wait, like, *something to drink*." He says those last three words in a different kind of voice, as if his words come in italics.

"Yeah," I admit quietly, feeling the shame creeping in.

"Keem, what happened?"

"I don't know," I say, racking my brain to find something to blame. But I come up with nothing. It could be some combination of stress and Eliza leaving, but explaining out loud that a girl who I have barely known for that long has that kind of pull on me feels somewhat embarrassing. "I went for a run, then came back, got a drink from the fridge. And it was just . . . *there.*"

"I see," Miles says. Then he asks, his tone a little more urgent than before, "Where are you right now?"

"Just in my bathroom," I confess, feeling even more exposed as I sit on the cold tiled floor.

"This would be the part where I would say that I'm coming over," he says.

We both share a moment of silence, the reality setting in.

"I think I just need to sleep it off," I say. "I'll be fine."

"Take care of yourself, man. And drink some water," he advises.

"I'm sorry, Miles," I say, feeling like I've disappointed him. "I don't want you to think that I failed."

"It's okay, Keem. You didn't fail. I'm just glad that you answered my call."

"I just don't wanna fall back into old habits, Miles. I don't wanna completely lose myself again. I don't wanna . . ." I gasp.

"Hakeem. Take a breath, man," he says, leading me through some breathing exercises. "Repeat your old mantra: I am not defined by my struggles. I am strong. I am resilient. I am worthy."

He's right. As I close my eyes, I repeat the mantra in my mind. *I am not defined by my struggles. I am strong. I am resilient. I am worthy.* And with that, I take the deepest of breaths.

I push myself up from the floor and splash some water on my face. The cool sensation helps ground me in reality. I hear some commotion downstairs, which means that Momma's home with Jorjah and Judah.

"Hakeem Lee!" I hear Momma's voice call for me.

"Coming!" I try to shout back, but my voice splits in a billion places.

"I'll call you back, Miles," I tell him. "Thank you for everything."

"No problem, man. I love you," he says.

I stand over the sink for a moment, taking his words in. "I love you, too, Miles."

When I click off with Miles, I stare at myself in the mirror for a moment. Long enough for Momma to call me a second time, with more urgency in her voice. I just want to make sure I look more alive than dead. I grab my toothbrush and toothpaste and brush my teeth as fast as I can so my breath is minty fresh if she asks to smell it.

After, I head downstairs to see what Momma needs from me, trying to put on the greatest act of the century by pretending to be completely sober in front of her. She's seen sober me and drunk me and every version of me in between. I'm just hoping I'm doing a good job with my performance.

Momma stands by the kitchen counter, a dishrag in her hands as she looks at me with a mixture of concern and suspicion. Jorjah and Judah are eating graham crackers topped with peanut butter and cut-up bananas at the dining room table.

"What are you upstairs doing?" she asks.

"Just working on an essay for my English class."

"Are you okay, honey?" Momma asks, her voice soft but filled with worry.

"Yeah, uh, just pretty tired," I say.

"You sure that's all?"

I nod, trying to force up a smile on my face to sell it.

She studies me for a moment, as if trying to read my thoughts through my expression. Finally, she nods slowly. "Well, all right. You've just been quiet around here lately. If something's going on, you know you ain't got to hide anything from me, right?"

"I know, Momma," I say, swallowing the hard lump of my secret.

She comes over and gives me a kiss on my temple. "You smell minty."

That beats her saying I smell like booze. "Just brushed my teeth," I say. "I went out for a run and came back all gross."

"I can smell that, too. But at least you won't have any cavities," she says jokingly. Her light brown hair is pulled back into a loose ponytail. When she wears her hair like this, it shows her fivehead that I inherited from her and angled cheekbones. "Stuffed peppers for dinner. Will be ready in an hour. Your dad won't be back, but he sends his love."

"I'll be down for that," I tell her. "But I should get back to my essay."

I get back to my computer, my copy of *The Catcher in the Rye* sitting next to me on the desk. I stare at both back and forth, but still no ideas come to me. This essay is worth a significant portion of my grade. If I don't come up with something to write, I could fail the class, which means I'll have to retake it over the summer.

Eventually, I give up. I slam my computer shut and throw my copy of the book on the ground. I check my phone to see if there's any news from Eliza, but there's nothing.

Later, in bed, I find a pirated audiobook of *The Catcher in the Rye* on YouTube. I listen to it, getting caught up on the book for Mr. Sanchez's class. I read—listen—until I fall asleep. My dreams that were once about Miles take a turn. Now I dream about Eliza.

In my dream, Eliza is standing in a field of wildflowers, her laughter echoing through the multicolored petals of the flowers. The sun is warm on my skin as I walk toward her, each step feeling lighter than the last. As I reach out to touch her hand, a gust of wind blows through the field, causing the wildflowers to sway around us, pollen blowing around our heads. Eliza turns to me with a smile that lights up her whole face, and I feel a sense of peace wash over me. We stand there together, surrounded by the beauty of the wildflowers. But then the dream turns dark. Storm clouds gather overhead, casting shadows over the wildflowers. The wind picks up speed, becoming more intense, causing the petals to whip around violently and the air to grow cold. Eliza's smile fades as she looks up at the darkened sky, her hand slipping out of mine. Panic rises in my chest as I reach out for her, but she begins to fade before my eyes. I call out her name, but my voice doesn't work. I scream, but no sound comes out.

The dream wakes me all the way at about 3:00 a.m. and I can't go back to sleep. When my eyes flicker open, I realize the audiobook is still playing. I pause it right as Holden says the greatest quote I've heard from the book yet. I stay up thinking about it and repeating it in my head until the sun comes out of hiding.

The mark of the immature man is that he wants to die nobly for a cause, while the mark of the mature man is that he wants to live humbly for one.

CHAPTER   TWENTY-TWO

Mr. Thompson is mid lecture on Manifest Destiny during fifth-period US History as I look over to Eliza's empty chair. Just like I saw the empty chair in Pre-Calc, just like I saw the empty chair in AP Chemistry, and just like I'm sure I'm going to notice the empty chair in Mr. Sanchez's English class next. All of it has me feeling like how I felt when I first noticed Miles's absence at school after he died.

"Manifest Destiny teaches us all something in the twenty-first century. It teaches us that we must forge our own paths, conquer our fears, and seize every opportunity that comes our way," Mr. Thompson says. "Carpe diem!"

As the other students scribble notes or doodle idly in their notebooks, I can't quite shake the uneasy feeling pooling in my stomach.

"Carpe diem!" Mr. Thompson repeats in a booming, low voice. "Anyone know what that means?"

Ximena, August's girlfriend, raises her hand.

"Yes, Miss Gomez?"

"Doesn't it mean 'seize the day'?" Ximena says, her voice soft and singsongy.

"Excellent! Seize the day!"

I can't concentrate on the drone of Mr. Thompson's voice as I picture Eliza walking through the sterile halls of the prison, her determination like a shield against the harsh reality awaiting her.

I look at the clock, noticing I've got only fifteen minutes before the bell. The words *seize the day* echo in my mind, a motto urging me to embrace each moment with purpose. But as I glance at the clock ticking away on the wall, I can't help but think that Eliza figured out what it meant to seize the day, to take every opportunity captive. Hell, even Miles did it before he died, was taking care of his family the best he knew how, even if it led to something he didn't expect. For a moment, I think about the story of my life. I wonder what it will all be for in the end. I think about the opportunities I've been given, the ones I've passed up, and the ones that I've yet to receive. I think about what seizing the day might mean for me. But I come up empty-handed. At some point, between grieving Miles's death, discovering the truth as to what really happened to him, and getting lost in spending time with Eliza, I lost track of where I'm headed. Instead of ironing myself out and focusing on my future, I've taken one step forward and three steps back. My old therapist, Dr. Chandler, once said to me that you can't judge a book by its cover, but you can by the opening line and the final line. You can make a judgment about a person, but only by the beginning and the end. My beginning is history, but my ending is not.

The bell rings, finally.

I grab my copy of *The Catcher in the Rye* and head to Mr. Sanchez's class, passing by Eliza's locker on my way there.

"Hakeem!" I hear my name from a ways away in different-pitched voices. I look back, seeing Mikki and August flagging me down.

I walk quickly to see them before the late bell rings. I hear a rumor in the hallways that tardy sweeps are happening again, so today's not a day I'm willing to be late to class, no matter how chill Mr. Sanchez is.

"Detectives are here," Mikki says, concerned.

Instantly, I lose my breath, wondering if something has happened to Eliza. Just when I think this, I see Principal Samuels escorting the detectives into the office down the hallway.

"What are they doing here?" I ask.

"They're asking questions about Miles," Mikki says.

"I overheard one of them asking Principal Samuels about his grades and what his behavior was like at school," August adds. "Messed up."

"Have they talked to either of you yet?" I ask.

"Nah," August says.

"Not yet," Mikki says, wearing a look of nervousness. "And I hope they don't."

For a moment, I think about why they're asking about Miles's grades, but then I remember a conversation I had with Dad a while back. There was this one time where I saw on the news that a kid down south was beaten to death by the cops and then the police turned around and made it seem like the kid was just some thug who wasn't anything but trouble because they kept talking about how the kid got suspended from school one time and had all below-average grades. I remember asking Dad about why that was, and he told me that sometimes people in power will do whatever they can to justify their actions, even if it means tearing someone down after they're already gone. He said it's a way to control the narrative and shift the blame onto the victim instead of taking responsibility for their own wrongdoing. It was the first time he told me that "all skinfolk ain't kinfolk" because sometimes it can be your own people trying to make someone look bad just so they can get away with something. I know the police didn't kill Miles directly, but in a way, the system failed him all the same. Detectives coming to school, snooping around, trying to find "dirt" on him makes me feel sick.

Ximena comes up to August, kissing him quick on the lips before walking away and heading to her next class. August makes a face at me, split between embarrassment and nervousness, as if to remind me of our secret pact.

"We should get to class, so we don't get detention," Mikki says just a minute before the bell rings.

I make it on time to Mr. Sanchez's class. As expected, there's no sign of Eliza. There's no message from her, either, telling me that she's okay. My mind goes to the worst-case scenario all over again and I can't focus on Mr. Sanchez's lesson on how the author uses imagery and metaphors to convey his central message.

Finally, the bell rings, signaling the end of class. "Don't forget rough drafts of your essays are due next week. We will do peer review in class before final drafts," Mr. Sanchez announces as people pack up. I grab my bag and rush out the door, scanning the crowded hallway for any sign of her.

Nothing.

It's only when I'm walking back to my car that I catch sight of her. As I approach the parking lot, my heart flutters, nearly skipping a beat as I recognize a vehicle parked next to mine that will always be etched in my memory: a hearse.

CHAPTER TWENTY-THREE

"Eliza!" I say, running to her, frogs leaping and doing cartwheels in the pit of my stomach. I feel like I'm looking at a ghost at first, but then it dawns on me that she's actually here and totally not a figment of my imagination's desperation.

Relief floods through me at the sight of her, but it's all quickly replaced by concern at her disheveled appearance. Her jacket looks like she's rolled around in dirt or sand. Her hair and skin look like she hasn't showered in months. Her face looks pale and exhausted.

She doesn't say anything at first. But after some time, she says in a quiet, soft voice, "Hey."

"How did things go? Did you get to see them? How was the drive? I was worried sick about you. I had no idea if you . . ." I stop to take a breath as her face turns like she's confused by what I'm saying to her.

"It was . . . a lot," she says after a brief pause.

"How so?"

"Seeing them there in those orange jumpsuits, chained up like animals, behind a glass wall—it did something to me. They wouldn't let me see them at the same time, so I had to take turns. The whole time, I just felt . . . *empty*. I felt like I was standing on the edge of a black hole, staring into the abyss of what could have been. Like I was staring into a mirror, seeing fragments of myself scattered across that terribly lit room. It was like looking back at the past, at the choices and mistakes that led us all to this point. And as I stood there, watching them behind that glass wall, I realized that they weren't the only ones serving a sentence."

I wonder if she's looking for me to comfort her, but all I can offer is sympathy because I have no words for what she's describing. But still, I attempt them. "I'm so sorry, Eliza."

Eliza starts crying. It starts lightly at first but then becomes like a flood, all the gates bursting down, crumbling into pieces. "Remind me I'm not a monster."

"You're not a monster, Eliza," I say, getting close enough to her to bring her into a hug. She sobs onto my shoulder, and her sobs become mine, my eyes becoming deep wells that never run dry.

Things are quiet between us for a beat. She seems different, almost like she left and came back as a shell of herself.

"You have a look on your face like you're not okay," I gently say.

"I . . ." she starts, but then tears choke her up.

"Did something else happen? You can tell me, Eliza," I say, trying to make her feel safe.

"I just feel like I have nothing to live for," she confesses.

Her words hit me right in my chest. "You do, Eliza. You do!"

"I don't!" she fights back, some amount of frustration in her tone. "I couldn't bear the thought of not confronting my father and brother, but while I was away, I couldn't bear the thought of being apart from you. It was the scariest thing I've ever experienced."

"We don't have to lose each other," I plead. "We don't have to give up on anything. We're together now and you faced your family head-on."

"But is that enough?"

"Listen, I shouldn't ask you to live for me, because even though that would be nice—because I think I am sure that I love you, and maybe you hate that I'm using that word because *I hate* that I'm using that word . . . but it's how I feel. I also couldn't stop thinking about you when you were away, worrying if you were safe or okay or if you were eating at all—I want you to stay alive for your own sake, because I believe there is an abundance of opportunities and wonders waiting for you in this life. You have so much that I see in you that is truly beautiful, truly magical, truly wonderful. You've got so much time ahead of you to explore and enjoy everything this world has to offer. You are deserving of all the good things that come with truly living, like smelling the freshly bloomed roses in a garden or feeling the sun kiss your skin on a warm spring day or experiencing all the highs and lows that come with the roller coaster that is life. I understand if you might not think so at the moment, but trust me, you deserve it all. Even though we haven't known each other for very long, being around you has brought healing to parts of me that I didn't even know were hurting. You're like a rainy day. So gloomy yet so beautiful up close. You're captivating even when you don't want to be."

She inches toward me, like there's a magnetic force pulling her nearer. She presses her lips against mine, kissing me like we have seconds to live, like the world is ending tonight, like I'm the one thing she wants so desperately at the end of a long journey.

The kiss consumes me, fiery and intense. Kissing her back is the best part.

When we break apart, she leans her forehead against mine, her breath warm against my skin. "I've wanted to do that again," she says.

"I'm glad you finally did," I say, meaning it with everything in me.

"The motel kicked me out because I haven't paid them, and I don't have much money left anyway. So . . . I have nowhere to stay tonight, and I don't think I should be alone," she murmurs in a dejected way.

"You can stay with me," I say kinda quick.

"I don't know, Hakeem," Eliza says doubtfully. "You have parents and siblings who might not like it."

"You said it's just for one night," I say. "You'll survive staying with me for one night. And so will my parents and my little brother and sister." Secretly, I wouldn't care if she stayed with me forever, moved in, never left. As long as I know she's safe and alive. That's all that matters in the world.

"Okay," she gives in. "Just one night. And I'll figure out where I'm going after that."

"If you need to stay longer, I understand. And I'm sure my parents will as well."

She follows me to my house. In my head, I replay the part of our conversation where Eliza said she felt like she had nothing to live for. I scream at her inside my head that it's not true all over again, hoping it sticks. I think of how everything with Miles—figuring out what really happened with his death and him coming back into my life through phone calls—has prevented me from really appreciating what I have with Eliza. I don't blame Miles for anything; I'm glad that I've been able to still talk with him, catch up like we used to, and have some sense of normalcy even though he's forever gone and things are definitely not normal. But Eliza is here, needing me, and I have a real chance to move forward with her in a way that I can't with Miles.

Back at home, I struggle to explain everything to Momma and Dad about Eliza, who she is, what's going on, and how she needs a place to stay for the night. The two of them exchange concerned glances, and I'm not sure where things will go.

Out of nowhere, Eliza blurts out, "I should probably explain more about myself. I don't have much family left, and, well, I've been on my own for a while now. Things just got a little rough lately."

"She's been staying at a motel," I add. "She shouldn't have to do that."

Momma places a comforting hand on Eliza's, her eyes brimming with understanding. "We're glad you're here, dear. You can stay as long as you need."

Momma ushers Eliza to the guest room, assuring her that she is welcome in our home. Dad pats my shoulder, offering his silent support. Then he sits down at the kitchen table and pulls out a newspaper, flipping through it until he gets to the obituary section.

Dad says, "I know your mom says she can stay for as long as she needs, but I'm gonna try and have someone look her up in our system tomorrow at work. Maybe we can get a lead about her family."

"No. Um . . . it's probably best if you don't do that," I say, still trying to keep secret what happened with her family.

"Why? There's a kid out here all alone, living in a goddamn motel. You don't see anything wrong with that?" he asks, some anger in his voice. I'm not entirely sure where his anger is coming from or where he's trying to direct it.

"I mean, yes, I know it's all wrong. But . . . I just think her family left her behind and she doesn't want to think about them anymore. Digging up info about them won't help her."

Dad looks at me, his face going from curiosity to acceptance. "Okay, I'll think about it. But now you've caught my attention."

Momma and Eliza come back, and Eliza looks around with awe and wonder.

"Such a beautiful house," she says, beginning to smile.

"Why, thank you," Momma answers. "This is what years of hard work and prayer gets you."

"I believe it," Eliza says. "Thank you for letting me stay."

Momma smiles at her and Dad nods from across the way. An awkward silence washes over the entire house before Momma inhales fast and hard and brings up how she made chicken-and-gnocchi soup for dinner with homemade garlic bread.

"Sounds amazing," Eliza says. "My mom used to make us gnocchi when we were kids." She stares at the floor for a moment, like she's reliving a memory, and then snaps out of it after a while. "When do we get to eat?"

Momma smiles. "I like this girl. Finally, someone who is eager to eat my food!"

Eliza and I promise to do some homework while dinner comes together, and although there's more cuddling than work that gets done, it almost feels normal to have her in my room with me. We spread our books out on the bed, but soon enough, we are both distracted by an old photo album that ends up falling off my nightstand. We laugh at embarrassing pictures of me as a kid, and even some of Judah, Jorjah, and Miles. One picture in particular of Miles and me catches her eye. In it, we're both covered in mud and wearing cowboy hats that are absolutely too big for our heads.

"Please tell me the story behind this picture," she asks.

"Nooo," I say. "It's too embarrassing."

"Okay, that only makes me want to know even more," she says. "You should know this by now."

"But what if we continue to just lie here," I say, wrapping my arms around her and squeezing until it's like we melt into the bed. We remain here, just enjoying each other's presence.

When dinner's ready, Momma brings out the steaming pot of soup and the warm loaf of garlic bread, filling the dining room with such a garlicky, buttery scent. We pass around the dishes and fill our bowls with soup and garlic bread. Dad asks for the hot sauce. It's where I get my love of spiciness from.

"Feel free to take however much you want, sweetie," Momma says to Eliza. "I can even save you some in a to-go container for when you leave."

"Thank you, Mrs. Hawkins. It all looks so delicious," Eliza says.

"Are you Hakeem's girlfriend?" Jorjah asks first thing.

I make a face at her, but she doesn't care. Eliza looks at me like she doesn't know what to say but offers a smile. "You'll have to ask your brother."

I try to make a face at her that says, *Wow. Way to throw me under the bus like that.*

"I hope she is your girlfriend. She is pretty," Judah adds, showing his missing teeth.

"All right, eat those vegetables in your soup, kids," Momma says as if she catches how awkward they're making things. But it also makes her laugh, like she's in quiet agreement with them.

"I'm flattered," Eliza says, smiling at Judah, who shoves a whole piece of garlic bread in his mouth.

It's one thing for Judah and Jorjah to embarrass me. It's a whole other thing for Momma and Dad to do it. I'm just waiting for it. I know it's coming, so I nervously take sips of my glass of water. Eliza's eyes flicker from person to person around the table, a warm blush creeping up her cheeks as she tries to navigate the unexpected attention.

"Eliza, did Hakeem tell you about the first girl he dated, named Daniella?" Dad says, putting hot sauce on a spoonful of soup.

"No, he didn't, actually," Eliza says, glancing at me, grinning.

"The answer is no. No because that was in, like, third grade. And it doesn't really count as dating," I say.

"He always came home talking about this girl named Daniella and how he wanted to do everything with her. During recess, he would sneak her all different kinds of snacks he would take from our pantry—Fruit Roll-Ups, Oatmeal Creme Pies, Oreos, anything."

My cheeks burn as Eliza turns to me with wide eyes, clearly finding this story amusing. "Oh, really? Seems like you've always had charm," she teases, a playful smirk tugging at her lips.

"She was a little cute thing with those thick glasses," Momma says. "I wonder whatever happened to her."

Judah pipes up while chewing bits of chicken. "Are you gonna kiss Eliza, too, like you did with Daniella?"

I nearly spit out my water in shock; my face would be turning beet red if I were a few shades lighter. And Eliza snickers, fist-bumping him from across the table.

"All right, all right," Momma says, reaching over to ruffle Judah's hair gently. Jorjah giggles and scoops another spoonful of soup into her mouth, clearly enjoying the moment. I can't wait to get them back one day when they're older.

After dinner, as Dad reclines in the living room to watch his shows and Momma does crossword puzzles in her room, I help Eliza bring some things from her hearse to the guest bedroom where she'll be sleeping. Eliza carries in a large, ornate wooden suitcase and sets it down gently on the bed.

"Thank you for the trouble," Eliza says to me.

"What trouble?"

"The trouble of getting your parents to let me stay here and just being a good person. You're one of the best people I've ever met. You're patient, you're kind, and you see me. The way you look at me is like a miracle even I could believe in."

I kiss her again, taking my time as I do it. I want to savor every moment, every second, every millisecond of our lips connecting, warmth running through my veins.

"Good night, Eliza."

"Good night, Hakeem. I heard you say it earlier and I've been thinking. I don't want you to be the only one. So . . . I love you, too."

CHAPTER TWENTY-FOUR

I wake up the next morning with a smile on my face, her name falling out of my mouth. I get dressed for the day—a *Stranger Things* graphic T-shirt, a plaid button-up, dark blue jeans, and my black high-top Converse. I grab for my backpack, stuffing everything I'll need for the day inside before slinging it over my shoulder.

As I'm on my way down the stairs, the smell of bacon and freshly brewed coffee wafts through the air. I find Eliza, Judah, Jorjah, and Momma in the kitchen. Momma hums a tune as she flips pancakes on the griddle. She looks up and grins when she sees me, her eyes scanning me up and down.

"I like the look today," she says. "I remember buying you the shoes and the button-up. I don't remember the shirt you have underneath."

It takes a minute to remember, but then it hits. "I got it from Miles. He bought it for my birthday last year. We watched the show together, and for a while it was both our personalities. We even started to play *Dungeons and Dragons* because of it."

Momma laughs. "You and that boy. Just silly, I tell you."

I glance at Eliza as she eats pancakes and shows Judah and Jorjah some card trick she knows. They look amazed, impressed by her magic. I notice that she has her packed bags already at her feet. I wonder if she's found someplace else to stay.

Dad comes downstairs in uniform. "Good morning, everyone," he says.

People say good morning to him as he walks into the kitchen, kissing Momma on the side of her face and then on her lips. "I'm gonna head out. I've got a long shift ahead. Chief's gonna announce promotions today, too."

"Wow, babe," Momma says. "You think you'll get one?"

"I hope for all our sakes I do," Dad says. "Prices for everything keep going up. A promotion would come with quite a nice raise, too."

"I'll be praying," Momma says.

"Good luck, Dad," I say. He hugs Judah and Jorjah, squeezing them tight, and then comes over to me to do the same.

"Good to meet you, Eliza," Dad says. He shakes hands with her and she thanks him for letting her stay in his house.

Eliza and I drive separately to school. We make it with five minutes to spare before homeroom starts. You can always tell when it's a Thursday at Center Grove High School because everyone looks tired and dead inside, already drained from the week, their eyes begging for the weekend, which will inevitably be filled with booze, parties, video games, and all the things high school kids can't do during the week.

Of course, it's pop quiz day in Pre-Calculus. If there's one thing Mrs. Li loves more than formulas and golden retrievers, it's pop quizzes. We have them so often, they really shouldn't be considered pop quizzes anymore.

Eliza sits on the other side of the room from me, so I give her a glance to offer her good luck. I don't know if she takes it that way or understands what I'm trying to do. But I don't even know if she needs luck. Eliza's smart and she seems like she knows about things that I don't. She might need to be the one wishing *me* luck.

Sameer taps me on the shoulder and whispers, "I hope you studied."

I shrug. I didn't study, but I also remember what we learned last being somewhat easy. I'll take my chances on bullshitting my way through this pop quiz.

Mrs. Li slams the pop quiz on my desk with all the might in her tiny body. "No talking!" she instructs. "Or you will earn yourself a zero."

I make sure to zip my mouth for the remainder of the quiz. I stare at it, and all the letters and numbers blur on the page in front of me. There are multiple choice questions, true-false questions, and even short answer ones. She puts a timer on the smartboard, giving us ten minutes to complete the whole thing. The ten minutes fly by and I've yet to answer a single question. I quickly randomly put C for every multiple choice and true for all the true-false. I write the letters *I-d-k* for the short-answer prompts.

"All right, class. I need you to stand up and trade your pop quiz with someone else," Mrs. Li says. People cheer that Mrs. Li decides to grade the pop quizzes this way because some people decide to cheat and change answers for their friends.

I end up exchanging quizzes with Eliza.

Mrs. Li leads us through what the correct answers are. "Number one is A as in Arthur. Number two is C as in cat. Number three is D as in David," she says. She goes on and on. When she makes it to the end of her answer key, Mrs. Li tells the class that she plans on grading the short answer prompts herself later on, but asks us to tally up how many questions they got right and circle it at the top.

Eliza doesn't miss a single question. It's amazing. She jumps right into school here and she's already way ahead of me and a lot of other kids in the class. I write 25/25 at the top of her paper, circling it like Mrs. Li asked. We give the papers back to the original person before turning them in to Mrs. Li.

I stare down at a 10/25 on mine. I failed. It takes a lot of effort, but I resist the urge to rip up the paper right here and throw it in the trash. Getting a 10 in the grade book is certainly better than getting a zero. I glance up and catch Eliza's eye, something in her expression softening. It's as if she can sense my frustration with myself.

The class goes on for what feels like way too long. Mrs. Li's voice drones on in the background as I tune her out, thinking back to what Eliza and I talked about yesterday.

The bell finally rings, signaling the end of Mrs. Li's lecture. I walk over to Eliza.

"Didn't do so hot, huh?" Eliza asks me. For a second, I can't tell if she's making fun of me, but then her warm eyes tell me otherwise.

"I've had better quiz scores," I say. "I can't believe I got so many answers wrong."

Mrs. Li overhears the conversation and butts in. "Math isn't about getting the right answers, my friend. It's about practice. The more you practice, the easier the math will become."

I nod at her as Eliza and I make a beeline for the door and into the hallway, where it's packed and smells like B.O. and corn chips. Eliza and I head to AP Chemistry, where we do some kind of experiment with a mixture of chemicals that ends up in a small explosion. The chemistry lab fills with smoke as the glassware shatters into pieces, but Ms. Eastman only laughs and mentions something about molecular compounds and ionic bonds—words that don't mean much to me, given that I haven't really paid much attention in Chemistry, either. To be honest, science and math are my least favorite subjects, but science makes math look like a walk in the park.

"Ms. Eastman can suck my dick," August says at the lunch table later on as Eliza and I arrive to the table with Bosco Sticks with marinara sauce and chocolate milk. "She gave me a zero for participation points in her class and she had the nerve to tell me that I'll have to retake the class."

"Damn, that sucks," I tell him. Ximena is glued to him, looking up at him like she's some kind of lapdog. She hugs his arm tightly, agreeing with everything he says.

"I used to like her, but now she's lost all respect from me," August explains, dipping his pizza in ketchup.

"She was really cool freshman year," Mikki says. "I had her for homeroom. She let us make TikToks in her class. But this year, she's been rude and bossy and just . . . extra. I think it's because her husband left her."

"What?!" Ximena mutters. "Her husband left her?"

"Allegedly for a girl who graduated last year," Mikki says, giving everybody the scoop.

"Damn," I say.

Eliza has been quiet for a while. She usually doesn't say much during lunch. But she looks up from her lunch now and says, "I wonder about the human psyche sometimes and what part of the brain or the chemicals that exist inside it causes us to do wicked and strange things." It causes the whole table to be quiet for a moment, her words lingering in the air. But I know that her words mean more than one thing to her.

"Anyway," August goes on, "I'm gonna just say *fuck you* to her lab report homework assignment she wants me to do tonight and watch the best movie ever made."

"Which is?" I wonder.

"*The Dark Knight Rises*, duh," August says.

Ximena sighs and rolls her eyes, and so does everyone else at the table besides Eliza, who nods like she respects his pick. Then Ximena says, "Actually, the greatest movie ever is *Ratatouille*."

August grabs his arm away from her, appalled. "What? The movie about the raccoon that makes human food?" He looks at her like she just grew a second head.

"First of all, he's a rat. It's in the name. And second, he's so cute. You can't tell me he isn't," Ximena says, defending herself.

"Both of you are wrong. We live in a world where *La La Land* exists," Mikki says.

"Whatever. You just have bad taste," Ximena tells August.

"Hakeem and Eliza, what are your favorite movies?" Mikki asks.

"I'm not really a movie girl," Eliza says. "But if I had to pick any movie to watch right now, I'd pick *Everything Everywhere All At Once*."

Then everyone's looking at me. I think about all the horror movies I've watched with Miles. Miles and I both enjoyed all of Jordan Peele's movies, but we agreed that *Get Out* was the best, most creative horror movie ever made. But some part of me feels like I need to pick an answer that isn't also Miles's. So I say, "Hard to pick one. I'll go with *Requiem for a Dream*. It's not horror, but it's the most realistic movie ever made."

Eliza glances at me, her eyes widening in surprise. August leans back in his chair, a smirk playing on his lips. Ximena raises an eyebrow, clearly not expecting my choice.

"*Requiem for a Dream*? Seriously, Hakeem?" Mikki exclaims, disbelief evident in her voice.

"Yeah, it's a classic. Jared Leto plays an iconic character."

Eliza leans closer to me. "I didn't peg you for a Darren Aronofsky fan," she says.

But all August hears is the words "peg you" and he makes a joke about it that has the rest of the table dying laughing. It takes a moment for me and Eliza to catch on, but eventually we join in laughing as well.

The rest of the school day flies by. As the final bell rings, Eliza and I meet up at my locker. I'm putting all the textbooks that I used all day back into my locker when she says, "I've been thinking a lot about a strawberry milkshake."

"Milkshakes sound good to me, too," I say. "Let's go."

Frankie texts me to come into the shop but I tell him that I won't be able to make it, that I'll pick up another shift later. Right now, the only thing I want in the world is a milkshake with Eliza. I make a deal that I'll buy if she drives.

At Shake Shack, we order our usual milkshakes, but instead of sitting in our usual spot, we decide to sit outside since the weather isn't bad. This weather reminds me of a time when Miles and I got to see Greta Van Fleet at the Ruoff Music Center.

Eliza sips her milkshake quietly. I know when she's got something on her mind. I've learned that about her now.

"You doing okay over there?" I ask, sucking in some of my shake.

She clears her throat, swallowing. "Uh, yeah. Just thinking."

"About anything in particular?" I wonder.

She's quiet for a long while, takes another sip of her milkshake, and then speaks. "Anne Frank wrote in her diary that despite everything she went through, she really believed that people were good at heart. I don't know if I see things like she did. I mean, how can you when this world is so uncertain, cold, and cruel?"

I nod, listening, trying to piece together what she's saying.

"How could she feel so optimistic about people, knowing what was happening to people like her?" Eliza says, some emotion in her voice. I can almost feel it. "After seeing my father and brother and giving them a piece of my mind, I thought I would come back the happiest little flower in the world, but instead I'm wilting, decaying, dying from the roots up. And I don't know if there's any going back. It's absolutely fucking heartbreaking to be convinced that you are what is wrong in this world."

There's a pregnant pause that slides between us for a while, the only sounds people chatting at nearby tables and cars driving past along the road.

I think about this one time I heard a sermon at church that helped me. Most things at church aren't very helpful, but I remember this one time when I found something that was, at least, somewhat meaningful to me. Dad reminded me of it recently, and now I want to share it with Eliza.

"There's a parable in the Bible about wheat and tares," I say. "One day, a farmer plants a bunch of wheat to feed his family and village. An enemy comes later on and throws out some fake seeds that will eventually become weeds. The crazy part of the story is that the farmer doesn't notice until the wheat blooms and gets choked up by the weeds. The tares look so much like the wheat that you can't tell the difference."

She looks at me like she's unsure what I'm saying, pushing her milkshake away. I watch her pull out a cigarette, light it, and take a big, deep puff of it, blowing smoke out the corner of her mouth.

"My point is that there's always a war happening inside us between the counterfeit and the real. We gotta learn to separate the weeds from the wheat. I think that's what life is all about, that's how we survive. That's how we make it through all the bullshit life throws at us that makes us feel like it's not worth living."

"But what if I'm all weeds and nothing else?" Eliza says, running a hand through her hair.

"You're more than that; you always were."

"But I have a pain within me that won't leave me, no matter what I do. It's been nice to have some joy with you, for once, but the pain keeps coming back to make me hate myself."

Tears build in her eyes and she wipes them away as if she doesn't want to cry in front of me.

She goes on, "No matter what, there's no anesthetic that exists that can take away this pain completely. You just have to learn to live with it and hope that over time, things hurt less and less and less. Samuel Beckett once said, 'You're on the earth. There's no cure for that.'"

"Wow, deep." There's something about the way she speaks that feels final, like she's made up her mind to do something about her pain. That if she can't escape it, she'll do something to end it. I know she's talked about killing herself before, but then I thought I'd convinced her to stay, to live, that she matters to me. I don't want to think about a world where she's not in it.

"I'm sorry for ruining our date . . . or whatever we are calling this," she says.

"You didn't," I say, almost pleading with her to believe me. "You don't ruin anything."

"If I could write a book about my life, it would go: Girl's born, she ruins things, she goes to school, she ruins things, she meets a boy, she ruins things. The end."

I say, "How about: Once upon a time, there was a sad boy living in a sad world and he met a sad girl and together they discovered all the secrets of the universe and happened to fall in love. The end. That's how our book would go."

"Bummer. The girl should totally die at the end," Eliza says, laughing.

"No way! This isn't some Shakespearean tragedy," I say.

"'To be or not to be, that is the question,'" Eliza says back, blowing smoke.

"You know, you're like who Taylor Swift sings about in 'Death by a Thousand Cuts,'" I say, knowing I absolutely despise Taylor Swift and feeling slightly embarrassed at announcing the fact that I've listened to her music.

"If I'm a sad love song, then you're fucking Edward Elgar's *Nimrod*."

"What did you just call me?" I clutch my invisible pearls.

She laughs. "It's a symphony, silly."

"*Nimrod*'s a symphony?"

"Yes. It's beautiful. And tragic. Listen to it sometime."

We finish our milkshakes, get into her hearse, and sit in the parking lot for what feels like hours. We stay there, talking, laughing, joking, bringing up memories, and listening to Edward Elgar's *Nimrod*. And she's right. The piece really does pack a punch. It's hauntingly melancholic, yet triumphant. It has a way of tugging at my heartstrings, for sure. We stay sitting in the hearse until the parking lot clears out and we're the only ones left.

"You're weird," Eliza says after a while. "By that, I mean cute."

"You think I'm cute, huh?"

"I mean, yeah, I do like your face."

"Aw, shucks. Thank you. I think your face is pretty good, too."

"I'm intentional about not wearing my heart on my sleeve. I'm a firm believer that the heart is sacred, not everyone should see it. But you come along and take it," Eliza explains. "Just like that."

The whole world mutes. She leans over toward me and then I lean forward toward her. We gradually slide toward each other until we're just centimeters apart, able to feel each other's breath, my skin tingling with excitement. And then we kiss. Every time we kiss, I feel like I'm floating aimlessly on a cloud of happiness that I've never felt before, a joy too deep for words. We kiss harder until tongue slips in. We kiss like if we stop, the planet will be set ablaze.

Eventually, she maneuvers her body over to the passenger seat, straddling me. She pushes the seat back, giving us more room.

Her hand searches my body as she kisses me, going down my chest, my stomach, and then my dick. She massages her hand there until I get excited—almost too excited, so I grab her hand and bring it back to the side of my face.

"We can stop if you want to," she says.

"But I don't," I say.

I want her. I want her like water when I'm dying of thirst. I want her like food when I'm starving.

I.

Want.

Her.

Here.

Everywhere.

Clothes off.

Nothing to separate our bodies.

I want our bodies to collide into the night and fireworks to erupt from within our anatomy, exploding and painting our story in the sky.

I pull off her shirt and bra. She pulls off my shirt as well. I kiss my way around her neck, then down her chest, stopping at her breasts.

"Do you have a condom?" she asks me. I think back to when Dad convinced me to keep one in my wallet. *Just in case*, he said. I'm thanking him silently.

"Yes, I have one," I say, nodding, pausing from kissing for just a brief moment. I reach in my back pocket for my wallet, pulling out the small golden package. I bite it open and pull out the condom. Condoms always feel kinda gross when you first pull them out of the package.

She grabs it from me, helping to take off my pants. She slides it on me, which sends me letting out a moan that nearly echoes throughout the hearse. And for the first time, I don't even care that I'm in a hearse. Our bodies collide and everything feels good and right and like it was meant to be. I could do this with her forever.

I tell Eliza she can stay over at our house again, but she insists she's come up with another plan, and she only wants to impose on my family when she absolutely needs to. I try to convince her, but she's stubborn and I let it go. Eliza drops me back off at home around nine, but not before we make plans to hang out over the weekend. We agree to talk more about it to figure out specifics, but right now, I'm riding the high of getting to connect with Eliza in the way we did. Sex was always an awkward thing for me—figuring out where your hands are supposed to go, constantly checking in with yourself, the voice in your head telling you that you suck at it. But with Eliza? It all seemed like things just came together. I ask her about where she's staying and she says she convinced the Motel 6 front desk receptionist to let her have a few more nights for half price. Which, knowing the charm that Eliza has, I believe.

I'm in bed, listening to Edward Elgar's *Nimrod* again, but on loop this time. Each time, I smile as I think about Eliza. At 10:30, my phone rings and I pause Elgar.

It's Miles.

"Miles, hey, man," I say.

"Yo, Keem! Are you alone?" Miles asks with some weightiness.

I sit up in my bed. "Yeah, I'm alone," I say. "What's going on?"

"Nothing, I'm okay. I just didn't want to interrupt anything if there was something going on. Wink, wink," he says.

"No, but if you would've called like a couple hours ago, you would've been interrupting. Wink, wink," I say back.

"What the fuck?" Miles laughs. "My boy is getting it in like that, huh?"

"Something like that," I say.

"Please tell me you wrapped it up, though. Unlike me," Miles goes.

"Of course, man. I'm always prepared."

"Yeah, when you used to be ho-ing around," he says.

"I was never a ho," I say.

"And I guess I'm the president of the United States," he says. "If we're gonna lie like that."

"Whatever, man," I say, trying to keep myself from laughing but failing epically.

"Remember what we did a year ago today?" Miles asks.

It takes me a second to remember, but when I do, it comes rushing back like a tidal wave. A year ago today, Miles and I skipped school to go watch the new Marvel movie that had just came out. After that, we ended up going to a nearby lake and went skinny-dipping . . . until we got caught by some upset old man who threatened to call the cops on us. Miles had a way of making even the simplest things feel extraordinary.

"That was some crazy stuff we did," I say. "I can't forget because we snuck into the theater and didn't have to pay for those tickets. And we cried seeing our favorite heroes get nuked."

"Wasn't that wild?" Miles says.

"Yeah, I've never had a thrill like that since," I say. Little did we know that our day of skipping school and mischief was just the beginning of the end of the series of adventures that would bond us for life.

Miles lets out a nostalgic chuckle. "I wish we could do something wild today to commemorate the anniversary."

"I wish we could, too, Miles," I say. "That would be pretty nice, actually."

A beat of silence, where we just listen to each other's breathing. For a second, his breath makes me feel like he's with me.

"Also, Hakeem, I've been doing some thinking," Miles says. I never know what to expect with that kind of a setup.

"Okay?"

"I think this should be our last call."

"Miles, what? What do you mean?" My heart skips a beat.

"I don't know how helpful it is to you that I keep calling you," he says. "I feel like you need to move on. And the more I call you, the more I'm stopping you from moving forward in your life. And I think maybe that's just a little bit unfair to you."

"No, Miles," I say, "that's not true. I don't feel that way."

"But I do! It's been dope getting to hear your voice and all, but I'm dead and you're alive. What good is it doing for either of us to be reminded of that every time we talk?"

Maybe there's something true about that, but I don't want this to be our last call.

"Every time I hear your voice, it's like a lifeline back to the days when things made sense, even if it's just for a moment. Please don't take that away from me," I admit, tears welling up in my eyes. "I appreciate your care for me, Miles, I really do. But you're a part of my life, even if it's in a different way now. Let's not make this our last call. I want to keep this connection alive," I practically plead.

"I don't know," Miles says. "I just know that our time together is running out. I want what's best for you, even if it means letting go of me."

I draw in a deep breath, thinking about what he says. Miles is right, of course, in his own way. Our connection is tethered to memories and moments long gone, a reminder of what once was. But I can't let go of him. Not yet. Not again.

"Forgive me, Miles, but I'll always wish we had more time," I say.

"You make it so hard to say goodbye," Miles says.

"Then don't say goodbye," I tell him.

Some silence breaks through on the other side of the line, followed by a good amount of static. Finally, Miles's voice comes back. "I will always be with you."

Beep, beep, beep.

Just like that, the call is over. I'm left saying his name over and over into the phone, not believing the fact that it's all done, like he can still hear me from this side, like I'm not ready to accept this being our last time talking.

I call him back. The line doesn't ring. An automated message talks back:

"You've reached a number that has been disconnected and is no longer in service."

CHAPTER TWENTY-FIVE

Eliza comes over Sunday morning when everyone's out at church. I still can't believe calls with Miles are a thing of the past now, I'll never be able to hear his voice again, casually catch up, or ask him for more encouragement to keep going. I think about how daunting it will be to go the rest of my days without him, how "moving forward," or "moving on," seems like such bullshit because, in my heart, I know I will never truly move on from Miles. How can you move on from someone who was such a huge part of your life?

I lie across my bed as Eliza sits on the floor near the foot of the frame, working on her essay. Seeing her type away on her school-issued iPad inspires me to type away at mine. For once, I think I've finally got some material to write in my essay. Writing about Miles and what he meant to me is a great way to start writing about Holden and the loss and grief he experienced throughout *The Catcher in the Rye.*

Each word I type feels like a drop of my heart's blood spills onto the screen. As the words begin to flow onto the page, I find myself pouring out all the emotions I've been holding inside since Miles passed away. The pain feels raw and overwhelming, but with each sentence I write, it's as if a weight is being lifted off my shoulders. Writing about him is cathartic in a way.

I take a sip of the peppermint hot chocolate that Eliza brought me from some local coffee shop chain. It's still hot, and is the extra motivation I need to keep going.

We write for about an hour, taking little breaks when we need to—to stretch, to kiss, to talk, to kiss some more. I run downstairs and make us a pseudo charcuterie platter with random snacks I find—crackers, peanut butter, cream cheese, grapes, apple slices, and kettle corn.

We take turns feeding each other grapes, playing games like who can hold the most in their mouth (I win), which feels like some scene from a rom-com movie.

After we call it quits with working on our English class essays, I lay my head in her lap, her fingers absentmindedly playing with my hair as she plays a different piece of classical music that I've never heard before. We're quiet, no words spoken for a while, but I put an end to it.

"This music is beautiful. Who's this?"

"Cello Concerto No. 1 in C Major by Joseph Haydn," she answers. "One of the best composers of all time."

I close my eyes, letting the soothing melody wash over me. Eliza's touch is gentle, comforting, and for a moment it feels like nothing else matters. As the last notes of the concerto fade away, a peaceful silence envelops us. I close my eyes, savoring the moment as Eliza's fingers continue to dance through my scalp. The warmth of her touch sends a shiver down my spine, and I can't help but get excited—nearly a little too excited, so that I have to cover my crotch with my hands.

"Let's dance," she says.

"Dance?" I say, knowing that's something I for sure can't do. There's a reason why I've always skipped school dances. Aside from the social anxiety and the awkwardness that comes with watching people twerk and grind up on each other, I decided why go to a dance if I'm going to stand in the back with a cup of water I'm anxiously sipping?

"Just follow my lead," she says, pulling me up from the bed. She changes the song on her phone. "Vivaldi's *The Four Seasons.*"

She grabs my hand and leads me through a waltz-like dance, giving me instructions when I need them. Her movements are fluid and effortless, a stark contrast to my clumsy steps and awkward sways. Even though she laughs at some of the movements I make, she makes sure I keep up with her. I didn't know she was a dancer, another layer of her I'm just discovering. As the song comes to an end, Eliza collapses onto my bed, breathless and smiling up at me. I fall on top of her, kissing her immediately when our bodies come together.

"I've got something to show you," she says. "I think you'll like it."

I wait in place, trying to think about what it is she possibly wants to show me.

"We have to drive there," she says, taking my hand. "I'll take us."

Eliza and I end up going on a spontaneous road trip. I watch her as the wind whips through her hair while we speed down the highway, playing pop songs and classical symphonies back-to-back. After what seems like hours, we arrive at a secluded clearing in the woods in some random small city just outside of Indianapolis, some place Eliza found and left her mark. Eliza parks the hearse and gestures for me to follow her. We trek through the forest, twigs snapping under our feet, goose bumps forming on my arms. Then we make it to our destination.

It's a huge field of wildflowers. All different colors, shapes, and sizes. This feels like her own personal planet, with everything that gives her life. She doesn't stop grinning from ear to ear, swaying around and dancing like we just were back at my house. She lies down among the flowers, patting the spot next to her.

I do the same and lie down on the flowers, the ground somewhere between soft and firm. Trees block out the sun's bright rays, but some light still manages to seep through branches, making the leaves glow green.

"Do you believe in Heaven?" Eliza asks me, her fingers positioned in a way like she's trying to take a snapshot of the way the sun breaks through the trees.

"Hmm," I say. "Maybe only on good days."

She turns her head to look at me and we lock eyes. "Good days?"

"Yeah, sometimes I don't know if I believe in it. Other times, it feels like it's the only hope we have," I say. "But the calls I had with Miles made me feel like at least there's some kind of afterlife. I just don't know if it's Heaven."

"I see. Do you believe in a higher power at least?" Eliza asks me.

For a second, I wonder where she's going with all this and why she's asking about Heaven and the afterlife, but I know that everything about her is impossible to figure out.

"Like God? I think so," I say.

"Why only *think*?"

"I mean, growing up, I always believed in God. I grew up going to church and reading the Bible and going to Sunday school. I was always taught that God had a plan for my life. That he has a plan for everyone's life. I can't quite wrap my head around why his plan for Miles ended up the way it did. Or why there are kids with cancer. Or people who have unimaginable tragedies," I say and draw in some fresh air, my lungs feeling tight. "I feel like all my life, I've been disappointed by God and maybe that's because he's disappointed by me, too?"

"I get that," Eliza says reassuringly. "I stopped believing in God at some point, too. Right around the time I stopped believing in my parents."

Damn. I can feel the power of her words, but I stay quiet, just taking it in.

"I just wonder what's on the other side of all those layers of sky," Eliza continues. "If there is no God, if there is no Heaven, then what? But, if there *is* a God and a Heaven, does that mean we are all just puppets in some divine play?"

"Exactly," I say. I feel safe talking about this with her. If Momma or Dad heard me talking like this, they'd be pissed, reminding me of all the ways God Himself would strike me down.

Eliza smiles, showing her teeth. She scoots closer to me and we kiss a couple times, until we pull away and remain staring into each other's eyes, communicating love without words.

"Can you hear my breathing?" I ask her. "I've always been told that I'm a loud breather. Sorry if that's annoying."

"Don't be sorry. Your breathing is my new favorite sound," she says.

"Really?"

"That might be the weirdest thing I've ever said to someone, but yes, I'm serious. It makes me happy every time I hear you take a breath. I'd miss it."

"Miss it?"

"Yeah, like if you stopped breathing loudly."

Hearing her say this sends a chill up my spine and causes a thick tingling sensation all throughout my body. I'm so glad I listened to Miles and gave us a shot. Being here with her feels like I'm on top of the world. We lie there in silence, the only sound between us now the faint rustling of leaves in the gentle wind.

There isn't anywhere else I want to be.

CHAPTER TWENTY-SIX

The following Monday at school, Eliza's not there. Yesterday after leaving the field of wildflowers, she told me that she was going to be at school to turn in her essay. I even asked her to hang out after school and we agreed. It feels odd that she's not here and hasn't said anything to me about it.

After homeroom, I send her a text.

Me: Hey. Where are you??

It takes a whole minute, but I finally get a response.

Eliza: Sorry. Woke up not feeling the greatest. I took the day off.
Me: Are you ok?
Eliza: I'm fine. Don't worry about me. 👍
Me: Are you sure? Do you need anything? Soup?
Eliza: Not that kinda sick.
Eliza: Maybe all those cigarettes are finally catching up to me? Idk.
Eliza: Just meet me after school.
Eliza: At the motel.
Me: Sounds good.

I hesitate on the next message that I send. But I send it quick and put my phone away.

Me: I love you.

I know we've said those words to each other already, but every time I say them, I still feel like I'm embarrassing myself. I don't check my phone again until after third period, when I see that she's said it back.

Sitting through all my classes today feels like climbing up the steepest mountain only to find out another mountain awaits. I can't focus in any of my classes, my mind drifting to thoughts of Eliza. Mr. Sanchez has us reading out loud during sixth period, popcorning around the room who reads. I zone out the whole time, so when Mikki popcorns to me, I have no clue where we're at in the book.

Mr. Sanchez shakes his head in disapproval and says, "The bottom of page 198."

I search the page until I find where we're supposed to be. I read the words but I don't hear any sound come out of my mouth. It's like I'm trapped in some trance, thinking about her.

When the final bell rings, I rush out of the school and head straight to the motel where Eliza asked me to meet her.

The familiar flickering neon sign casts an eerie glow over the empty parking lot as I spot where Eliza's room is. I run up the stairs and knock on the door. She doesn't answer.

I knock harder, nothing.

I knock even harder, this time saying, "It's me, Eliza. It's Hakeem."

Still, nothing.

Finally, I twist on the doorknob and the door clicks open. It creaks as it widens, revealing a neat and organized bedroom. I see her suitcase; her toothbrush is still in the bathroom and her shoes are on the floor near the bed. The air even still smells like her. But she's not here. I check everywhere—the shower, under the blankets, under the bed. She's gone.

I text Eliza again, telling her I'm at the motel. I don't get a response.

I check my phone to see if I can get a glimpse of her location, but she still has it turned off. Then I notice something white on top of one of the pillowcases on the bed. It's an envelope. I grab it and open it quickly.

HAKEEM,
I'VE ALWAYS LOVED HAIKU.

IN A FIELD OF BLOOMS,
LOST AMIDST THE WILDFLOWERS,
LIES A SOUL SET FREE.

E

I head back down to my car, realizing her hearse is gone. I don't know why I didn't notice that before I went up. Hopping in my car,

I'm not sure where to look for her. I don't know what the poem means and have no way to ask her about it. I read and reread the poem over and over again, taking my frustration out on my steering wheel when I get too stressed. Then, after what feels like the hundredth time of reading the poem, something stands out. I focus on the word *wildflowers* and think back to where she brought me yesterday. I wonder if she's there and trying to take me on some kind of journey. That feels like something she would do.

I start my car up and head for the highway, attempting to retrace the turns and exits that Eliza took when she brought me to her secret place. The air is heavy with the scent of rain, and thunder rumbles in the distance. I go faster, trying to make it to her before a storm rolls in. I drive with the radio on so that I don't get trapped in my thoughts. The radio plays some '80s rock music that makes me feel hopeful. Bon Jovi. AC/DC. Journey. Billy Idol.

As I approach the place we parked at last time, I see Eliza's hearse. The front door is open. I walk up to the door and look around inside. On the driver's seat sits a copy of *The Collected Poems of Emily Dickinson*, a note hanging out from between some of the pages. Underneath the copy of the book is her essay for Mr. Sanchez's class. I pull out the note from the book.

HAKEEM,
IF YOU ARE READING THIS, IT'S BECAUSE YOU FIGURED
OUT MY HAIKU. I HOPE YOU LIKED IT. I'VE BEEN
READING SOME EMILY DICKINSON LATELY.
HERE'S A LINE THAT I LOVE:

BECAUSE I COULD NOT STOP FOR DEATH—HE KINDLY
STOPPED FOR ME.
YOU ONCE ASKED ME WHAT I WOULD DO ON MY LAST
DAY ON EARTH. I NOW HAVE AN ANSWER FOR YOU. IT
WAS TO SPEND IT WITH YOU. I'M SO GLAD I DID THAT. I
WILL HOLD IT IN MY HEART FOR ETERNITY.

WILDLY YOURS,
E

My heart suddenly pounds in my chest—hard, so hard I hear ringing in my ears. I race through the woods for the field, the whole world seeming to move in slow motion. My lungs feel heavy and my hands shake. I silently pray to God for the first time in a long time, asking him to not let what I think is going on to be true. I run like my life depends on it, because my life and her life are the same right now. I get to the field of wildflowers and see her there, sprawled out on the ground, her body lifeless and stiff, eyes closed.

I fall down at her side, feeling a deep sob erupt from within me. I shake her violently but she doesn't wake up. I shake her even harder, trying to pry her eyelids open, but she doesn't move. Her body is cold, despite it being warm outside. I put two fingers to the side of her neck, confirming my suspicions.

"Eliza, no," I say. "No, no, nooooo. This can't be. Live, Eliza! *Live!*"

Her body lies here, lifeless.

Her black backpack is next to her, by a tree. I reach for it, emptying out the contents. An empty pill bottle falls out.

My hands tremble as I pick up the empty pill bottle, a sinking feeling settling in the pit of my stomach. Tears blur my vision as I stare at the bottle in disbelief, each breath feeling like a struggle. I collapse onto her, sobbing into her chest, not wanting this to be real.

I try to lift her but I'm too weak, I don't have the strength to carry her body.

I dial 9-1-1 and explain our location as best as I can. They tell me to stay put, and at first I hold her, crying and crying as I rock her in my arms. Then I panic, imagining all the questions the police will have, and what it will look like if I'm here. I picture the local cops calling Dad, and know I can't stay. I will spend the rest of my life explaining, and there isn't anything I can do for Eliza now. I run back to my car, feeling my heart hurt as if it'll burst into pieces. I desperately need someone to talk to. Once I'm a safe distance away, I pull over and call Miles's number again, hoping he'll answer despite telling me we won't get to talk anymore. I hope he senses my desperation, wherever he is. I hope he understands that it's all hitting me now—how I lost him, how I've lost her. How I don't have the strength to cope with both.

But yet again the line doesn't ring.

"You've reached a number that has been disconnected and is no longer in service."

CHAPTER TWENTY-SEVEN

I drive as fast as I can back toward my house, doing way beyond the speed limit. At some point, I look down and see *120 mph* on my speedometer. I pound away at my steering wheel in disbelief. "Fuck, fuck, fuuuuuck!" I shout, tears welling in my eyes and blurring the road. I can't believe she's gone. They're gone. I can't believe it.

I can't lose her. I don't want her to be gone.

God, please! I plead. *Not Eliza. Not after Miles.*

I swerve in and out of traffic, narrowly missing collisions as I cut across lines carelessly. The world around me blurs into a frenzy of lights and sounds, but all I can see is her face, his smile, her laughter.

I make it back home, and I'm all alone. I pace everywhere in the house, upstairs, downstairs, my bedroom, my parents' bedroom, the kitchen—thinking, wondering, crying, weeping, wanting to die. Eliza saved my life. She saved my life in more ways than she ever knew and in more ways than anyone else ever could. Why couldn't I save hers? I can hear her now, telling me that she's not the type of girl who needs saving, but still I wish. That's all I'm left with now—the wishing. Wishing things were different, wishing it was me and not her, wishing time away at this unforeseen crossroads.

I call her number. If Miles could pick up, maybe she can pick up. But it just rings and rings, until I get her voicemail. Her voice, alive. Her voice, a lie.

I scream at the top of my lungs. I know no one's home, but I don't care either way. I imagine cops and paramedics arriving to gather up Eliza's body. Thinking about Eliza's dead body makes me sick to my stomach, something turning in my gut. A feeling building and building, like thickness coming up my esophagus. I run for the bathroom and lift up the toilet seat, bending down to hover over the bowl.

I throw up everything I've eaten and more into the toilet. I throw up so much that my head hurts. I start dry heaving.

I go downstairs to the kitchen, furiously ripping through items in the freezer to find the Crown Royal. I grab it out and take a big swig. That big swig is followed by another and then another, until the bottle is empty. The burning liquid trickles down my throat, leaving a trail of fire in its wake. The room spins around me, but I welcome the disorientation. It helps me forget, helps me numb out just a little bit, but I want more—I want more than just to feel numb.

I slam the empty bottle onto the counter, accidentally shattering it. I walk back upstairs, nearly tumbling up each stair. I head for my parents' room, which is off-limits when they're not home. I open every single drawer, hoping to find something, *anything* to take. I empty out dresser drawers, the nightstands, and even try to break into Dad's safe. No luck. I open Dad's closet and notice a box with a bunch of things inside it.

I empty it out on the floor, not thinking or caring about the fact that I'm leaving a trail behind for Momma and Dad to see when they come home. I rapidly pull things out of the box, looking for something to do just the thing I'm needing right now. At the bottom of the box, hidden beneath old letters and photographs, I find a small baggie of white pills.

I grab the baggie, unsure of what they are, and head to my room, shutting the door behind me as if to give myself more privacy. I sit at my desk and crush up the pills in the bag. It takes a minute, but I finally turn the pills into a powdery white substance.

I make lines along the desk, snorting it through my nose. The powder burns as it enters my nostrils, making my eyes water and my head swim. I lean back in my chair, the room spinning around me in a hazy blur. The effects hit me almost instantly—a rush of euphoria followed by a wave of dizziness that threatens to consume me.

It takes a moment to kick in the full effects, but when they do, out of nowhere, I feel raptured into the clouds. My body feels weightless, hands tingly, mind at ease. It feels like I'm standing on top of the world and nothing I do or think matters. I can't think about anything, just floating aimlessly, like pure freedom. And it all happens so fast.

Everything is so beautiful, so good, I don't feel like I even need to breathe air anymore. I feel good. I feel so good. I feel so *fucking* good.

I notice there's still a little bit left on the desk. I scoop it all up and snort it out of my hand, making sure I take every last drop.

Suddenly, my heart is pounding in my chest so hard I can feel it.

Then I feel like my lungs stop working. I wheeze for oxygen.

Within seconds, everything goes black.

CHAPTER TWENTY-EIGHT

I wake up to a bright light blinding me. My eyes are blurry and no matter how much I blink, nothing comes into focus. I hear voices, but everything is muffled and I can't tell what they're saying. I don't immediately recognize any of the voices, either. For a second, I think that maybe I've made it to Heaven or Hell.

I try to move, but I can't. I try to open my mouth to talk, but I can't. It takes a while and a lot of energy trying, but my vision comes back to me and I feel like I have some feeling in my hands and feet. I look around the room, at the flushed, stale light, the monitors all around me, the wires coming out of several different parts of my body. I'm in the hospital.

As I lie here on this bed, I try to remember back to what landed me here. But I can't recall anything. I don't know what happened, which causes me to freak out inside. I feel like I'm frozen in place, stuck, trapped in this bed. I look down and see that there are cuffs tying me to my bed, like I'm some kind of violent monster.

Eventually, I get enough strength to wiggle them, but they're on tight. Panic continues to rise within me as I frantically search around the room, seeing nurses and doctors talking with each other. A nurse notices that I've woken up. She darts over to me and cheers, "You're awake! Amazing! A miracle! Not many live to see another day with the kind of overdose you had."

I try to say something, but I can't. Looking down, I notice

there's a tube down my throat preventing me from making any words. I can only grunt and groan.

Machines beep faster around me. "It's okay. You're okay. Just stay calm and you'll be better in no time. You've been on a ventilator for a few days now, so it'll take a little bit of time to regain some of your strength," the nurse explains.

A ventilator?

The nurse's words echo in my head as I try to process the information. How did I end up on a ventilator? It takes some time, but slowly bits and pieces start to come to me. Losing Eliza, driving home, finding alcohol in the fridge, and taking whatever pills I found in Dad's closet.

Doctors come in, look me over, and remove some of the wires from my body and pull out the tube from down my throat. It feels strange as it comes up.

I cough and spit up as the tube is removed, my throat raw and aching. The nurse hands me a cup of water, and I take small sips, grateful for the cool relief it brings. As the fog in my mind begins to lift, I remember the pain of losing Eliza on top of the pain of losing Miles, the crushing grief. In my darkest hour, I had turned to anything that could numb the pain, even if it meant risking my own life.

"Your parents would like to see you," the nurse says. "Is it okay if I go and grab them?"

I nod at her. I can't move my head much because my neck feels stiff, but she gets the point and disappears out of the room with the other nurses and doctors. Minutes pass by and Momma and Dad come walking through the curtain. Dad holds Momma close at his side as they walk in. It looks like she's been crying extra hard, her makeup messy and scattered everywhere. Dad looks like he hasn't slept in days.

I try to say hi to them, and it comes out extra raspy. My throat stings.

They rush over to my bedside, tears welling up in Momma's eyes all over again as she clasps my hand tightly. Dad's jaw clenches, his eyes filled with a mixture of relief and worry.

"Oh, Jesus Lord! Thank you, God, my baby is awake," Momma whispers as she looks up, her voice breaking with emotion. Dad just nods, unable to form any words as he squeezes my hand gently.

I look into their eyes and see the pain reflected there, the fear of losing me etched in their faces. Guilt washes over me like a large ocean wave, knowing that I put them through this, knowing that I almost left them behind, knowing that they were close to having to bury their own kid.

"I'm so sorry," I manage to croak out, tears welling up in my own eyes now. Momma pulls me into a tight embrace, her sobs muffled against my hospital gown. Dad rests a hand on my shoulder, offering silent support and understanding, feeling as present as ever.

"We love you so much, honey," Momma says between sobs. "We're just so grateful you are still here with us."

I hear footsteps approach and the sound of people talking on radios. Before I can blink, two cops and a detective come walking through the curtains of my hospital room.

"I'm Detective Hugo. This is Officer Smitt and this is Officer Meinerding. We just want to ask this young man some questions about Eliza Fitzpatrick," the detective says, looking at me intensely.

"This isn't a good time," Dad says, going up to them to explain the situation.

"We promise we'll be quick," Detective Hugo says, pulling out a pen and notepad from his brown jacket. "With your permission."

Dad looks at me and then back at them and then at Momma, who hasn't taken her eyes off me. I try to put up my hand, but when I can't, I settle for trying to say, "It's okay. I'll talk."

As I try to clear my throat, my parents exchange worried glances before reluctantly stepping back to give us some space. I can sense their anxiety, the tension in the room thick as the detective pulls up a chair next to my bed. Officer Smitt and Officer Meinerding remain standing, their eyes scanning the room alertly.

Detective Hugo clears his throat before flipping open his notepad. "Thank you for agreeing to speak with us. By the way, you're not in any trouble. We know that Eliza's death was a suicide. We are just trying to piece together the full story. We just have a few questions about her. Can you tell us about your relationship with her?"

I take a deep breath, trying to gather my thoughts despite the fog of confusion that still lingers in my head from my coma. But eventually, it all comes flooding back. Everything.

The detective scribbles down things in his notepad furiously as I talk. It takes about five minutes until the interview is over, and I'm crying. At first, I don't realize it but when I feel the tears roll down my cheeks, I know that I'm crying. I cry for Eliza. I cry for the way this world wasn't good enough for her. I cry that I couldn't get to her in time, or Miles in time. I cry for my parents. I cry for me.

Dad escorts the detective and police officers out of the room, having a word with them in the hallway. I can't hear anything but it sounds like Dad is yelling.

I stay in the hospital for a couple more days because the doctors think I need more time before I can be released. One of my parents sleeps in a chair next to the bed while the other goes home to be with Judah and Jorjah. Each day, I get visitors—Mikki, August, Mrs. Angela and Mr. Rodney, even, like, Mr. Sanchez. I get flowers, cards, my favorite snacks, and lots of ice cream.

When I finally get released from the hospital, it's a Friday. My parents help me into the car after I'm wheeled out in a wheelchair, their expressions a mix of relief and fear. The drive home is quiet, but I know it's because we are all trying to process the last several days, weeks. The familiar streets pass by outside the window, but everything feels different now. *I* am different.

As we pull into our driveway, I see colorful balloons and a banner that reads *Welcome Home* strung across the porch. Tears prick at my eyes as I realize how loved and supported I am. Momma turns off the engine, and we all step out of the car, taking a moment to breathe in the cool evening air.

"Welcome home, Big Bro," Judah exclaims, giving me a hug.

"I've missed you," Jorjah says, also hugging me. "I was really scared."

I hug them back.

The next several days, I stay home, Momma taking time off work to take care of me and keep an eye on me. As the days pass, I slowly start to regain my strength, both physically and emotionally. I spend my days watching horror movies, listening to Edward Elgar's *Nimrod*, thinking about Eliza, thinking about Miles, but also thinking about my future. Indiana State University invites me to visit on a weekend for incoming freshmen, and I almost want to laugh at how oblivious they are. College is the last thing I want to do right now.

It's not an easy several days, because I end up dreaming about Eliza and the memories we made, waking up to cry when I need to. I feel some type of way about the fact that I relapsed in such a major way. I wonder who took care of her funeral arrangements, and if I'll ever know where she's buried. Or even if she got buried at all. She could've been cremated. Who can I ask? I don't know anybody in her life. It was only us when it was us.

On Monday morning, I wake up to the sound of Dad singing a Bruno Mars song at the top of his lungs in the kitchen. It means he's called off for the day. The scent of pancakes wafts through the air, mingling with the aroma of freshly brewed coffee. I make my way downstairs, feeling a sense of gratitude wash over me for the normalcy of this moment. Dad looks up from the griddle, a wide smile spreading across his face. Clinging to my family has been nice lately. They haven't even judged me or made me feel bad about relapsing.

Dad slides a plate of fluffy pancakes in front of me when I make it to the dining room table. Judah and Jorjah are already going to town on theirs, covering them in peanut butter and maple syrup.

"How'd you sleep?" Dad asks.

"Good," I say, swallowing hard. My throat still isn't back to 100 percent yet.

Momma sashays into the kitchen and kisses my forehead. "I'm glad you slept well."

I dig into my plate of pancakes. The taste of actual cooking and not hospital food makes me happy. "These are delicious, Dad," I say.

"Thanks, Son. I have a secret ingredient," he says.

"Secret ingredient?" Momma wonders as she bites into a plain pancake. "What is it?"

"I can't tell you, then it wouldn't be secret anymore," Dad says.

But I know that the secret ingredient is cinnamon. I see it sitting on the counter next to the pancake mix.

After breakfast, Dad tells me that after the twins go to school, he, Momma, and I are going to hike at the nearby nature reserve. He insists that we need to get out of the house more, but I know it's all because of me and what I did.

The sun is shining bright in the sky as we make it to the park Dad drives us to in the family van. As we trek through the park, I can't help but think about the woods that Eliza led me through, the ones that I found her in with no life in her body. I find myself breathing in the fresh air deeply, letting it cleanse me from the inside out.

We reach a clearing overlooking a peaceful lake and pause to catch our breath. Dad gives out tiny bottles of Gatorade and granola bars to sustain us, to keep us going. Momma takes my hand in hers, her eyes filled with unspoken understanding and love. "You're my brave boy, Hakeem. You know that?"

I don't feel brave. I feel like the furthest thing from that.

"I'm sorry if we contributed to your . . ." Momma can't even get the words out. She stops and has to take a breath, blinking back tears.

I know what she means, so I just interrupt. "It's okay," I say.

She brings me into a hug, squeezing me tight. "When you go to college, you'll be able to start fresh. You'll meet new people, explore new ideas, and find yourself in ways you can't even imagine right now," she says, her voice filled with hope.

"In the meantime," Dad says gently, "you need help. You're going to have to go back into treatment, and also start going to your meetings regularly. Do you understand?"

"Yes," I tell him. And I mean it. I know what I have to do. I've done it all before.

I couldn't save Eliza from making the wrong choice. I couldn't stop Miles from getting involved with the wrong people. But I can avoid both things for myself.

I want to live for Miles and I want to live for Eliza, just as much as I want to live for my family. I know it's going to be hard and there are going to be days where I want to give up, but I will try to remember the lesson Eliza taught me that she didn't listen to herself: People are easily knocked down and destroyed, but wildflowers are not. They always persevere. *We* always persevere.

ONE WEEK LATER

CHAPTER   TWENTY-NINE

Rumors at school ruin my week when I return. Someone mass-messaged the whole school that the new girl killed herself. I feel powerless against everything because they're not wrong, but the rumors sting all the same. And there are the rumors about me—people whisper around in the hallways and between classes that I got suspended, that I overdosed, that I was in a coma, that I was in a mental institution because of what happened to Eliza.

I get dirty looks at times walking in the hallway because in some way I'm like a bad-luck charm. Whoever gets close to me dies. I'm the boy who should be wearing a scarlet letter—a letter signifying to stay away at all times, that I'm dirty, broken, or to be feared. I walk around the halls with my head down, telling myself not to make eye contact with anyone. I can almost feel the judgment in locking eyes with some people as they pass by. Mikki and August and even Ximena are extra nice, as if to compensate for everyone else.

In English class, we've moved on from *The Catcher in the Rye* and now we're studying *The Picture of Dorian Gray* by Oscar Wilde. We go from studying one book by a depressed author to another, but I'm not entirely complaining. I know how much Mr. Sanchez loves this book. He's described it as his favorite novel of all time at least seven times and clutches the book tightly to his chest.

Mr. Sanchez walks around the classroom as everyone fidgets

with their copy of the new novel. He explains the gist of what it's about and why it means so much to him as a queer Latino.

He grabs the pen to the smartboard and writes on the board. *Behind every exquisite thing that existed, there was something tragic*, he writes. Then Mr. Sanchez turns to the class and asks, "What do you think Oscar Wilde meant by that?"

The class is quiet. I read and reread the quote on the board. I copy it down inside my notebook, swearing to try a lot harder in school this time.

"Hakeem," Mr. Sanchez says.

It catches me off guard, but I know he wants to call on me just to check in and see if I'm paying attention. But maybe also because he knows I've had my fair share of tragedies.

I think nice and hard. I think about how Eliza would answer the question. "I think Oscar Wilde was trying to convey that beauty often arises from struggle and suffering," I begin, my voice confident. "Just like a diamond is formed under pressure, maybe beautiful things in life are also born from the depths of tragedy."

Mr. Sanchez nods thoughtfully, a hint of pride flickering in his face. "Wonderful interpretation, Hakeem. It's almost like you traveled back in time to interview Mr. Wilde about the meaning of his novel."

"Thank you," I say, giving him a look of gratitude.

Mr. Sanchez walks around, weaving between the rows in his classroom. He continues to lecture the class, which feels more like he's gushing. "Oscar Wilde was a master at weaving together the threads of beauty and tragedy, entwining them in a play as

296

old as time itself. In every stroke of Dorian's portrait, in every line of his story, there lies a profound truth about the human experience."

The bell rings right after Mr. Sanchez assigns us to read the first three chapters for homework and prepare for a class discussion tomorrow. I slide the book into my backpack and head for the door.

"Wait up, Hakeem. Can I have a moment?" Mr. Sanchez asks.

I hang by the door as my classmates filter out into the hallway, darting to their next classes.

"I know how close you were with Eliza," he says, reminding me of the same conversation he had with me after Miles passed away. It feels like my life is cyclical and I'm reliving the same moment all over again like some dumb movie. "Part of the reason why I picked this book for us to read in class was to give you a chance to explore and maybe find solace in the themes of beauty and tragedy within its chapters. I know it's not much, but literature has a way of offering us a mirror to reflect on our own experiences."

"Thank you, Mr. Sanchez," I say. "It means a lot."

"Also, I graded your *Catcher in the Rye* essay. You did a nice job. You earned yourself an 88 out of 100. You're a good writer, but I know you can take yourself to another level if you set your mind to it," Mr. Sanchez says, handing me back my essay with red markings all over it.

I look at him, waiting for anything else he might add.

"I know things have been tough for you lately, and I want you to remember that there are people here who care about you," he says softly. "If you ever need to talk or if there's anything on your mind, my door is always open."

"Thanks," I respond, feeling a lump form in my throat. It's been difficult to think about Eliza's passing, let alone open up to someone about it, but Mr. Sanchez's genuine concern makes me feel a little less alone in my grief, which I'm thankful for.

The rest of the school day is the same old, same old. Teachers teaching things I'll never use in the future. Students gossiping about one another and spreading rumors about me that aren't true. Me avoiding the cafeteria because I'm not ready to sit at a lunch table without Eliza and Miles.

At dismissal, when I make it to my car, I sit in the parking lot reading the poem Eliza wrote for me before she left to see her father and brother. Now that I've had time to sit with it and know more (but never enough) about Eliza, I read between the lines. Maybe that's what you do with all poetry: You read between the lines for the meaning between words.

IN THE DUSK'S EMBRACE, WHERE SHADOWS LOOM,
MY HEART, A CHAMBER OF IMPENDING DOOM, GLOOM.
IN FIELDS WHERE WILDFLOWERS BLOOM AND SWAY,
I PEN THESE WORDS, MY SOUL'S ANGUISH AND DISARRAY.
BENEATH THE MOON'S COLD, UNFORGIVING LIGHT,
I WANDER LOST, CONSUMED BY ENDLESS NIGHT.
AMONGST THE BLOOMS, WHERE BEAUTY HIDES ITS STING,
I MOURN THE LOSS OF EVERY FLEETING THING.
OH, LOVE, A SPECTER HAUNTING MY DESPAIR.

AN ABSENCE LEAVES ME GASPING IN THE AIR.
LIKE WILDFLOWERS, WE BLOOM AND THEN DECAY,
IN THE GARDEN OF DREAMS, WE FADE AWAY
YET IN THIS DARKNESS, A FLICKER STILL REMAINS,
A FRAGILE HOPE, A THREAD THAT SOFTLY STRAINS.
BUT SHOULD IT SNAP, AND ALL MY WORLD DESCEND,
LET WILDFLOWERS MARK WHERE MY JOURNEY ENDS.

I make a return to group, just like I promised Momma and Dad. (I'm also scheduled to see Dr. Chandler in two days.) I haven't been to group in a while, so I imagine things will feel a little weird stepping back in there, especially with what I'll see as an empty chair for Eliza. It takes me a bit to get out of the car. I think back to meeting Eliza here, our first conversation, the few times we talked here, the first time I watched her smoke a cigarette, the first time I noticed just how beautiful she was up close.

Finally, I build up the courage to get out of my car.

Taking a deep breath, I push open the door and step inside. The familiar scent of lit candles, mildew, and coffee greets me. I immediately spot the empty chair where Eliza used to sit, causing a pang in my chest. I sit in the seat next to it, saving it for her as if she's going to come walking through those doors at any moment.

As I settle into my seat, Yolanda sees me, pauses, and then nods in greeting, her warm eyes filled with understanding. I'm glad she never judges. I know that's kind of her job and that's kind of how NA groups function everywhere, but it's like we just pick up right where we left off. The discussion starts, and though it takes too much effort, I push through thoughts of Eliza to focus on what we're learning about today.

Yolanda leads the discussion, saying, "I used to think that recovery was a destination, a place you arrive at and then everything is fixed. But it's not like that, is it? Recovery is a journey, full of twists and turns, highs and lows. It's about progress, not perfection." Her words resonate deep within me, reminding me of things Miles said and things my parents have said, too. But it's still good to be reminded of it.

It's so quiet you can hear the wind blowing outside, people listening intently on what she has to say. Some people even jot down notes. Others nod along and blurt out that they agree.

"Does anyone here have anything to say? Anything they want to confess? Anything they want to celebrate? Any glows or grows?" Yolanda asks, looking around the group.

Aram raises his hand and shares that he just encouraged a friend of his to seek out an NA group and even invited him to come to ours.

Another girl, Rena, shares about how she was tempted to use heroin again but found that if she listens to Frank Ocean's *Channel Orange* album, she can resist the urge to use.

As others in the group share their own struggles and triumphs, I find myself opening up, too, letting out the pain and guilt I've been carrying once and for all. I share about how I didn't believe in love, how I found it in Eliza, how it's a terrible thing to love someone so much and not be able to keep them from dying by suicide. I talk about how I used because I couldn't handle life. How the whole world became a wave that swallowed me up. One minute I was standing up, fine. The next, I was under that huge wave, fighting for breath, fighting to make it back up to the surface. Using helped me escape. It freed me up. It helped me not panic when it was almost impossible for me to ever make it back up for breath again. Using made me feel intensely good. And sometimes, that's just the greatest desire of my heart. To feel good.

But I know there are other things out there that will make me feel good, like stargazing at night, like visiting the Grand Canyon, like swimming with dolphins in the Pacific Ocean, or simply playing video games with a friend like Miles or sharing a milkshake with a friend like Eliza. I know I'll have to do a lot of work to find the fruit of living, but I know it exists. It has to.

E P I L O G U E

It's a Thursday, two months since the world lost the loveliest wild-flower on the planet. The days feel longer, the sun doesn't shine as brightly, and the birds don't sing as sweetly. There is an undeniable void in the universe that no one and nothing can seem to fill. I wake every morning for school and think, *Just one more day.* Just one more day and I will have the strength to face the world without her and Miles. But that day never seems to come. As I walk through the halls, faces blur together in a sea of indifference. The world moves on, but I am frozen in time, unable to let go.

"Tell me a story," Dr. Chandler says.

I take a deep breath and nod, gathering my thoughts before I begin my story. I start all the way at the beginning, from when I was born, talking about when I met Miles, when I started school, when I started using, when Miles got hit by that bus, all the way up to meeting Eliza and the journey of a lifetime she took me on. The only thing I keep to myself are Miles's phone calls. No one but Mikki will ever understand, and I'm fine with that.

Dr. Chandler leans in, her eyes fixed on me with a mix of curiosity and concern. I can sense that she's analyzing every word, every pause in my story. As I go into the details of the adventures Eliza and I embarked on, the landscapes we traversed, the secrets we gave to each other, the memories we made, I see a flicker of recognition in Dr. Chandler's gaze. She pulls her glasses down and holds them in her right hand, narrowing her eyes at me. I stare at her and she stares back at me, a silence coming in between us that causes me to hold my breath.

She studies me as if she can see into my soul, into my heart, into my thoughts.

"I understand," she finally says, her voice soft yet assured, adjusting her seafoam-green blazer. "You've been through so much, seen so much. It seems like you've come to realize that the journey shapes us in ways we cannot always comprehend at the time, but later we understand."

Something like that, is what I want to say. But I don't. Instead, I get choked up, tears pooling around in my eyes as I think about the things I learned from Eliza and Miles. I'm realizing that talking about them will never become easier. That every time I have to talk about them it will feel like opening up a door over and over again, expecting to see someone on the other side. Except the door is my heart and on the other side is a reminder of the person I'll never, ever be able to see again.

I miss them.

I miss them so much.

Falling in love with Eliza Jane Fitzpatrick saved me. She was my favorite story, my favorite song, my favorite lyric, my favorite memory. The deeper I fell for her, the more I felt myself healing. I guess that's the thing about love. It has its way of making us whole in time.

"You're learning," Miles tells me. Not on the phone, but still in my head. Always with me.

For now, I'm stuck in the place between sleep and awake. The place where you can still remember dreaming. Maybe Eliza and I can meet there sometime, among some field of wildflowers. Go on another adventure of our own. Explore more secrets of the universe. Tell each other stories of the waters we've parted and the seas that we've crossed.

I think back to Miles and what he said about love. But love isn't a feeling. It never was. Love is people.

Though I'm here all alone, left to get older and grayer without my best friend and the only girl I ever truly loved, I know the beauty of love is that it never truly fades away. It lives on in the memories we hold dear, in the stories we share, in the way it shapes us into who we are meant to be. This is the thing that makes me feel like if I can't go on, I'll go on. I think through the days, weeks, months, years I've spent searching for wholeness. I think about the times ahead where I'll be tempted to use again and the times where I won't. I think about my family and how they welcomed me back and nursed me back to health. I think about my high school graduation and the last summer break before college, if I choose to go. I think about how no matter what, there's always going to be a light at the end of the tunnel.

Though I might be an addict, I have learned to love through the ruins that addiction leaves behind. Eliza's absence on top of Miles's absence has carved a hole in my soul, one that can never be filled. But it's a hole that teaches me the value of every fleeting moment, of every beat of my heart.

Eliza and Miles, I promise to make the most of this second chance. You have faith in me, don't you?

ACKNOWLEDGMENTS

First and foremost, thank you to my Lord and Savior, Jesus Christ, for getting me through writing the toughest book of my career. When so much doubt crept in, I'm thankful to have been comforted by His peace and love. I truly couldn't—and wouldn't—have done this without Him.

Special thanks to . . .

Elli Coles, I know I already dedicated the whole damn book to you, but you deserve to be thanked more. Thank you for sticking by me all this time and for loving me unconditionally. Thank you for letting me read you snippets of this book without context and ask questions about whether things sounded too cheesy or too much like a Shakespearean play. I appreciate you more than words can contain. I love you!

My parents, for bringing me into this world and doing their very best. We might not have always gotten along or seen eye to eye, but each of you will always have a special place in my heart, Mom and Dad. You both taught me that there can be beauty in the ashes, that hope does come, if I let it. I love you guys and thank you for always allowing me to write part of you both into my books.

My grandmother Charlene. I know you're in Heaven, but it always still feels like you're here with me, whispering how proud of me you are. You were always bragging on me to anyone who would listen—your doctors, friends, and even random delivery men. I hope

I'm living a life worthy of you continuing that in Heaven. I miss you dearly.

Lauren Abramo, my ridiculously talented and wise agent and friend. Thank you for ALWAYS being my champion and helping this book become what it is. I know I've promised you my firstborn before, but I'm truly serious about how much I owe you! I'm lucky to have you in my corner.

David Levithan, my extraordinary and genius editor and friend. Thank you for acquiring this book despite how much it changed from my original pitch. You have helped me tell one of the most vulnerable stories I've ever told and helped take it to the next level, as you always do. I'm so thankful to be teamed up with you at Scholastic and look forward to many books to come.

The crew over at Dystel, Goderich & Bourret. Thanks for cheering me on behind the scenes as much as you guys have over these years. It has been the honor of a lifetime to be a DG&B author. Cheers!

CJ Johnson, thank you for crafting a truly stunning yet haunting cover that made me cry instantly upon looking at it. It's powerful and tells a story of its own. Thank you, Maeve Norton, for dreaming it up and putting it all together. I said this to David Levithan, but I truly am blessed by the cover god for continuing to give me the most awesome covers.

Hugest thanks to everyone over at Scholastic who's had a hand in this book, especially Melissa Schirmer and the entire production team, Rachel Feld and the entire marketing team, and everyone in publicity and sales.

Steven, Emily, Jonah, and Rio Portillo, I'm really thankful that you all have been so much like family to me over the years. I look up to you guys and hope that you know that I feel your love for sure and love you each so much right back.

Meghan Kirkpatrick, thank you for being the best "sister" I could have asked to have through marriage. You are strong and courageous and brave. I know you're a fan of my books, but I'm also a fan of you! Let's grab a matcha soon?

My "married into" family—Andrea, Shane, Kadee, and everyone. Thank you for loving me and cheering for me since the beginning. I praise God for you guys.

In no particular order: Reginald Hayes, Christopher Glotzbach, Brittany Glotzbach, Iesha Alspaugh, Tony New, Marci New, Bekah Whelchel, Zach Whelchel, Carly New, Mitch Schussler, Anna Park, Brandon Clemens, Jenna Clemens, Courtney Bishop, Zane Bishop, Logan Arnold, Paul Butler, Peyton Trowbridge, Rory Sullivan, Daniel Trone, Nick Smith, and so many others—thanks for all the love, encouragement, and drinks as I wrote this book. It takes a village to write a book, and I'm grateful for this village of love.

My author buddies who make this job less lonely and more worth it: Mason Deaver, Farrah Penn, Mark Oshiro, Nic Stone, Adam Silvera, Angie Thomas, Scott Reintgen, Dave Connis, Eric Smith, Adi Alsaid, Randy Ribay, Emily X. R. Pan, Simon Curtis, Leah Johnson, Gayle Forman, Dhonielle Clayton, and so many others. (Sorry if I left you off this list, it's not intentional, I promise. There are SO many of you!)

Big thanks to my family and loved ones who have celebrated with me along the way. I'm thankful for each of you, especially my two sisters, Diamond and Taya. I love you both more than you know and can't wait to see you two do some incredible things in your life.

And to my amazing readers—new and OG—thank you for picking up this book. My mission is to write books that serve as mirrors and windows. I hope you enjoyed reading *Your Final Moments* and that it leaves a mark on you—in a good way. You are so, so loved!

ABOUT THE AUTHOR

Jay Coles is the acclaimed author of *Tyler Johnson Was Here* and *Things We Couldn't Say*. He lives in Indiana. You can find him online at jaycoleswrites.com.